MORE PRAISE FOR
Karen Kay

"Captures the heart and soul of the American Indian."
—*The Best Reviews*

"An exciting historical romance." —*Midwest Book Review*

"Kay blends legend and fact into a beautiful love story . . .
She enhances a magical, passionate plot with historical
detail and just a touch of magic." —*Romantic Times*

"Enchanting . . . Will capture your attention quickly and
never let go!" —*Huntress Reviews*

"Terrific . . . Fans will appreciate this fine tale."
—*Paranormal Romance Reviews*

RED HAWK'S WOMAN

KAREN KAY

BERKLEY SENSATION, NEW YORK

THE BERKLEY PUBLISHING GROUP
Published by the Penguin Group
Penguin Group (USA) Inc.
375 Hudson Street, New York, New York 10014, USA
Penguin Group (Canada), 90 Eglinton Avenue East, Suite 700, Toronto, Ontario M4P 2Y3, Canada
(a division of Pearson Penguin Canada Inc.)
Penguin Books Ltd., 80 Strand, London WC2R 0RL, England
Penguin Group Ireland, 25 St. Stephen's Green, Dublin 2, Ireland (a division of Penguin Books Ltd.)
Penguin Group (Australia), 250 Camberwell Road, Camberwell, Victoria 3124, Australia
(a division of Pearson Australia Group Pty. Ltd.)
Penguin Books India Pvt. Ltd., 11 Community Centre, Panchsheel Park, New Delhi—110 017, India
Penguin Group (NZ), 67 Apollo Drive, Rosedale, North Shore 0745, Auckland, New Zealand
(a division of Pearson New Zealand Ltd.)
Penguin Books (South Africa) (Pty.) Ltd., 24 Sturdee Avenue, Rosebank, Johannesburg 2196, South
Africa

Penguin Books Ltd., Registered Offices: 80 Strand, London WC2R 0RL, England

This is a work of fiction. Names, characters, places, and incidents either are the product of the author's
imagination or are used fictitiously, and any resemblance to actual persons, living or dead, business es-
tablishments, events, or locales is entirely coincidental. The publisher does not have any control over
and does not assume any responsibility for author or third-party websites or their content.

RED HAWK'S WOMAN

A Berkley Sensation Book / published by arrangement with the author

PRINTING HISTORY
Berkley Sensation mass-market edition / June 2007

Copyright © 2007 by Karen Kay Elstner-Bailey.
Cover art by Robert Papp.
Cover design by George Long.
Handlettering by Ron Zinn.

ISBN: 978-0-425-21603-3

BERKLEY SENSATION®
Berkley Sensation Books are published by The Berkley Publishing Group,
a division of Penguin Group (USA) Inc.,
375 Hudson Street, New York, New York 10014.
BERKLEY SENSATION is a registered trademark of Penguin Group (USA) Inc.
The "B" design is a trademark belonging to Penguin Group (USA) Inc.

PRINTED IN THE UNITED STATES OF AMERICA

10 9 8 7 6 5 4 3 2 1

This book is dedicated to:

Wendy Lieberman
A very sweet and dear friend

My favorite cousin,
Dewey Earnest & his mother, Beatrice

Effie, my maternal grandmother,
whom I never knew

My good friends,
Wendy Ettricks & Joanne Snitzer

My mother-in-law,
Joyce Bailey

And my husband, the love of my life,
Paul Bailey.

Thank you all for your help and your inspiration,
in the past, in the present,
and may the future be filled
with all good things.

Red Hawk's
Woman

PROLOGUE

New York, 1848
Midnight

Lightning crashed through the rain-soaked air, while below, the ground and everything on it appeared huddled together, as though seeking strength to withstand the howling wind and the heavy deluge. People scurried to get out of the downpour, but it was useless. The wind had increased tenfold and was blowing so passionately, that had one believed in such things, it would have appeared as if the gods themselves were angry.

However, inside the lush Thirty-Fourth Street home, except for an occasional hint of the weather outside, all was quiet. A man was dying. He was a great man, a good man, a man of wisdom. But his time on this Earth was drawing to an end, and he knew it.

It was this awareness that had caused Trent Clark, a well-known professional archaeologist, to summon his best friend, Walter Rutledge, to his side. That Rutledge was younger than Clark by perhaps thirty years held little significance; not when the matter at hand was trust, friendship and a devout attempt to secure history.

"This way, please," said Fieldman, Clark's butler. "Mr. Clark will see you now."

"Aye, of course," replied Rutledge.

"Is that you, Walter?"

"Aye, that it is. That it is," said Rutledge, dropping his hat and coat into the butler's arms and rushing into the room.

"Come closer," said Clark as he reached out as far as he dared, clutching at Rutledge's hand. "Come closer." Clark's utterance was low, more of a croak than a normal tone of voice. Hearing it, Clark knew a moment of regret. What he wouldn't give to be young again, to be vital . . . to be able to find the treasures himself.

But it was not to be. Clark sighed. *Enough.* He must clear his mind of all distraction. The matter at hand was too important.

"That will be all, Fieldman," said Clark, when the butler lingered. "I will call for you when we finish."

Fieldman nodded, backed out of the room and shut the door.

As soon as it was closed, Clark began to speak again, and he said, "Please come closer, my friend." He coughed, wondering if his voice could be heard over the competition of the weather.

Luckily, Rutledge must have heard the command, for he obeyed at once. Bending down, he came nearer.

Clark signaled his appreciation by a quick dip of his head, and he hardened his grasp on his friend's hand. "This is serious, Walter. Listen carefully."

Rutledge nodded.

"Do you see this box?" Clark gestured toward the highly

polished nightstand, where sat an intricately wrapped container.

"Aye, sir, that I do," said Rutledge.

Again Clark gestured toward it. "Take it."

Rutledge hesitated, hand midair.

"Take it," Clark demanded again, and this time Rutledge hastened to do as bidden.

"Open it."

One-handed, Rutledge obeyed, though his fingers shook. First, off came the string, then the swaddling that surrounded it, until at last he held a red, ornate box in his hand. At length, as though with misgivings, he peeked inside the case, only to gasp aloud.

But it was exactly what Clark had expected. "Go ahead," said Clark. "Touch it."

"But sir, this be . . . this be . . ."

"A quartz nugget," whispered Clark. "That I know. The figure carved within it is from the gold vein that runs through the quartz. As you know it is quite rare to find this in nature, much less to be fashioned as it is. It came into my possession most unusually, make no mistake."

"A dig?" asked Rutledge, referring to an archaeological adventure in uncovering the history of an area, by means of a shovel and trowel.

"Aye," said Clark. "A dig. There be quite a story that accompanies that piece," he added as he settled back against the pillows. He drew in a shaky breath and let it out twice, seeking the means to gather together the strength to say what must be said. But such routine actions weren't as easy as they used to be. After several brief pauses, whereupon he was more than aware of the rattling in his respiration, Clark continued, "The piece is now yours. I give it to you . . . as a trust."

"Thank you, Clark. But a trust? Surely you have not stooped to becoming a *collector*?"

"Mayhap, I might have done so . . . in this one instance. But do not judge me so harshly."

Rutledge shook his head. "I am surprised is all. We are professional archaeologists, not treasure hunters. After all, it was you who lectured me time and time again that the artifacts we discover do not belong to us, that the history we uncover is for all men who would but reach to know it."

"Aye, that I have. But you must allow me to explain, my friend." Clark's voice was weak with frailty, yet stern with determination. "I have little time left on this Earth to tell you what I must. Now please. Sit."

Rutledge paused, looking highly uncomfortable. Then as though suddenly making a decision, his features became blank. He sat back down. "I am sorry," he said. "I should not be judging you before hearing you out. I am certain that you must have your reasons for keeping this to yourself. And I will hear them, for you have always been one of the most ethical men I have known."

Clark breathed out with relief, then sank back against his pillow. "Thank you. Now, I have a request to make of you, my friend."

Rutledge gave a quick acknowledgment with his head, as though to say he had expected as much.

"It is believed that there are three additional pieces that match this one," continued Clark. "All of them are legended to be of the same material, quartz with solid gold figures etched within. They are a set, so to speak. Or perhaps I should say they are brothers and sisters. I have only the one piece and I hold it in trust. Not for myself, no mistake, but rather I have held it for a friend who bestowed the thing upon me."

"But surely you could have told him that it was impossible, if not unethical to keep it and—"

"The man was an American Indian."

"An Indian?"

"Aye." Clark nodded. "When he delegated this into my care, he charged me to find the others, for the set belongs not to history, not to me or to you or even to a museum. Rather the artifacts—when you find them—belong to a clan of American Indians . . . the Lost Clan."

"The Lost Clan? I have never heard of them."

"There is no reason why you should know of them," Clark said. "Now, bend down toward me, my friend, for I do not have the strength to speak up to be heard, and it is important that I tell you a story, the myth that is attached to this piece. Hear it well. For I am about to discharge a duty that I have carried with me these long and many years."

"A duty?"

Suddenly, Clark clutched Rutledge's hand. "Promise me that if you accept my challenge, and if you find the matching artifacts, you will not keep them or give them to a museum."

Rutledge hesitated, clearly troubled.

"Promise me." Trembling, Clark glared into Rutledge's eyes.

"Trent, I—"

Clark gasped, heaved, then began to shake. "Promise me, for I cannot tell you the legend until you do."

Still Rutledge hesitated, while a myriad of emotions flickered over his countenance. At length, however, he capitulated. "Aye," he said, "I promise."

At once, Clark's teeth stopped chattering, the shaking subsided, and with a long, scraping breath, the elderly gentleman fell back against his bed. And since there was little time left to debate, he began at once. "No mistake, the artifacts must be returned as a set to the Clan, for only in doing so will a powerful enchantment be lifted."

"An enchantment? You mean . . . like a curse?"

"Aye, a curse. The story I am about to tell you is a fantastic story, an unbelievable story. And yet I believe it to be true, and no lie." He stopped, drew in air, then went on to say, "For you see, the old Indian who gave me this piece—and it be many years since he did so—was a man who had seen much in his younger days."

Arms straight out in front of him, the old man lay his hands, palms down, against the sheets. "This artifact, and the three others that are yet to be found, are very valuable—and not because they are made of gold."

Rutledge nodded.

Clark glanced at Rutledge, again gestured toward the object, then said, "You, my friend, call that piece an artifact, because you believe it to be made by a human hand."

"That I do, right enough. It is carved, meaning that it must have been created by—"

"But do not be so hasty. Examine the piece in your leisure if you must. I have done so, and I do not believe the piece to be made by a human being."

Rutledge's mouth dropped open. "But . . . but that is impossible, no wind or rain or natural occurrence could have—"

"It was not carved," said Clark. "That is, no one man sat and fashioned this statue. The piece that you hold there is one of the Thunderer's children."

"The Thunderer? His children?"

"Aye, the god of thunder. He be a part of American Indian mythology. At times the god takes on the form of a bird, sometimes that of a man. But long ago, the Thunderer lost his children . . . forever . . .

"Come," Clark continued, "it is a long story, and I am tired. I make only one request, my friend."

"And that is, sir?"

"Locate the matching set. And once found, they must be returned to the Lost Clan."

"But how can I do that if the Clan is lost? I have never heard of them before this moment."

"When that time arrives, you will know what to do. This is what the old Indian told me. You will simply know. Now, tell me the truth, and no lie. Do you promise to do this?"

Rutledge bobbed his head up and down.

"Speak up, my friend," demanded Clark. "I must hear you say it."

"I promise I will do all I can, Clark, barring any natural occurrence or disaster."

"Good, good, please God," replied Clark on a sigh. The sudden burst of light into the room, followed by an earsplitting explosion of thunder, seemed almost a cliché. Perhaps the natural occurrence would have been trite, as well, if it weren't for the graveness of the occasion and the matter at hand. At last, however, Clark spoke up and said, "Then all is well. Aye, all is well. Now, let me tell you about a time when the people were closer to the land, and to the gods; a time when the Thunderer used to take on human form. For this is a story of that god and a clan. It is a story of greed, of war, of murder. But, as they say in native mythology, I go ahead of myself. Let me begin at the beginning . . ."

And so the story began, with Clark's voice droning on and on. Hour upon hour ticked by unnoticed, until at last it was done.

"Now you understand, my friend," whispered Clark huskily. "I am passing on to you more than an artifact. That piece represents the many lives that are at stake. What you hold 'tis a sacred trust. For many years I have had to bear this burden alone. But now"—his hand tightened its grip on the younger man's—"you are a part of it, too."

And with these final words, Trent Clark left this world.

Chapter 1

Eyes wide open, eight-year-old Effie Wendelyn Rutledge quietly flipped over in her makeshift bed, her attention centered on the two adults who were crowded close together. Their voices were hushed as they spoke, quite difficult to hear because of the fire that crackled merrily outside their tent. It caused Effie to concentrate all the harder. Holding her breath, she pulled the covers over her head, remaining as silent as possible. In truth, she feared that if she uttered a sound—any sound—she would miss something vital.

On the far side of the tent, Effie's mother, Alice Rutledge, and her dearest friend, Wilma Owens, reposed in a corner. Both appeared to be dozing, unaware of what was being said.

Beside Effie lay Lesley Owens, a girl four years her senior. Lesley was also asleep, and this fact was odd, since it had been Lesley's idea to stay up and listen to the adults.

Outside, in the distance, a coyote howled, an owl hooted and the incessant wind wailed through their camp, adding more distraction to Effie's quest in eavesdropping. The wind was another oddity out here, she thought, for it never ceased, and the sounds of its gusts reminded her of a person, as though the air itself were alive and conversing in a language all its own.

On that thought, Effie sighed and opened her eyes to the darkness that is attendant when one hides beneath the covers. But the shadowy vision that met her matched the mood of the night, for the blackness outside their tent lent an atmosphere of foreboding to this place. Perhaps it was because there was no moon.

However, though many children might fear the murky aura of evening, not so Effie. *This* was her family, this her life, and she considered herself as much a student of archaeology as anyone twice her age. Vaguely—if she tried really hard—she could hear her father's soft voice. She concentrated . . .

"It happened," she heard her father, Walter Rutledge, say, "so long ago and is so completely mysterious that no one knows if the legend of the Lost Clan be fact or fable."

"Yet, you must believe it to be true, Rutledge," replied John Owens, Effie's father's best friend, colleague and Lesley's father. "Otherwise, we would not be here now."

"Aye," agreed Effie's father. "That I do. As I have already said, a figurine was given to Trent Clark, whom we know was a highly skilled conservator. It was he who restored the piece to its original luster before his untimely death—"

"Only a few years previous, wasn't it?"

"Aye," said Rutledge. "That it was." Walter Rutledge

became silent for so long that Effie feared her father might not continue. But in due course, he began again, saying, "Clark not only entrusted the piece to my care, he gave me reason to believe that the legend might be true. In particular there was an old Indian whom Clark had interviewed—a man who had lived to see an entire group of people restored to flesh and blood. According to Clark, that old Indian had witnessed a people appear out of a heavy 'mist.'"

"Humph!" said Owens. "Have a care, my friend, where you place your trust, and perhaps your credibility. If you seek my opinion, I believe that you are speaking of things too fantastic to be believed. Legends are good for telling on a dark night such as this, but to put one's faith in them . . ."

"That be a bold statement you make. And I am not sure I agree—"

"You must realize," interrupted Owens, "that we are interested only in facts, and the Indians embrace all sorts of bizarre ideas, all of them attributable to a supernatural consciousness. Yet what proof do we have that such notions exist?"

Rutledge sighed. "And what proof have we that they do not?"

Owens paused. "Touché," he offered up at last, but there was a smile in his voice.

After a time, Rutledge must have come to terms with whatever notions Owens was trying to impart, for Effie's father laughed, then said, "I would ask that you pay me little mind. Perhaps there be a bit of witchcraft in the air this night, and it is this that makes me speak so. For in truth, your arguments against such a thing are sound. Scientifically sound. And yet I cannot help but notice that, though you caution me, you are here with me now."

Owens hesitated. Then, he said, "Yes, that I am. But after all, I cannot be letting you have this dig all to yourself, now, can I?" Once more, there was amusement in Owens's tone. "I may not believe the legend . . . but I'd like to, and if there's any adventure to be had in a dig, you know I will be there with you." Owens paused a beat, then continued, saying, "Do you have the piece with you?"

"No," said Rutledge. "I have placed it in a sealed box, safely stored away, for it is made not only of quartz, but of solid gold. To be sure, there may be other natural elements occurring in the piece, but if there are, they are not to be seen by the naked eye, and are certainly not in the majority."

"Who do you suppose made the thing? The Indians?"

"Perhaps. But in my experience, the Plains Indians do not value gold like those people who are to be found way to the south of us . . . in Mexico."

"Hm-m-m . . . Strange."

"Aye, that it is. I do have a theory, however. Consider this," said Rutledge. "If the myth is to be believed, then according to legend, it was the Creator who made the images."

"The Creator? More legend? . . ." Owens let out his breath, as though in disbelief. "My friend—"

"More legend, to be sure," Rutledge went on to say. "For the Thunderer had four children who were killed. Now, Clark told me on his deathbed that he believed the Creator would not let the children die, but rather placed the spirit of each child into the gold of these rocks, there to await a time when a hero would come forth to gather them up, and to place them all together again. There were four in all, and it is said that when the four are again a set and are given back to the Clan, the Clan will be freed."

Owens hissed, the sound reminding Effie of a snake. Who was he, thought Effie, to sit in judgment?

"It's not really so odd," continued Rutledge. "The images, after all, look as though they could be the Thunderer's children. Half bird, half human. And they are intricately made."

Nothing was said or done, as a lengthy silence ensued. But after a time, Owens asked, "I think I would like to hear the legend again, if you would humor me."

At those words, Effie felt herself grin. *This* was what she had been waiting to hear. *This* was why she was still awake, even when her friend was not.

Not daring to move, lest she be discovered, Effie settled in to listen. And at last she was rewarded, for her father began, "In a time so long ago it has been forgotten, a clan killed the children of the Thunder god. It is said that this act was done because of the Clan's greed for more food and more power than it would need to simply survive.

"Now, the Thunderer in Native American mythology, you must remember, is an angry god; he is a god of revenge, of sudden death, of lightning and thunder. But he is also a god of bodily lust. And so in retaliation for the Clan's deed, the Thunderer stole some women from the people, three or four, then he began to wage war on the entire tribe. He might have killed all within the Clan, too, but for the Creator, who intervened on the people's behalf.

" 'Nay, they shall not die,' the Creator had said." Walter Rutledge's voice was dramatic, and lent the story a believable air. "But though the Creator spared their lives," he continued, "the Clan were to pay for their murderous crime. And pay they did, with their very existence . . . their eternity. Thus began the tribe's plight, for the Creator banished the people to live in a mist, or a very heavy fog.

"It was an unearthly world," he continued, "not real or substantial, and the Clan was trapped there, may still be trapped there, neither dead nor alive. But the Creator is nothing if not a god of justice, and he bestowed upon the people a chance to end the curse."

"Oh? And what is that chance?" asked Owens skeptically.

"It is said that within each generation—about once every fifty years or so—the tribe emerges from the mist that binds them, but only for a single day. However, on that day, a boy is chosen from each band in the tribe. This boy is charged with the duty to go out into the world, to grow up within another tribe so that he might learn of the world that is now in existence, so that he might have his chance to try to undo the curse."

"And you believe this? That the Creator," Owens jeered, "would be putting such a responsibility onto a young lad? It would be quite an undertaking for a youngster, no doubt."

"Indeed," said Rutledge, "you are right, especially since the only clue given to each of the boys is that he must show kindness to an enemy, offer help to a foe.

"Now, many have tried to undo the curse," Rutledge carried on, lowering his voice dramatically. "But according to the legend, most have died in obscurity, shamed at their defeat . . ."

Silence ensued after this statement, broken only by the fire's crackle and sputter. It was some time thereafter before Owens spoke up, asking, "How so that they have died in shame?"

"Apparently," said Rutledge, "the chosen boy has only until his thirtieth birthday to reverse the curse. If he has failed in his quest by then, he will live out his life, still flesh and blood, but forever to carry the knowledge that he failed his people. Most of those chosen—so goes the story—have died trying."

Utter quiet followed in the wake of this explanation, and then Owens asked, "Is it so hard to show an enemy mercy?"

"It does seems incredible, does it not? I can only suppose that there must be more to the undoing of the curse than simply this, for of course it would appear to be such an easy thing to do. But there is more."

"More?"

"Aye," said Rutledge. "I have said nothing about this last, not even to my dear Alice, for even I find it too incredible to be believed . . ."

"Too incredible for you?"

"Aye." Again, Rutledge hesitated, and Effie held her breath. Her father, however, still not knowing of his young audience, went on to say, "My dear friend, Trent Clark, mentioned that the tribe reappears in the flesh for one day about every fifty years—once a generation . . ."

"So you have said."

"And if his calculations were correct," continued Rutledge, "it would be about now that the tribe might reappear."

"Reappear?"

"Aye, the people would become real again—for only a day."

Owens let out his breath in a loud slur, which sliced through the air, magnified because of the silence in this place.

But though the action might have been meant to put Rutledge off, it did not have that effect, for Effie's father continued, "We are here at the right time and in the right place. We might see it . . . we might see them . . ."

Effie caught her breath, then placed her hand over her

mouth, in an ineffective attempt to block out the noise of her gasp. But the sputtering of the fire must have hidden her mistake, for the two adults seemed oblivious to anything but their own conversation.

Might see them. The idea was profound, thought Effie, and even she, an eight-year-old, could envision the outcome, the honor, the excitement of such a thing.

It was a long time before Rutledge spoke again, saying, "Can you imagine what a find it would be to discover those people?"

"Aye," agreed Owens, "that it would be. But who would believe us . . . you, might I ask? If the Clan only surfaces once a generation, and then disappears just as quickly?"

"Humph!" replied Rutledge. "Is it so important to be believed? Think for a moment of the opportunity if it were true . . . think of the questions we might ask those people, the knowledge we might acquire . . ."

"Aye," agreed Owens. "It would, indeed, be an unusual find. But we are not here to locate a *live* people. We are here to determine the past of this place, and to find those artifacts. And if it is a truth that the Lost Clan comes to light in this location, we will find evidence of it."

"But, don't you see? They would be of the past . . . and of the present . . ."

Owens snickered.

Effie's father, however, seemed unaware of his colleague's displeasure, and he said, "Come, and let us go away to our beds. I believe our wives and our children are already fast asleep, and we must be up at the first light. Not only is there the history of a people to uncover, there is a chance that we might discover them in the flesh."

Owens laughed, but it was not one of pleasure. "I cannot say that you have convinced me," he said, "but I am

willing to believe in you, and since you judge that this is
so, who am I to refute you?"

"Indeed!"

Effie heard the two men laugh. She could even imagine that they shook hands. Excitement twisted through
her young body, making sleep all but impossible.

Turning over, she gazed at Lesley. Too bad the elder
girl had missed the story. But Effie felt certain that on the
morrow, Lesley would taunt her until the entire thing was
told.

Maybe she wouldn't relate it.

The thought made Effie smile, since it was exactly
what Lesley would do, were their positions reversed. Effie
yawned and, with the resilience of youth, soon drifted off
to a dream filled with adventure.

CHAPTER 2

Mahkwiyi Istikiop, or Wolf Creek,
Montana Territory
Spring, 1850

Twelve-year-old Red Hawk awoke to the darkness of a new dawn. Reaching out from his sleeping robes, he pulled up the edge of the tepee's bottom, and with a quick motion, glanced outside. As expected, the early hours were painted black, the only color discernible being a misty gray haze that hung over every organic and inorganic thing. The air was still, dull and uninviting, seeming to urge one to slither back into bed. But Red Hawk fought the impulse. There were chores to be done, responsibilities that were his alone to do.

He crawled out from under the tepee's entrance flap and stood. The fog was heavy this day, lingering, as though it refused to give way to day. Striding forward into that mist, Red Hawk cut a glance upward.

It was eerie, he decided, but such things worried him

not. In truth, days like this lifted his spirits. He breathed in deeply.

The dewy air felt refreshing, not gloomy, and he relished its wet touch on his lungs. Truth be known, this was his favorite time of day, when life was awakening, when his heart was fresh and pure, when he was attuned to his environment. It was also a time that allowed him to be alone, and he savored each instant . . . for it was in the leisure of morning that he could dream, wish, hope and plan for a better day.

Aa, that things could be different, thought Red Hawk, for today was a special day. Not for him, never was it so for him. Instead, it was a day for the glory seekers, and perhaps for the old men and women, too.

To be sure, today was the day when the elders would choose the defenders for their people. On this day, another few boys would be selected from the last of the tribal bands; they would go out into the world, to seek their duty to their clan.

If only he could be one of those boys picked. *Haiya,* the battles he would wage, the honor he would bring to his clan, which was the Yellow Shawl Band of his tribe.

"And why not me?" he uttered to no one in particular. "Why cannot I be the chosen one?"

Imagine, he thought, there he would be, venturing forth into a new world. Picking up a stick, he pretended it was his bow, and with several imaginary arrows, he staged a mock battle. Quickly, he shot arrow after arrow, each lodging into the Thunderer's heart.

"I will seek you out, you terrible, murderous Thunder Being," he mumbled. "We will engage in furious battle. A strike here, there a plunge with my spear, and out will pour your coldhearted blood. And then there will be one less evil in the world."

No doubt, the people would consider him a hero, as well, thought Red Hawk. His name would be revered by the women and children, and spoken of in adoration. Songs would be sung to him in camp, praises sent up to the Creator. And lastly, but most importantly, Red Hawk would discharge an obligation he held, a duty to his parents.

"One bad deed for another," grumbled Red Hawk. "And who better to do it than I? Is it not because of you, Thunderer, that my life is in ruin? Is it not because of you that I have no parents? Is it not you, Thunderer, who is the cause of the women in camp calling me, 'Poor Orphan,' a name I despise?"

Red Hawk thrust out his chest with pride and squared back his shoulders. "I will have my day with you, Thunderer. Be not deceived."

But the feeling of having accomplished great deeds was as fleeting as a scattered rain cloud across a desert sun, and Red Hawk slumped forward. Alas, there was little chance of his dreams becoming a reality. For, though Red Hawk, more than anyone else, might merit the right of revenge, it would never be.

Was he not an outsider here? Was it not true that by blood he didn't even belong to this clan, let alone to any particular band in the tribe? All those years ago, it had simply been his parents' bad luck to be visiting the Clan at the time when the people had made battle with the Thunderer.

His mother and father had been part of those killed in the Thunderer's first sweep across the camp, leaving Red Hawk alone. And his fate might have been dubious indeed, for Red Hawk had been practically a newborn, with great need of a mother.

But as chance would have it, an old man had taken Red Hawk in, had found a means to engage a wet nurse, and the boy had been raised by the man he now called "Grandfather." True, Grandfather had adopted Red Hawk officially into this tribe, but this was not the same as being born to it.

And Red Hawk knew the difference.

Impatiently, Red Hawk kicked out at a rock at his feet, his face alive with fury. He hated the Thunderer; hated him for all he had done, for all he did now. Make no mistake, given the chance, Red Hawk would kill the deity.

But enough. For now he would control his impulses, as Grandfather had so painstakenly taught him to do. He would channel his anger, take it out on his chores, as soon as his morning bath was finished.

Bending down, Red Hawk grabbed hold of a long stick, and swishing it out in front of him, as if it were a spear, he cut through the air with it, imagining the Thunderer out in front of him.

"Take that," he said, while quietly jabbing the stick in the air. Serious now, Red Hawk skirted forward, one jump after another, his stance challenging, stick raised. As he did so, he lifted his face and arms upward, and he swore, "I will best you, Thunderer. I promise. Be I champion or not, I will best you."

But there was no answer in the sky, not even a rumble to answer the hopes of the youth.

At last Red Hawk lowered his arms. "I am tired of being called the orphan, the homeless boy, the poor boy," he muttered to no one in particular. Then, raising his face toward the heavens again, he said, "My name is Red Hawk. Remember it, Thunder Being. Red, for the color of war, for the blood shed by my parents. Hawk, for his power, his magnificence, and for his sharp eye. It is a good name. It was my father's name. But it is now mine . . . not 'Poor Orphan' . . ."

When no one arose to challenge him, Red Hawk assumed he was still alone, and he continued, "My father was a heroic man, a good man who died defending a people who were not even his own. Red Hawk was his name. Before he died, my father bestowed the name on me. And I accept it. Someday," he muttered, looking over his shoulder, "everyone in this camp will sing praises to that name."

Red Hawk made another pass with the stick, only to throw it down in disgust. What was he doing playing a child's game? He was twelve winters in age, almost a man. He had best start acting like one. Pushing aside his emotions, Red Hawk took a step forward along his path to the river.

"Grandson." A heavy hand fell to Red Hawk's shoulder.

Red Hawk jerked his chin up and turned to stare behind him. There stood his grandfather, the man's whitened hair held in two braids at each side of his weathered face.

"Yes, Grandfather?" said Red Hawk. As was custom, and because he held the utmost respect for his elders, Red Hawk said no more, though he longed to know why his grandfather was up and about so early. Normally, his elder awoke with the rising of the sun, and that time was still far away.

"The council of the elders has already been held," said Grandfather.

Red Hawk nodded. He knew what that meant, of course: Champions had been chosen. His insides twisted. Yet Red Hawk pretended indifference; it had little to do with him.

But Grandfather was speaking, and he said, "It is important that you learn what has been decided."

Why? thought Red Hawk. Why should he desire to participate in some other boy's glory? Wasn't it enough that most of the other boys in camp chided him? Why should he celebrate their victory?

Still, he could not bring himself to put these questions to his grandfather—to do so would be the height of dishonor, since it would show disrespect to a man who had given Red Hawk nothing but love.

And so the boy let Grandfather lead him to White Claw, the Clan's wisest of men. Throwing back the flap of White Claw's lodge, Red Hawk's grandfather stepped into the tepee's quiet interior, and Red Hawk followed.

White Claw was seated against his backrest, which was made of willow branches. White Claw looked perceptive, yet worried. Suspended from a tripod close to hand was White Claw's medicine bundle, as well as his quiver, decorated blue and white with porcupine quills. Arrows, meticulously fashioned to be straight, filled that quiver.

A lining, painted red and yellow, skirted the entire circumference of the tepee. In the center of the lodge was the ever-present fire, though its embers at this early hour were low.

Once seated, Red Hawk covertly glanced around him, taking in those assembled here. And though no boy's countenance showed the results of what had occurred only moments ago, it was plain that a council decision had already been made. Why was *he* here?

The boys from Red Hawk's own tribal band were Talks-straight and Shows-the-enemy. Both were seated near places of honor. Neither spared Red Hawk a glance.

Also present in the council was a boy, Runs-with-his-horse, from the Black Fire Band of the tribe. That one looked proud, distinguished. Not so Talks-straight or Shows-the-enemy.

At last White Claw picked up his great pipe, filling it

with the sacred tobacco, a combination of not only ordi-
nary tobacco, but also the inner bark of the red willow.
Hesitating first, he took a puff, then passed the pipe to
Red Hawk.

As soon as Red Hawk had smoked and delivered the
pipe back to its owner, White Claw spoke. He said, "You,
Poor Orphan, have been chosen as champion for the Yellow Shawl Band."

For the beat of a moment, Red Hawk forgot to breathe.
He? Was this possible?

And though this news both shocked and excited him,
as was the way of most American Indians, Red Hawk
kept his emotions as carefully hidden as possible.

"Perhaps it is well that you understand that you are our
last choice," spoke White Claw. "Both Talks-straight and
Shows-the-enemy were first looked to as the Yellow Shawl
Band's champions. But Talks-straight fell, upon entering
the lodge this morning, and it appears that he has broken
his arm."

Glancing toward Talks-straight, Red Hawk noticed first
the grimace of frustration on the other boy's countenance.
Then he gazed briefly toward Talks-straight's arm, which
Talks-straight was trying to hide from view.

But White Claw wasn't finished; he went on to say,
"We then looked to Shows-the-enemy. But Shows-the-
enemy contracted a fever early this morning and must be
attended to here. Though he assures us that he could still
represent his band, we cannot send him on a task such as
this when he is sick."

Red Hawk said nothing. Good manners, however, dic-
tated that he give his elder a nod, that he might indicate
that he had heard, and had understood what had been said.
This, he did.

"Therefore we have no choice," continued White Claw,

"but to enlist your aid in representing your band of the tribe in this, our most desperate need. Though you do not belong to the Clan by blood, it is still the family in which you have been raised. We look to you, Red Hawk, to do your best. It is an honorable thing that we ask. But know that there will be much danger. As in all deeds, no man, no lad, need go where he does not will it. What say you? Will you accept the challenge?"

Red Hawk opened his mouth to speak, but found to his horror that he could not. His tongue felt stuck to the roof of his mouth.

White Claw repeated, "You may refuse if you wish. It is your right."

Still Red Hawk found that his speech wouldn't coordinate with his will, and all he could do was sputter.

"What say you?" prompted White Claw. "Do you wish more time to consider?"

When Red Hawk's trouble persisted, he did the only thing available to him: He nodded, using signs and gestures to communicate his acceptance. It was only when White Claw said in response, "It is well," that Red Hawk found he could at last utter, "Honored . . . I would be honored."

Grandfather smiled, but not so any other man in the council. In truth, most of the elders looked disgruntled, perhaps a little stunned. The two boys, however—those who might have been chosen, were they well enough—appeared angry and dispirited.

White Claw, however, had more to say to both Red Hawk and the other lad present, Runs-with-his-horse. Said White Claw, "Remember that you will each one go out into the world and become a part of another tribe. Runs-with-his-horse, you will seek out the Crow. Poor Orphan, you will go to the Southern Pikuni, our brothers. Learn who are their enemies, study your adopted tribe well, and remember the words of the Creator, 'Show kindness, help your enemies, understand them.' For had we as a clan done so in the past, we would not now be enslaved."

Both Runs-with-his-horse and Red Hawk nodded.

"Remember, Poor Orphan," continued White Claw directly, "that you are your band's champion. You are not on an errand of revenge. Study the Pikuni people well, learn who are their enemies, show their foes mercy, give aid, but most importantly, do not engage in battle with the Thunderer, even if you are challenged." White Claw focused on the young boy, and, as though drawn by his elder's glance, Red Hawk gazed into the medicine man's eyes.

"I must seek your word on this, Poor Orphan."

Once more incapable of speech, Red Hawk simply nodded.

It was enough.

"Very good," said White Claw. "You each one have until your thirtieth birthday to lift the curse. Your people are depending on you. Know this: The curse *can* be broken, for there are now three bands of our people who are no longer with us, having been released out of the mist. Learn well and quickly. Do not be diverted by things of the flesh or of revenge." He stared at Red Hawk. "If you are successful, you will be honored by your people for all time. If you fail—as many others have done before you— you will live out the rest of your life in the flesh, knowing that you failed your people in their most urgent time of need. Remember to show kindness, give mercy, help an enemy. We look to you as our hope . . . our only hope."

With this said, White Claw emptied the ashes of the ceremonial pipe into a shell directly in front of him. It was a signal that the council was at an end. "That is all."

The boys, all four of them, along with Red Hawk's

grandfather, rose up and as a single body exited White Claw's lodge.

Once gone, White Claw sighed deeply and turned to the chief of the Yellow Shawl Band. "Have hope, my friend. Although I realize that it is a bleak day when we must choose Poor Orphan as a champion for your people, perhaps he will rise to the challenge."

"But to send such a one?" said the chief. "He, who exhibits many of the same traits as the Thunderer himself?"

"*Aa*, yes," replied White Claw.

But the chief of the Yellow Shawl Band was not finished, and he said, "Is it not true that Red Hawk is quick to anger? That he is hard to forgive others, and even when the chance has been presented to him to show mercy, he has never yet given another quarter?"

"*Aa*, yes, it is so. But what else could we do? We could not send those who are sick or injured. And think well, my friend. Is it not true that in the past, all of the boys you have thought would qualify for this honor have failed?"

When the chief nodded, White Claw continued. "Maybe the boy will come into his own. Perhaps he will find the strength to conquer the evil that at times possesses him. We can only pray that it will be so. For, my friend, the deed is now done."

The chief of the Yellow Shawl Band grunted, frowning. He said, "*Aa*, it is done. But, though you are wise, I do not share your optimism."

White Claw merely smiled before saying, "Fret not. Remember that there is always the chance to end the curse within the next generation."

However, the chief of the Yellow Shawl Band was not to be so easily placated. With a look of utter disgust, he shook his head bitterly. Then at last, he rose up to take his leave of the council.

White Claw, last to exit his own lodge, sat for many moments in reflection. But then, he, too, arose. There was much to be done today to prepare these youths. He had best make ready for the next council.

CHAPTER 3

Setting down her trowel, redheaded Effie Rutledge knew the time had come for a break. She exhaled deeply, and straightening up, wiped her brow of perspiration. Having helped her parents at the site of the dig throughout the early morning hours, she had done her duty, at least for awhile. It was time for a bath.

"I am so hot," she whined, started to pout, but then thought better of her actions, and in a more adult voice asked, "May I go swimming?"

With a quick nod and a sweet smile, Alice Rutledge endorsed the action. She did advise, however, "Stay close. It's still quite hazy out this morning, and I don't want you missing a step and falling."

"I won't do that, and I will stay close," Effie responded, and immediately her spirits lifted. If there were one thing that Effie liked most about accompanying her mother and father on these excavations, it was the sense of freedom she enjoyed. No one—outside of Lesley Owens—treated her as if she were too young to know her

own mind. And perhaps it was in response to her parents'
trust that Effie behaved herself uncommonly well.

Tantrums were an unknown affair. Truth be told, Effie
considered herself as adult as the next person. She was
simply trapped inside a child's body.

"Is Lesley going with you?" Alice Rutledge asked her
daughter.

"No," replied Effie. "She's left with one of Father's
students, someone named William, I think. They said they
were going to survey the lay of the land."

"Oh," responded Mrs. Rutledge. "That's nice."

Effie sighed. "Yes, Mother. Now, may I go swimming?"

"Of course, dear."

"Thank you."

Deciding to leave before her mother changed her mind
or asked more questions, Effie padded toward her favorite
spot. She could almost see the place from the excavation
site.

Caught off to the side of the Big River—or the Missouri River—was a splendid water hole. Not too deep,
not too shallow, the place was hidden from view by long,
green prairie grasses, as well as pine, cottonwoods and a
magnificent willow. In the distance—and able to be seen
from the pool on most days—were white-capped mountains, which favored the land with a fairy-tale appeal. It
was the ideal place for a quick dip.

Of course Effie knew it was dangerous to swim
alone—and briefly she wished that Lesley were a little
more friendly toward her, for it would be fun to have a
swimming companion. But Lesley's attitude in regards to
Effie was far from amicable—except, of course, when
Lesley wanted something.

Perhaps Lesley thought Effie too young; certainly,
Effie was the younger by four years. But in attitude, Effie

considered herself to be the more mature of the two of them. Alas, if truth be told, Lesley exhibited more tantrums than Effie had ever witnessed in anyone.

As Effie trod toward the water, she couldn't help but notice the profusion of pink wildflowers whose fragrances filled the air with a sweet scent. She touched their soft, dewy petals as she passed by them, her fingers coming away wet from the encounter.

Odd, she thought, in places this morning, the fog was so thick, she could barely see her hand as she flattened it over the grasses and flowers. But in other areas, the haze was starting to dissipate, lending to the land a cathedral-like profusion of golden streams of light slanting through the mist.

For an instant, Effie caught her breath, so beautiful was the sight—so profound. The moment felt sacred, as though she were close to something . . . something wonderful. Perhaps it was the Creator that she felt so near, since such beauty could not be by accident.

She let out her breath. It was a good way to start the day, and as she stripped off her dress, her petticoats and chemise, throwing them to the side, peace filled her soul. She left her square-toed boots on her feet, however, so that her tender toes need not tread on any sharp rocks; her pantalettes also remained in place, since she couldn't bring herself to strip to bare skin from the waist down. Her drawers were green, not white, as a woman's pantalettes might be. Green, because her mother had made them from the canvaslike material of an old tent.

At last Effie was ready to swim, and unafraid, she waded into the water.

In truth, there was little need for fear. The swimming hole was close to her parents' dig, well within earshot were there to be any trouble. And Effie was an experienced swimmer, her parents having schooled her in the techniques of lifesaving when she was so young, she could barely crawl. Thus, Effie felt safe and quite exuberant.

The water was only ankle deep at the shoreline, but it was cool and refreshing, as she had known it would be. Soon, Effie plunged into the water completely, wetting herself from the top of her very red head to the bottom of her heavy, wet boots. Surfacing, she grinned.

What pleasure!

As Red Hawk trod a path to the water, a few rays of golden sunlight had pushed their way through the fog. In response, the ground came alive, welcoming the warmth of those beams. Here, and as far as the eye could see, the lush, green earth was covered with a misty haze. Mother Earth was awakening.

The early morning scents of grass and pine were bursting with aroma, sweetening the atmosphere. The terrain was solid and firm beneath Red Hawk's feet; and the air enveloped the boy in a cool embrace. But Red Hawk barely noticed the Earth and all her scents and secrets, so inward was his attention.

In truth, he was confused.

This was to be his last day in camp. On the morrow, he would awaken, never to see Grandfather or any of the people again, unless he were successful in lifting the curse . . . which might be many years in the future. And though Red Hawk had often wished for this very opportunity, the reality of it was more than he could easily assimilate.

He would have eighteen years in which to break the curse. Surely, he could accomplish this. For truly, it seemed like a great deal of time had been allotted him.

However, if that be true, why was the spell proving to

be so hard for others to break? So many champions before him; so many failures.

Would he be successful? He certainly hoped that he
would be, although . . . Without even starting his mission,
he was disadvantaged, and he knew it. Alas, if given a
choice between breaking the curse or seeking the revenge
that was so rightfully his to take, what would be his
choice?

If he were to be honest with himself—and he must be
truthful—Red Hawk would admit that he was unable to
answer that question. And it was this fact, all by itself,
that worried him, for he had given his word to White
Claw to forego seeking revenge on the Thunderer.

But perhaps, he assured himself, he would never be required to make the choice, in which case such meditation
was foolish.

"Remember Grandfather in all things," he muttered to
himself. "Remember Grandfather."

And so it was that Red Hawk was grumbling when he
saw her.

There, sitting on a rock at the edge of the pool, was the
most unusual, but perhaps the most beautiful creature he
had ever witnessed. He stared. Was she a vision?

She could be, for he was unable to see the girl as well
as he might; the ever-present mist that swirled around her
made her appear dreamlike. Yet, for some unknown reason, he felt certain she was real.

Was she part fish?

No, she must be human, he thought. She looked
human . . . well, at least she did from the waist up. But
she was certainly like no other being he had ever seen.
For one thing, her hair was a dark shade of red, not black
or brown, and the locks of her mane were curling about
her head in cascading spirals. Her skin color was a shade

or two whiter than that to which he was accustomed, as well, but not enough to draw a great deal of notice.

From her waist upward, she wore nothing, but this seemed a usual sort of happenstance. Most of the children in the village ran naked, and she was a child, he determined, since, from his view of her, she had thus far developed nothing which, due to modesty, must be hidden.

But . . . did she have legs?

Red Hawk couldn't be certain. From the waist downward, it appeared that she no longer grew skin. All he could see from there downward was green. Surely most forms of human beings were not green on the bottom, were they?

Was she a white person? Had there not been rumors in the tribe about such people? Stories that the tribal medicine man, White Claw, had seen such people and had talked to them? Were white people half fish?

Slowly, as silently as he could, Red Hawk crept toward the girl, and was almost upon her, when she moved, stretching. Her hands came up to push back her hair, as though she were combing it with her fingers.

Without warning, she turned toward him. Her eyes were big, he noted, a light shade of brown, and she stared straight at him.

He froze.

She grinned.

What happened then Red Hawk could never explain, nor did he ever wish to. One moment he was on his feet, the next, he was tripping all over himself. Suddenly he was all hands and legs, and they seemed to be going in all directions at once. The result of course was that he landed on the ground none too delicately, and quite on his rump.

"Hello," she said, when things had settled down. "Who are you?"

But Red Hawk had no conception of what she said, or

even if her words were part of a language. Was she singing? She might be; her voice was that beautiful.

Looking up at her, for he had yet to arise, he said, *"Oki,"* deciding that it was best to greet her politely.

But she frowned, clearly not educated in the great language of his people.

"Who are you?" she repeated. However, since he didn't understand her, and vice versa, he used sign language to help impart his meaning.

Yet, even in this, a most basic form of communication, she seemed adrift, for she frowned at him, clearly not understanding him or what he said. But the scowl on her face seemed unable to take permanent hold on one so bright and cheery, and very soon the grimace had transformed into an easy smile.

Maybe that was his undoing, he thought. The grin. It is said that there are people whose faces glow when they smile, as though lit from within with magic.

She might be such a one. For when Red Hawk looked into her eyes, he thought that surely he had eaten something bad this day. His innards were awash in butterflies.

"Well, no matter who you are," said the girl after awhile, "would you like to swim with me?" Then she bestowed upon him yet another of those beguiling grins.

He froze, gaping. He knew of nothing else to do but stare at her.

When he didn't respond to her question at once, she made hand motions at him, giving him to understand that she was about to fly into the air . . . or at least that's what he thought she said.

Was she a goddess, then? he wondered.

He frowned at her and she giggled, and with a single hand motion, she invited him to join her. Then, as quick as all that, she slipped into the water.

Was he to follow? Was she a water being, after all?

Blackfeet legends told of such beings. There were said to be nymphs, sometimes monsters, who were sent from the water's depths only to lure a man to his death.

Perhaps she was such a one. Mayhap he should use caution.

Red Hawk, however, ignored any prudence. He was curious about her, after all, and she was . . . different. Besides, though he was only twelve winters old, at this moment he felt very much the male of the species.

With nary a thought for personal danger, he followed the girl into the water. If she were a siren leading him to his death, he wondered, why would some men fear it?

But she wasn't about death, he soon came to understand. She was about playing . . . and fun. And there was no great need to translate languages when the object of the game was to decide who was "it."

"Catch me," she said, as she tagged him with the slightest brush of her hand. He watched as she dived underwater, then he followed her, letting her take the lead.

She is not a fish, he came to understand as he opened his eyes underwater. *Nor is she a siren, or a goddess.*

She swam by use of hands and legs, not fins, he observed. And what he had thought might have been scales from her waist down were nothing more than the ugliest sort of leggings he had ever seen.

Why would a girl swim in such things? And with her footgear still on? He, himself, was dressed only in his breechcloth.

Catching up with her, he tagged her.

Still underwater, she spun around, and though they were both beneath the surface, she smiled at him. But then, as quick as that, she lunged toward him, her arm extended.

He backed up, but his heart wasn't into retreating from her, and he let her touch him. Her hand was soft, delicate, and he was pondering the experience, when all at once, she struck out, away from him.

They both surfaced.

"I am the better swimmer of the two of us," she taunted him, before she giggled. And though Red Hawk couldn't discern the words, her meaning was clear. She was playing to win.

He realized his mistake at once. If he were to earn her respect, he would have to prevail in this game. However, he was wise enough to realize that he best not shove defeat at her too soon; *saa*, he would need to win this game with her blessing and goodwill. Not an easy feat for a boy of twelve.

"*Kika*, wait," he called out in the Blackfeet tongue. "*Poohsapoot*, come here! Let us define this game."

But she paid him no heed, and not because she didn't understand him, language barrier or not.

He followed her, tagged her, but he didn't at once retreat. Instead, opening his arms, he invited her to touch him back. To this end, he swam around her, leaping to and fro, but always at her arm's length.

Tentatively, doubtfully, she reached out toward him. And she had almost grazed him again, when he extended his hands toward her instead. He tickled her.

"No fair," she laughed, doubling up. "Your arms are longer than mine. Now, no tickling."

He didn't understand her words, though he was fairly certain he comprehended exactly what she wanted. Grinning at her, he repeated the action.

"No!" she said, and there was no mistaking the intent of that word. He wasn't about to end the game, however, not yet, and so he danced around her once again, his arms wide open and tempting her to make him "it."

"What are you doing?" she asked, her gaze following him as he swam easily around her.

But he didn't answer. Instead, reaching out, he tugged at one of her curls.

"Stop that!" she ordered sharply; nonetheless, she was laughing.

He repeated the action.

"Oh, this is not fair. You are bigger than I am and your arms are longer." She leaped toward him suddenly. But he backed away, just in time, his arms still open as he trod water, offering her a clear target.

She laughed and he joined in with her.

And so it was that the morning hours wore on. Back and forth they played, Red Hawk allowing the beautiful water spirit to win the game of tag. But never more than he.

"Oh, you are too much for me," she declared, smiling up at him. "Unfortunately, I must pronounce you the winner, though I think you have a terrible advantage over me." As if to compensate for the inequality, she reached down in the water and pulled off each of her shoes in turn. She said, "Why did I not think of this before now? These awful pantalettes I am wearing get in my way and my boots drag me down, while you have only your breechcloth to restrict you. No wonder you are able to taunt me."

Taking aim, she threw first one boot at the shoreline, and then the other. Her hurl wasn't accurate, he noted, and one by one, each shoe fell short of the shore, plopping into the water, their hard leather causing them to sink swiftly. At once gallant, Red Hawk propelled himself forward, capturing one shoe, then the other.

She followed, wading right up to him, where she extended out her hand, asking for the boots. One by one, he presented the shoes to their owner, his hand lingering over the last boot before dropping his arm to his side.

"Thank you," she said, looking up at him. Smiling, she held her shoes against her breast and pointed to herself, saying, "Effie. Can you say that? Effie," again she indicated herself.

"Eh-h-h–eee," he repeated.

She nodded. "Close enough. And you are?" She indicated him.

Words and gestures aside, he knew instinctively what she asked, but it was beyond his means to tell her what she desired. Somewhat alarmed—for an Indian would never ask another his name—Red Hawk tried to justify her action. She was not from here, he decided. She might not know the protocols of his polite society.

For one, a man never spoke his name aloud. Not only was it a taboo, it was also considered boastful, for names often told of great deeds.

Also, Red Hawk was reluctant to willingly utter the name that the others in the Clan called him. His name was Red Hawk, not "Poor Orphan." And even if she wouldn't understand the words, he could not bring himself to say them.

He gazed away from her, prompting her to try again. Pointing to him, she said, "And you are?"

This time Red Hawk shrugged, and, turning away from her, he swam back toward the middle of the pond. There he waited, motioning her forward, asking her with signs to continue their game.

But she shook her head. "Aren't you going to tell me your name?" she asked. "After we have spent such a remarkable morning together? What am I to call you?"

Red Hawk feigned misunderstanding, saying nothing.

"Oh, very well," she uttered, clearly exasperated. "It's

not very much to ask, though, is it? I'd just like to know what to say if I'm to address you. Will you be here tomorrow?"

Again, he remained silent, not understanding her words, though he did motion her once more to join him in the center of the pool.

But she shook her head. Turning, she began to wade closer to the shoreline. "I can't," she said. "Don't misunderstand me. It's not because you won't tell me your name or anything, but my parents might become concerned if I am gone too long. Already I've been here for several hours, and so I must return to them. I have enjoyed your company, though." And with a grin that was half apology, she turned to leave the water.

A feeling of loss swept over Red Hawk, and he swam in toward the shoreline, following her. Coming up behind her, he touched her gently on the shoulder to get her attention, then taking hold of her hand, he guided it to his shoulder, where he allowed her to "tag" him.

Averting his gaze, Red Hawk started to draw back from her, but she held on to him tightly. Curious, his glance met hers, became lost in hers.

"I have enjoyed my morning swim with you," she said earnestly, the honest appeal in her eyes intriguing. At last, she let go of him, and reaching her hands up behind her neck, she unfastened the necklace that she wore—one made of a gold-colored substance. Placing the necklace in her small hand, she extended the jewelry toward him.

"Take it," she said, when Red Hawk didn't immediately reach out to capture it. "Take it," she repeated, motioning toward it and then to him.

At length, he nodded and reaching out, grasped hold of the prize.

"There," she said, "that wasn't so hard, was it?"

But he didn't understand her meaning; the words were not easily discerned.

Looking down at himself, as he stood before her in only his breechcloth, he searched his body for a gift he might give her.

But what? There was little that he owned.

Time seemed short as he pondered the problem, and he had almost given up the idea altogether, when he remembered . . . his earrings. The white shell earrings he wore were of some value.

Once they had been his mother's. Now they would be hers.

Unfastening them, he placed two white shells in his palm, extending his hand toward her.

"For me?" she said, and he nodded.

Her tiny fingers slid over his palm as she reached for the prize. Red Hawk was amazed that a simple touch should make him feel as if he were suddenly falling through space.

"I don't know why I should say this to you," she said, "for I know that you cannot understand me—and perhaps that is why I feel I *must* say this—but I think I have fallen in love with you." Her hand briefly clasped his.

And then it was over; she turned away, and hurrying off in a direction opposite to that of his own camp, she was almost out of sight, when she suddenly spun back. Running toward him, she came right up to him, said, "I almost forgot," and standing on the tips of her toes, she brought her face up to his, where she placed a kiss on his cheek.

She giggled and said, "I hope to see you here tomorrow." Flashing him one last grin, she fled.

She didn't look back, and maybe it was good that she hadn't. For, in response to that kiss, slight though it was,

Red Hawk had taken a few quick steps toward her as if to reciprocate, when suddenly, he became so uncoordinated, he tripped over himself.

Once again, the earth cushioned his fall. Once again, he lay flat on his fanny.

But though she had not spared Red Hawk a final glance, he watched her, looking at the place where she had disappeared for a long time, as though her impression still remained there.

"*Otahkohsoa' tsis*, Red Hawk," he said to the air, as if it might carry his words to her. "Red Hawk is my name." And so distracted was he that he didn't notice White Claw and the chief of the Yellow Shawl Band appear beside the stream and step toward him.

Luckily, so befuddled was Red Hawk that he didn't hear the chief of the Yellow Shawl Band say, none too gently, "This is the chosen one?"

The elderly gentleman shook his head. "Oh," continued the chief, "that we had another . . ."

CHAPTER 4

**The mining settlement of Virginia City,
Montana Territory
May 1867**

Effie stared at her reflection in the broken mirror before allowing her gaze to alight on the starkness of the room behind her. One single bed, one broken chair, one oval-shaped, dirty rug and nothing else to decorate the cheap hotel room, except perhaps the grime left by the last resident. Dust, which looked to be months deep, covered everything, and the scent of mold was enough to cause even a strong heart to weep.

Was this shabby arrangement the best they could do? Sighing, Effie realized that it was.

"'Tis my least favorite element of a dig," she told her reflection. "Why is it that the beginning of an expedition must entail staying in cheap quarters and eating food not fit for a dog?" She shook her head in resignation.

And yet you love the adventure, her reflection seemed to reach out to her and say.

"No, I don't," Effie muttered back to the mirror. "Oh, I must admit that I would rather be here than tied to some man who might force me to stay home, attending to his needs. That kind of life would be a sort of slavery for me." She drew in closer to the mirror, as though to study in more detail the light brown of her eyes, as well as her upturned nose. "Not that I haven't felt the urge to marry and raise a family. But at least, the desire has been only occasional, thank God.

"However, at the age of twenty-five," she continued to lecture herself, "I may have missed my chance at marriage . . ." Her voice trailed away. Then, clearing her throat, she carried on, saying, "No great loss. After all, the position as a teacher is a good one, and it is a trade that allows me to work in the field of archaeology. Besides, this excavation may very well be the most important one of my career."

Reaching into one of the drawers of the hotel room's vanity, Effie extracted a knapsack and unfolded the leather to reveal two objects heavily wrapped in protective brown paper. Out of habit, she glanced quickly around the room before unwrapping the two pieces of quartz, which were about four inches in height, and two and one-half inches across. Though recently polished, the artifacts were ancient. Gently, she ran her fingers over the intricate gold moldings that were forever etched within the niche of the quartz. The impressions were figurines, half bird, half human.

The first relic had been bequeathed to her father long ago by Trent Clark; the second her father had found . . . quite by accident, having discovered the piece while digging for worms for fishing. Exuberant over his find, Walter Rutledge would have planned more explorations long ago, but something unforeseen had happened. The War between the States had broken out, and Rutledge, as determined to join the fight as the next man, had spent his energy in the war.

Sadly, there had been no further expeditions since Walter Rutledge had sustained permanent injuries.

Effie breathed out deeply in resignation as she returned her attention to the pieces of ancient sculpture. Both objects were light, probably weighing no more than two pounds each, but they were valuable. Not in terms of the amount of gold to be found in them, but because they were ancient, rare and the effects of a legend.

In truth, if she'd had her way, she would have left them both back East, safely locked in a security box. But this wasn't entirely her decision to make.

Her father and mother, though both were still situated back East, held sway over the particulars of this excavation. And it was her father who had determined that the artifacts were safer traveling with her than staying back East. That there had been two attempts to steal them had given him cause to believe this, and he had not relented in that viewpoint.

Knock, knock.

Effie jumped, so lost had she been in past reflections. "Who is it?"

"It's Lesley," said a voice on the other side of the door. It was Lesley Owens-Smith. "May I come in?"

"Yes, but allow me a moment, please," Effie replied. Hastily, she rewrapped the figurines, placed them back into the knapsack and gently returned them to the vanity drawer. "All right," said Effie, "come in."

The door opened and in walked a woman who was probably the most beautiful person of Effie's acquaintance. As was common with Lesley, she looked as stylish as if she had stepped off a Godey's fashion plate. Her dress was a tomato red silk tartan plaid with velvet trim, the skirt stylishly flatter in front than in the back. Her flaxen blond hair was caught back in a snood, and instead of a hat, she wore a ribbon on the crown of her head.

It was early morning, and Effie glanced down at herself, as if in comparison, her own figure still enwrapped in a green silk morning gown. It was something she usually refrained from doing—comparing herself with Lesley, since in Effie's opinion it was a useless endeavor. She simply didn't measure up to Lesley's standards.

However, even the best intentions can go astray, and Effie found herself still focusing on the differences between the two of them. While Lesley's eyes were a deep blue, Effie's were light brown. Lesley was taller than she was, as well, and older, but only by a few years.

Both women were slender, but Lesley's figure was on the voluptuous side, whereas Effie's curves, while still hourglass, were smoother and more gradual. The two women both loved archaeology and had deemed the field worthy of their endeavor; they had grown up with parents who were not only fast friends, but also companions and colleagues. By all rights, Effie and Lesley, too, should be friends.

But they weren't.

Oh, they liked each other well enough, Effie supposed. But even as children, they had never taken much pleasure in each other's company.

Effie considered herself the more serious student of archaeology. While Lesley, in her opinion, tended to dabble—according to her interest, which fluctuated. It wasn't that Lesley didn't have the knowledge of what to do or how to do it, it was that she lacked the discipline so necessary in this field. Always something besides the matter at hand would catch her eye, and, truth be told, even marriage hadn't seemed to tame the coquette in her behavior.

Effie sighed and cautioned herself against such negativity. Lesley was a friend. It wasn't her fault any more than it was Effie's that the two of them were simply not close.

"It's a dull morning, I'm afraid," said Lesley as she sat down on the end of the bed.

"Is it?"

"Yes, quite dreary, actually. It's foggy out again. How I would have loved to stay abed this morning. But you know how Henry is—this being his first expedition—and he has to be up and on the go long before even the birds awaken. Sometimes his enthusiasm dampens mine."

Effie smiled.

"What are our plans for the day?" asked Lesley, and without awaiting a reply, she went on to ask, "And have you heard from my parents?"

"I have not heard from your parents, but I still expect them to join us in a few weeks' time, and I'd like to have all our supplies settled and our guide hired so that when they do catch up with us, we will be ready to go."

Lesley nodded. "Please, refresh my memory. The purpose of this dig is . . . ?"

"To uncover evidence that the legend of the Lost Clan is real, and if possible to find the missing artifacts, and if we do, to return them to the Clan."

"Hells bells," said Lesley, "it is a rather unusual dig, isn't it?"

"In what way?"

Lesley slanted her a look before saying, "Well, ever since I can remember, my parents have drilled into me the ethics of not keeping artifacts, but rather turning them over to a museum or some other similar institution. 'We are not collectors,' they would say to me. But really, we don't intend to do that in this case, do we?"

"You know that we don't," said Effie.

Lesley lifted her shoulders. "Then you must grasp what I mean about the unusual nature of this dig."

"Yes . . . but you do remember that my father gave his word to Mr. Clark, don't you? And—"

"Don't get me wrong," said Lesley, interrupting. "I'm not disagreeing, I'm simply of the opinion that this dig is . . . different. It's more in the field of anthropology than archaeology, since we're hoping to study a people not only by means of the things they left behind, but also by meeting them face-to-face . . . if that's even possible."

Effie shrugged. "I admit it doesn't seem very plausible. Yet, I am committed to continuing my father's work—and your father's, too."

Lesley sighed. "Yes, yes. It's all rather dull, though, isn't it? Oh, did you see the bathing suit that I brought with me? It's the very latest thing."

Effie grinned pleasantly. "No more swimming in a blue gown for you, then?"

"Have you seen these new suits?"

"Yes, I believe I did notice them in a fashion magazine or two."

"Oh, they are the sweetest things," said Lesley. "Trousers, much like knickerbockers, and a blouse-tunic with a belt. Mine is in blue flannel. Would you like to see it?"

"Oh course." Effie smiled. "But you should wear it so that I can properly admire it."

Lesley beamed. "Yes, yes, I agree. And that would

be fun, wouldn't it?" She rose to her feet. "I will return momentarily." And with this said, Lesley swept out of the room.

Meanwhile, Effie returned her attention to the task at hand before the interruption, and stepping toward the vanity, she assured herself that the artifacts were still intact and well wrapped. She shut the drawer.

It was strange, really, that her father had entrusted the care of them to her and not to his best friend, John Owens. It wasn't that Effie didn't like having the responsibility— in truth, it was a point of pride that her father trusted the valuables to her—it was simply that, outside of the two students who accompanied her, Effie was the youngest member of the team—and yet she was the one in charge of the entire affair.

She could only hope that John Owens would not resent the fact.

Still at the mirror, Effie looked up and smiled at her reflection. *How glad I am to be back in the Montana Territory. Alas, I was beginning to despair that I might never see this country's beautiful mountains and wide-open spaces again.*

The knock at the door was expected, and glancing up, she called out, "Come in."

Lesley came into the room, modeling the bathing suit, turning this way and that.

"Oh, it's wonderful." Effie chuckled pleasantly. "Look at how it effectively covers you, yet it is evident that you will have freedom when you swim. Have you tried it in the water yet?"

"No, I haven't," said Lesley. "But I am anxious to do so. Would you like to come swimming with me today?"

"I would love to," said Effie, "but you know that I can't.

I must hire a guide as soon as possible. I really do want to be prepared so that when your parents arrive, we will not be delayed because of me."

Lesley made a face. "They wouldn't mind. They are used to me delaying them."

"Yes, I'm sure they are quite forgiving," said Effie. "But still, this is the first time I have been the director of a project and I am anxious to prove myself. I only hope that your father is not upset that it was I who was put in charge of it."

Lesley made a face. "Far from it. You know how studious he and my mother are. They are simply happy to be coming back to this territory."

"As am I," said Effie.

Lesley tilted her head to the side. "I guess I am, too. But I had better go and change before Henry comes back from his breakfast. Heaven forbid I keep him waiting." With another smile and a wave of her hand, she opened the door.

Effie waved, as well. "Till later, then."

Lesley disappeared in a rush of flannel swimming wear.

Effie closed the door. What she hadn't told Lesley was that she, too, had brought a swimming costume with her. But hers lay at the bottom of her trunk, unworn and unused, since she had not yet found the courage to wear it in private, let alone in a public place. Nor did she presume to wear it here, since the world at large still considered such things scandalous.

And she of all people needed to keep up a professional appearance. But this was, after all, Montana . . . would it really be such a risk?

She exhaled on a sigh. She had best be about her business.

The longer she delayed, the more costly the project. And goodness knows, she'd had enough problems funding this excavation. Indeed, if not for her father's influence, she might still be seeking the means.

But her father's name was well known in the field of archaeology, and that alone had helped her to raise the funds. Of course, John Owens and his wife had helped in their own way, too, by lending Effie encouragement.

Therefore, it had been no strain when Effie had granted Mr. Owens his one request: to allow him and his wife to accompany her on the dig. Effie had already been intending to ask them both to be part of her crew, especially since John Owens's experience would make him an ideal field supervisor.

Again, she worried over Mr. Owens's possible resentment of her position, if only because, due to his age and background, he should have been the one to have it.

Frowning, Effie returned to the vanity, where she again checked the safety of the artifacts . . . an unnecessary precaution. There they were, still wrapped in their little knapsacks.

She really had to find a more secure spot for them. But where? If she carried a locked box in her possession, others might become suspicious. Especially when thus far she had tried to give the members of the project the impression that the artifacts were stored somewhere else—safe, hidden.

Of course they all knew that she would have to carry the valuables with her once they were en route to the digging site. Even her students were aware of this.

After all, the main purpose of this expedition was to find the remaining two artifacts, place them with the two she carried and return them all to the Lost Clan. Although exactly how she was to go about that, she didn't know. Her father had said it would be evident at the time. She only hoped that were true.

Mindlessly, she shut the drawer and picked up her brush, wiping it on her skirts to ensure its cleanliness before stroking it through the reddish waves of her hair. Gently, she patted each curl neatly into place.

At least she and her students, who were here to relocate the site of the dig, were to be in this dull mining town for a short while only—not more than a few weeks. By that time Mr. Owens and his wife should have caught up with them, and their party would be complete and on its way.

But while in Virginia City, it would be her crew's job—well, mostly hers—to enlist a guide who was trustworthy, since she and her party would be traveling over unknown and dangerous territory. She must also ensure the project possessed the proper equipment, as well as a supply of rations that would carry them through the winter months, if need be. There would also be trowels and shovels to buy, shears, brushes, knives, plus many journals for their various reports.

Placing the hairbrush back onto the vanity, Effie rose and stepped softly toward the lone window, which was, at present, pushed open. Dust-laden curtains were pulled back by a single tie, and they covered only one far corner of the window. Effie took a position opposite those drapes.

Gazing outward, her eyes were met by a fog that seemed to hang over everything, animate and inanimate. Its wetness threw a damper over the morning, as though the day itself were urging one to remain indoors.

Yet oddly, the scent in the air, the feel of the atmospheric moisture and the lethargy it might induce had the opposite effect on Effie. In truth, such conditions as these brought back remembrances of another place, another time.

It had been hazy that morning, too. Strangely, those

few hours seventeen years ago had left an undeniable impression on her.

Why?

Inadvertently, Effie reached up to her chest, her fingers seeking out the warm, gold chain that lay nestled between her breasts. Taking hold of it, she drew it out, away from her clothes and her body, her gaze fastening onto the two perfectly rounded white shells that were strung there. Those shells had once been earrings, had once been owned by someone whose memory, to this very day, was precious.

Briefly, she allowed herself to speculate on the boy who had given the trinket to her, a boy who would now be a man.

At once, a feeling of nostalgia washed over her. Why? Why did she recall those moments with such a feeling of longing? It wasn't as if she had known the lad well. That one day was all that they'd ever spent together; she had never seen him again.

Still . . .

The two of them had connected on a personal level, one that felt magical, mystical, more spiritual than physical. As the years had gone by, she had even imagined herself in love with the lad, had spent years weaving childish dreams around him.

Effie sighed. Sometimes she wondered if *he* might not be the reason she had never aspired to marry. Was she the sort of woman who, having once given her heart away, was of no use to another?

"Are you out there now?" she addressed the mist as though he were there in it. "And if you are, do you ever think of me?"

For a brief moment, a vision materialized before her, one of a future that had never been, and would never be. Deep in thought, she drew her arms over her chest and hunched forward. What would her life be like, she wondered, if she and the boy had engaged in more contact with one another?

That he was American Indian, that their life together might have been difficult, would have held little sway over her. To Effie, such things were immaterial, especially when the heart was involved.

Effie blew out her breath in self-disgust. For all she knew, the man was probably married now, with three wives and ten children.

Briefly, her gaze turned outward again, and despite her own good sense, her spirits reached out toward the mist. Sometimes she wondered if they had both been enchanted that day.

Enough. She was no longer a child who could afford to engage in immature imaginings and dreams. There was work to be done, and the good Lord knew that if she didn't do it, it would most likely go undone. Ah, yes, the morning awaited.

In terms of territory, a good many miles separated them. There was nothing to tie them together, not even a similarity in custom, culture or way of thinking. And yet, they each one shared a common peculiarity: They both loved the dawn's early gloom.

Instead of the mists of morning taking away one's vigor, it acted as a catalyst, oftentimes bringing back to mind for each of them that one moment. It is said that in all humanity, there is at least one single instant in a person's life when all the world's vectors converge to make a particular time, and everything about it, perfect.

And so it was for these two; their time together, seventeen years earlier, was such a one.

Thus, as Red Hawk trod toward the water, there to engage in his usual morning prayers, he greeted the haze as another might welcome the first rays of golden sunlight. His spirits soared, and opening his arms, he began to sing in the new day, to give his thanks to the Above Ones and to *A'pistotooki* for the dawn.

> "Haiya, Haiya, *a new day begins.*
> Haiya, haiya, *though the daybreak is murky, my heart is light.*
> Haiya, haiya, *will this be the day that I will learn your secret?*
> Haiya, haiya, *have pity on me, Old Man,* Naapi.
> Haiya, haiya, *time grows short, and my people await their freedom.*
> Haiya, haiya, *is there not some clue? Some spirit guide who will help me?*
> Haiya, haiya, *have pity on me, Old Man.*
> Haiya, haiya, haiya . . . "

Red Hawk's voice droned on and on. Always he asked the same thing. Always there was no answer, no sign to point him toward the right path.

Was *A'pistotooki*, the Creator, listening? It was a difficult thing to determine, for in all these many years, there had been nothing to guide Red Hawk, nothing to show him the path he must take, if he were to aid his people and end their curse. In truth, in this quest, Red Hawk was floundering.

Still, the cloudy morning beckoned, and though he meant no dishonor, Red Hawk's mind wandered off the matter at hand. Perhaps the morning vapors were at fault, for it seemed to him at times as if the mist itself were pulling him in a certain direction.

Where was *she*? he wondered. What was she doing?

Had the girl married by now? Did she have young ones? Did she love her husband?

"Ehh-fee," he said her name aloud.

He had never seen the girl after that one day, though he had stayed by the pool, waiting for her to return. But she had not come back, and he . . . he had a mission of importance to attend to. Besides, the elders had awaited him; there had been more counseling to be done, rituals to be adhered to, plus there had been Grandfather's needs to placate. Alas, when the sun had advanced beyond the midday point, Red Hawk had left their lagoon.

Taking in a deep breath, he tried to drag his attention back to the present moment, and looking forward, he smiled, as though she stood before him. Sometimes, the mist simply had that effect on him.

Hunching over, he began to prepare for his daily bath, and he drew off his moccasins and breechcloth that he might stand naked, trusting, before the Creator. Opening his arms in welcome to the early morning fog, he began:

"Thank you for the new day, A'pistotooki," he sang out, though this time he spoke his prayer. *"Thank you for your wisdom. But I would ask your pity. I come to you humbly, for you see before you a desperate man. I have but one full winter remaining to discover the way in which to end my people's curse. And* A'pistotooki, *I have no better knowledge as to how to end this enchantment now than I did when I was but twelve years old. As you know, I have sought out the enemy in fight after fight. Always have I shown my foes mercy. I have even abandoned my desire to revenge myself against the Thunderer.*

"A'pistotooki, *I have little to offer you. My needs are simple. I ask only this. I seek a helper,* A'pistotooki. *Some sign as to what I must do. Will you not take pity on me and hear my plea?"*

Red Hawk paused, but when nothing happened, he continued, *"Creator, why do my prayers go ignored? Why is it that in all this time, there has been no sign to guide me, no vision, no teacher pointing me in the right direction? Have I not done all I could? Have I not continued on this path, alone? Creator, I am but a simple man. I would ask for a helper, a sign, anything."*

However, as always seemed to happen, there was nothing but the silence of the countryside to respond to him.

"A'pistotooki," continued Red Hawk, *"is it because I was the last choice as a champion? If this be so, I ask your patience. For, whether my people desired to have me as their defender or not, I am yet here, and I am doing all I can to help my grandfather's people. I would see them again, I would be reunited with Grandfather if I could. I yearn for his wisdom. I ask only this: Send me a message, a messenger, anything, so that I might learn how to end the curse of my people. That is all."*

With this said, Red Hawk wasted no time, and he executed a dive out into the middle of the stream, the water being little more than shoulder deep. One strong stroke after another, and he could sense the blood beginning to flow within him. At last, he reasoned that he was warm enough to stand on both feet. Reaching down, he picked up a bit of sand from the river's bed, to scrub his arms, face and neck.

This done, he felt clean, and expecting nothing more than a good rinse, he dove underwater, his strong legs kicking out to propel himself forward. On he swam, out toward the deepest part of the river. It was then that it happened.

Suddenly, he stopped midstroke.

It was she. There before him.

Using his hands to keep himself beneath the water's surface, as well as to hold him steady, he stared.

What was this? A vision at last? Or was *she* here with him now? Smiling at him, tempting him?

"Ehh-fee?" He mouthed her name, watching as a bubble of oxygen formed. He rubbed his eyes. But when he gazed forward once more, no one was there.

His spirits sank. However, a voice spoke up from behind him. It was a deep voice, and it said:

"Seek out the water being. Seek what the water being seeks."

Red Hawk spun around in the water.

Who was it that addressed him? He looked outward, then swam forth gently.

"Seek out the water being. Seek what the water being seeks."

Red Hawk rubbed his eyes yet again.

Was it a fish or a monster that confronted him? If it be a fish, it was the largest one he had ever seen, bigger even than he was. If it be a monster, it might be one of the "sea dogs" that were rumored by the Blackfeet to exist. Whatever it was, it was about seven feet long from head to tail.

Mouthing the words, Red Hawk asked, "Are you my helper?"

But the monster/fish didn't answer, it said instead, *"The Creator has given you many clues, but you have not recognized them."*

"What clues?" asked Red Hawk.

Again, the sea dog did not answer, except to say, once more,

"Seek out the water being. That which you must find is that which the water being seeks."

"Water being? Is that you?"

"Four golden images,
When all in a row,
Slaves, your people will be,
No more."

"I don't understand. What images? All of what in a row?"

"Seek out the water being. That which you must find is that which the water being seeks."

Red Hawk's lungs were almost at the bursting point, and he knew he required air soon. But he was unwilling to surface. Not yet. He mouthed again, "I don't understand."

But the sea dog had nothing more to say, and with a flip of its tail, it spun around and swam away.

The water being? thought Red Hawk. Who was the water being? He knew of no water being.

And what else was it the sea dog had told him? That the Creator had already given him many clues . . .

What clues? Red Hawk was aware of no earlier hints given him that would indicate what he must do . . . unless . . .

Could it be that the early morning mists were the Creator's way of giving him help? It was certainly a time of day that he loved most, for always it reminded him of *her*.

Could that be the sign for which he hungered? If it were, he had been foolish, indeed, to have ignored it these many years.

He carried his conjectures further. Pretend for a moment that the mists were the Creator's way of speaking to him, what would they have shown him?

That the mists raised his mood? That they allowed him to feel closer to . . . something . . . To her, perhaps?

Was she the water being? What if all those years ago,

the Creator had sent the young girl to him on the very day
that he had been picked as champion? What if she had
been more than a girl whose company he enjoyed? If she
were his vision come to him in the flesh?

At last Red Hawk's lungs protested too much, and the
need to breathe blocked out further thought. He surfaced
at once, gulping down the life-giving air. But his attention
was as far removed from concern over his physical well-
being as if his body no longer existed. Instead, he heard
again the words of his spirit protector, who appeared to
be a sea dog:

*"Seek out the water being. That which you must find is
that which the water being seeks."*

"Ehh-fee," he mouthed her name.

Could it be? Had he not thought at first that she was
part fish? Had not their entire encounter occurred in or
near the water?

Effie. All at once, as though struck, he was certain of
it. It *was* she.

Odd, how the realization calmed him, and he relaxed,
until another thought struck him: *Where was she?*

It was seventeen winters since they first met . . . a long
time in which to have gone their separate ways. She could
be anywhere.

Treading water to relax his muscles, Red Hawk closed
his eyes, letting his mind drift, searching, if possible, a
spiritual connection with this girl whom he had never forgotten. With his mind, he asked, "Where are you?"

No response.

He inhaled deeply, then again, silently, he asked,
"Where are you?"

He waited, then, faintly, came an answer. *"I am here."*

Red Hawk's heart lifted.

It was good. Time and distance faded. They were, at

this moment, as attuned to each other as though their time together had been yesterday.

Perhaps it should be said here that another, in another culture, might express doubts, wondering perhaps if this were all Red Hawk's imagination, that he only "thought" he heard her speak because his was a desperate soul. But then one would not be taking into account that such things as conversations with the spirits, with the Above Ones and with all of creation, was commonplace to the American Indian's heart.

"Where is here?" thought Red Hawk.

No answer, except to say, *"Here."*

Short. Sweet. Nonetheless it was enough.

Suddenly Red Hawk smiled, for she had answered him in the best way possible—with a vivid image of her exact location. What was more, it was a place he knew, vaguely. But he knew it.

Opening his eyes, Red Hawk realized that it was time to bring his meditation to an end, while at the same time beginning his journey. With this purpose in mind, he swam toward the shore.

Though life might have thus far handed him a good bit of disappointment, Red Hawk was at this moment happy. Effie had returned to this country.

He would go to her.

CHAPTER 5

Click!

Effie's eyes flicked open.

The room was dark, but she knew she was no longer alone.

Fear shot through her instantaneously. She froze, fright taking its toll.

After a short while, however, her mind began to function; reason asserted itself. And though panic leapt through her, she knew she could not give rise to it. She must stay calm. Slowly, so as not to make any sound, she turned her head on the pillow.

A figure in black stole through her room. It was a man; a slender man. What did he want?

That's when it came to her. *The artifacts.* Someone had broken into her room to steal the artifacts. It was the only thing that made sense.

But how would anyone know of them? Let alone that she carried them on her person? The only people who even knew of them were in her crew . . .

"You will not discover them here." Perhaps she was

insane, but Effie found herself speaking to the intruder as though she might, with simple words, change his mind. She continued, "Do you really think I would be so stupid?"

The figure turned, faced her, even advanced toward her. But he said nothing.

"Who are you?" asked Effie. "How do you know of them?" She didn't name what it was that she referenced, certain that they both knew exactly of what she spoke.

Silence.

Slowly, timidly at first, she sat up in bed, picking up an object that always stayed close to her.

"I should warn you," she spoke slowly, "that I sleep with a gun. I have done so since I was a child."

Holding the weapon with both hands, she cocked the pistol to give emphasis to the fact. The sound of the catch was loud in the otherwise silent room.

She continued, "I have this pretty little Colt revolver pointed at your head. If I were you, I would leave as silently as I came. For if you don't, you will soon not have the means to do so."

The figure made no further movement. However, the sound of another pistol being cocked shot through the room.

Effie's heart leapt into her throat. Summonsing her courage, she kept her voice steady as she said, "On the count of ten, I promise that I will shoot you. One . . . two . . ."

The black figure crept closer.

"Three . . . four . . . five . . ."

The figure darted to the side, but in doing so, had come one step closer to her.

"I am not pretending a skill I do not have," Effie elaborated. "I may be a woman, but I have no reservations about shooting you. Six . . . seven . . ."

The man in black leapt forward, but was still too far away to reach her.

Shocked, but with the gun held steadily in front of her, she counted down more swiftly, "Eight . . . nine."

A blast filled the room, but not from her revolver. Her assailant's bullet must have hit the bedding close by her; feathers flew everywhere.

Pretending a calmness she was far from feeling, Effie said, "You missed. Ten."

Effie pulled the trigger, and the sound of the explosion was deafening.

Had she hit her target? She peeped around the bedpost. *No.* But then what should she have expected? She had not aimed to kill, only to hurt, to disable.

But the intruder, as though a mere shot had taken away his boldness, turned, and executing a rather classical pirouette, opened the door and disappeared beyond it.

Gun still clutched with both hands, still pointed toward a now absent "guest," Effie sat quietly in the aftermath. She let out her breath, hardly able to account for it.

How had this happened? How had news of what she intended doing leaked out to society's unsavory element?

A few moments must have passed unnoticed, and Effie became aware of the sounds of people—probably other hotel guests and her crew—who were on the other side of her door. However, it was beyond her ability to move, let alone speak or explain what had happened. Briefly, she was glad they were out there, not in here.

She was unnerved. True, she slept with a gun. True, she knew how to use one.

But never had she been forced to take action against another human being with one. She found the experience far from pleasant.

Gradually, someone opened her door—it wasn't, after

all, locked—not anymore. It was one of her colleagues, Carl Bell, who was followed immediately by another one of her associates, Henry Smith. Then came the rest of her crew, Lesley and Madeline, who were followed by a few others that Effie didn't know. As people began to filter into the room one by one, it did occur to her that the worst thing that could have possibly happened to her just had.

Not only were the artifacts no longer safe, *neither was she*.

I . . . we need protection.

On this thought, she steeled herself to talk, to explain, as best she could, what had transpired only a moment earlier.

The very next day the man she had hired as their guide quit, stating that she had misinformed him of the exact sort of danger her project entailed.

Dear Lord, Effie wondered, how on God's green Earth had the man heard about the raid against her so quickly?

"Bad news travels fast, ma'am."

"Within hours?" Effie stared at the gentleman who called himself Sheriff Hopkins, the only law in this town. He was seated before her in his office, his booted feet propped up on his desk.

"This is a very small town, ma'am," said Hopkins, whose mustache was so long, it appeared as if he had no upper lip. "Who was the first person that you told about your nightly visitor?"

"There were several people staying at the hotel, Sheriff, including my crew. All were awakened by the shots. And of course I had to make a report to the manager of the hotel. I believe he said his name was Mr. MacDermitt." Effie swept her full, blue-striped silk dress in front of her as she advanced farther into the room. On her head was perched a little hat with a plume that hung down over her chignon in back. And because there was still a chill in the fresh, Montana air, she wore a shapeless peplum thrown over the dress. She continued, "But I only told him of it first thing this morning. There was no manager on duty last night."

The sheriff raised his shoulders as if to say, "Well, that explains it." Meanwhile he lit his pipe.

Watching, Effie exhaled, exasperated. "Aren't you going to do anything?"

Taking a few puffs on his pipe, Sheriff Hopkins extinguished a match, then glanced up at her.

"Tell me, ma'am," said the sheriff without answering her question. "Why is a pretty little gal like you here? All alone? And in a country that's wild and unruly."

"I wasn't aware that it was a crime to be here. And, for the record, I am not alone."

"Now don't go gettin' all sassy with me. Just askin'." The sheriff removed his boot-clad feet from the desk. "I'm tryin' to understand the reason why some man would break into your room in the middle of the night."

Effie shrugged.

"Jealous husband?"

"I'm not married."

"Lover's quarrel?"

"No."

"Irate father?"

"I am over twenty-one."

The sheriff drew a long puff on his pipe, set it to the side, then slowly shifted his weight in the chair. At length he stood up, as if only now remembering his manners.

"Now, ma'am," he said, skirting around the desktop. "I have to ask myself—and you—again, why is a pretty

gal like you here? I know you said you was goin' diggin'
in the mountains—"

"I'm an archaeologist."

"Yes, ma'am, I heard you the first time, but any digger
I've ever heard tale of didn't look like you—young, pretty,
even if a trifle overdressed."

Overdressed? Effie pressed her lips together before she
said, "Then I expect your experience is very limited?"

Heaven forbid that the man should smile. Yet, he did,
and Effie was struck at once by the fact that the sheriff
did, indeed, have an upper lip.

"You're sure a cheeky little thing."

"And you're not helping me, though I'm certain you
mean to. Now, Sheriff Hopkins, what I really need to know
is what is going to be done to discover who entered my
room last night—and also where I might hire myself another guide?"

The sheriff took a step toward her; Effie backed up.

"'Fraid I won't be able to assist you, ma'am, lessn'
you tell me what it is someone might be lookin' for. And
as far as a guide, you'll just have to ask around town . . .
but don't expect much."

"Don't expect much? What does that mean?"

The sheriff backed up to lean against his desk. "It
means," he said, "that no one here wants to take on a job
that's jinxed."

"Jinxed? Who said the job was jinxed?"

Sheriff Hopkins shook his head. "Too much bad luck,
ma'am. Someone breaks into your room in the middle of
the night and shoots at you. Then your guide quits on you
right sudden. What's next? Shootin' your guide?"

"But—"

"We have a sayin' here in the West that goes like this:
Trouble comes in threes. Don't rightfully reckon you're

goin' to find many folks here who want to take on that kind of liability. What you really need isn't a guide, ma'am. It's protection."

"I see." Hadn't she had a similar thought last night?

"Do you?" The sheriff squinted at her.

"I think so," said Effie. "And you're going to provide me with that 'protection?' "

"No, ma'am, I'm not," said the sheriff. "My job here is to keep the peace. I figure I'm doing that by informin' you that there's a double whammy sittin' over you. If goin' into Blackfeet country isn't dangerous enough for a white man—takin' you and your party through savage and per-ilous mountains where many men have got themselves lost—you also need someone to act as both lookout and sharpshooter."

"No, sir, I don't. I can shoot, and we can post a watch."

"Yes, ma'am, I reckon you can. All I'm sayin' is that you're asking a lot of a man."

"Am I?"

"I believe so, ma'am. Now, if I was you, I might start lookin' elsewhere than here for a guide. Some place where they don't know you."

Effie's chin shot up in the air. "Was that an insult?"

"No, ma'am," said the sheriff. "Just speakin' the cold, hard truth." The man rose to his feet, then returned to his chair, and it wasn't long before his feet had once again found his desktop. He said, "You might try Helena. You might find more men there who'll have experience in them mountains. Nice makin' your acquaintance, ma'am," he smiled, then tipping his hat, he placed it over his eyes, while he slouched back in his chair.

Effie stood aghast, hardly believing she had been dis-missed so rudely. However, seeing that there was little point in making more conversation with the man, she turned and let herself out the door.

Determined that the sheriff would come to realize his mistake, Effie marched toward the general store. Within moments, she opened the door to the establishment, let herself in and walked straight to the counter.

"Excuse me," she addressed the man there, who had been engrossed in a ledger. Absentmindedly, he looked up at her, then he smiled. Effie returned the gesture.

"May I help you?" the clerk asked.

"I hope that you can," said Effie. "I am looking to hire a guide who can lead myself and a few other people to the Gates of the Rocky Mountains country."

"The Gates of the Rocky Mountains, you say?"

She smiled at the man. "Yes, that's right. My name is Effie Rutledge." She held out a gloved hand. "I am the person in charge of the archaeological expedition that came into town a few days back." She added another grin when the man accepted her hand. "Do you know of any man who would be willing to hire on as the guide for the project?"

"Clyde Herman's my name," said the man, "and I'd consider it a real pleasure to help a pretty little gal like you, ma'am, but that's Blackfeet country, isn't it?"

"Yes, that it is, but you see we've been there before, although many years ago, and—"

"Don't reckon," Mr. Herman interrupted, "that your task it going to be an easy one, ma'am. Word has it that them Gates of the Mountains is terrible dangerous." He scratched at his bearded face. "What happened to the guide you hired yesterday?"

"He . . . hmmm . . . he quit this morning."

"Did he now?" The clerk shook his head back and forth. "Yep, thought I heard somethin' about that, and I'm right sorry."

"You heard about that already?"

"I did, ma'am."

"Goodness," she exclaimed, "news certainly gets around here."

The clerk raised an eyebrow, then leaned over the counter, as though he were a co-conspirator. "Nothin' else to do, I'm afeard."

She sighed deeply. "I suppose you're right. But to return to my original question, dangerous though it might be, do you know of anyone who would be willing to take on the position? Someone who might perhaps yearn for adventure, for risk?"

The proprietor didn't answer at once, though he did look thoughtful. After a time, he said, "If you don't mind my asking, ma'am, why did Jake quit? It was Jake, wasn't it, that you hired on yesterday?"

"Yes, it was," she said. "And he quit because . . . well, because he is not a brave man, and when something happened last night that—"

Again, Mr. Herman leaned in close to her. "Heard tell your room was broke into."

"Yes," said Effie, wondering why the man's knowledge of her personal affairs had surprised her. Apparently one had no privacy in this town. "But you see," she went on to say, "I can explain that, and I—"

"Don't envy you none, ma'am, poor little thing that you are. It's gonna be awful hard to find someone to help you now."

"But why? There are lots of men in this town, and among them I should be able to find one who—"

"You see, ma'am, it's like this," said Mr. Herman. "When one of the fellas quits, it's as good as sayin' that they all quit. We're a mining town, ma'am. Close-knit."

"But—"

"See, there's precious metal that's been found in these here hills—all around Virginia City—and a man's gotta protect his stake. If 'n you want him to walk away from his means of livelihood, then . . ." He left the rest unsaid, as though anything else that followed were self-evident.

Effie cleared her throat. Then, strictly on the off chance, she leaned over the counter, and, as though she were seeking a tête-à-tête, she said, "Are you certain that 'protecting their livelihood' is the real reason I might have trouble finding someone to help me? It wouldn't be, perchance, that the men here have been told that my project is jinxed?"

The man gulped. "It might've been said a time or two, but me? I don't believe in jinxes."

Tightening her lips, Effie nodded slowly. "I'm certain you don't," she said, but her meaning was clearly the opposite.

For an instant Mr. Herman appeared uncomfortable, and straightening up, he adjusted his collar. This done, he said, "Look, ma'am, I'd like to help you, but I can't. I run a store, that's all. Have you tried over at the sheriff's office?"

"Yes, I have," said Effie. "Most certainly."

"Well . . ." The proprietor let the word trail away, as if the rest of the sentence needed no saying. However, brightly, as though he'd only realized this, he added, "Are there more in your party?"

"I am not alone in this venture," said Effie, "if you think that might make a difference. There are four others traveling with me who can shoot."

"Hmmm." Mr. Herman hesitated, scratched his chin,

then gazed at her over the rim of his spectacles. "And are all your crew female?"

"Why, no," said Effie. "Does it matter?"

"It might."

"Well, then," Effie continued, "I have one male and one female student; they are a married couple. And there are two other friends, who are also married. Why do you ask?"

"More superstition, I'm afraid, miss." The proprietor looked downright crestfallen. "The more women in a party, the more likely that party is to get wiped out."

"What?" Effie stared at the man, uncertain she had heard that correctly. But when the clerk didn't elaborate or say anything else, she replied, "Why, that's ridiculous. I can assure you that we have been on several expeditions throughout the States, and—"

"It's also Blackfeet country you're lookin' to travel into, ma'am. Them Indians is just plain mean. Around here," he glanced behind him, "them Injuns is called the 'tigers of the plains.'"

"Are they? But . . . sir, this expedition is not about those Indians, it's about . . . I . . ." Effie's voice trailed away. What was the point? Mr. Herman had made it clear that not only couldn't he help her, he wouldn't.

With a sigh that spoke of frustration, Effie found herself saying, "Well, I thank you anyway, but I guess I'd better be goin'."

The clerk nodded, smiled and turned away to wait on another customer.

Effie spun around, one arm coming down to sweep her blue-striped silk skirt with her. Unwarranted, the swishing sound of her dress as it grazed over the hardwood floor reminded Effie of the sounds of her intruder last night.

For a moment she froze. But after a short while, reason

returned and, picking up the front of her dress, she stepped toward the door.

Mr. Herman—at once the gentleman—met her at the entrance, and opening the door for her, he smiled a final apology. "Wish I could have given you better news."

Effie paused, returned the smile and was on the verge of adding a further comment, when she realized it was unproductive. Holding out her gloved hand to the man once again, she said, "I thank you, Mr. Herman."

She beamed up at the man, unaware that in this neck of the woods, the way she was dressed, because of the shapeless peplum thrown over her dress, she had identified herself as a woman of "masculine" taste. But perhaps the fault with the observation was not Effie's; maybe the men in Virginia City were not accustomed to the latest in women's fashion, or perhaps they had grown used to the look of the local "for hire" girls, with their curvy figures and high-combed hair.

Whatever the case, Effie was aware that she was not accomplishing anything of use. And despite what these two gentlemen had confided to her, she was still saddled with a problem: She needed to hire a guide.

Apparently, this left her with no alternative but to solicit each man's cooperation personally. All right, she thought, so be it.

Intending to do that at once, Effie swept off down the street.

CHAPTER 6

Effie's boots staccatoed over the sidewalk's puncheon logs. Things weighed heavily on her mind. Even the events of the previous evening—frightening though they might have been—were fading in significance against this newest problem: Where was she going to find a guide?

She supposed the first thing to do was to find the rest of her crew. Lesley and her husband, Henry, had left on errands with the student and his wife, Carl and Madeline Bell. The reasoning, which had been sound at the time, was that they could all accomplish more if they each one worked at different tasks.

That was before Effie had talked with the sheriff. Now, her viewpoint had changed, and she realized that they needed to band together to resolve this one problem. Of course, their finances would be stretched because they wouldn't complete as many tasks if they were all concentrating on only one assignment. However, there was nothing for it, since there would be little point in any expedition at all, were there no guide.

Now where had she sent Henry and Lesley? Oh, yes,

to the hardware store to purchase the shovels, axes and trowels that would be required for the dig. Madeline and Carl had gone off to the livery, to buy or hire the wagons needed for the journey.

She would try the livery stable first, and since the hardware store was in the same direction, perhaps she could accomplish two things at once. Changing direction, she set off at a steady pace.

Involuntarily, a thought came to mind. *Jinxed.*

Drat! Who had started the rumor? And how did she go about changing it?

It simply wasn't true—why, she and her students had hardly begun this expedition. How could it be jinxed so soon? Outside of this problem of finding a guide there had been no trouble, no bad luck . . . nothing.

She climbed down a set of four steps in preparation to cross an alley between buildings.

That's when she saw him.

Standing across the main thoroughfare, he stood watching her. He had wrapped himself in a blanket, making it difficult for Effie to discern much about him, except that he was, indeed, American Indian. The blanket he wore was a colorful one. Made in geometric hues of reds and oranges, browns and pinks, it covered him completely, except for his moccasins and the bottoms of his leggings.

His hair was caught and held at each side of his face with braids. Two eagle feathers, which must have been affixed at the back of his head, had been pushed forward and were twirling in the wind. However, the style of his hair was different than what she would have expected. Instead of his mane being simply parted in the middle in front, as she had always supposed was the more common Plains Indian fashion, a forelock of his hair had been caught and brushed up high over the forehead, pompadour style.

Also, she could discern a white, looping necklace around his neck, which fell down over his chest. Or at least she thought it did. His blanket hid the bottom half of the jewelry.

Around his neck was a white and blue choker, and hanging from his ears were white shells on a string; they were similar to the ones that were suspended from a gold chain around her neck.

The man wore no war paint that she could discern. And he stared at her. Indeed, he seemed to frown at her.

She caught her breath. Unquestionably, he was magnificent.

She should glance away. But she didn't.

In truth, she couldn't quite explain what drew her toward the man, or the fact that she found herself crossing the road without having willed herself to do so. It was as though her feet knew the way toward him, and she was simply traveling along for the ride.

As she drew level with him, she smiled. After all, it seemed the polite thing to do.

He did not return the gesture. Instead his eyes flashed at her dangerously.

But she ignored his look, and coming to stand in front of him, she found herself saying, "I am seeking a guide to take me into the Gates of the Rocky Mountains country" before she could stop herself. Perhaps that was what had drawn her to him. Need.

But he didn't answer, and she fretted. Had she forgotten her manners? Or maybe he didn't speak her language? She bit down on her tongue, then began again, "I'm sorry, sir, but do you speak English?"

He didn't say a word, though he did narrow his eyes at her.

Perhaps his silence should have made her uncomfortable, but it didn't. Curiously, she found that she was at ease with him, and she continued to speak to him. She said, "Excuse me, let me begin at the beginning. I don't mean to accost you like this, but I am desperate to find a guide for my archaeological expedition."

She shot a smile at him again, but he might as well have been a boulder for all the good it did her. "Let me introduce myself," she continued. "My name is Effie Wendelyn Rutledge, and I . . ."

Something in the man's demeanor changed. It wasn't so much a look as an impression that some emotion within him shifted. For a moment, he appeared unsteady on his feet. But then he uttered, "Ehh-fee?"

"Yes," she confirmed, with a slight bob of her head. "That is what people call me. You speak English, then?"

He nodded and drew his arms out of the blanket, as though he needed his hands to speak the words. He stepped forward. But something went wrong with the simple movement. One moment he was on his feet, as solid as a stone, the next he was falling backward, although he salvaged the move and caught himself before he crumpled up completely. However, his pipe fell to the ground.

She glanced at him strangely. Had he tripped over his own blanket? She said, "Why don't we take our conversation to the sidewalk in front of that store." She pointed toward the establishment. "We will be out of the way of the wagons and buggies there." She graced him with what she hoped was a cheery grin. "If you would be so kind, I would like a moment of your time."

Again, he nodded, started to move his hands with the sign gestures that Indians frequently used, changed his mind and instead, he stooped to pick up his pipe. But he must have been thrown off balance, for once again, something happened, and instead of grasping hold of the pipe, he lunged for it, missed it and plummeted forward.

Effie stared at him, aghast. Weren't Indians noted for their unwavering composure?

Deciding to overlook the entire incident, she turned her back on him and walked to the sidewalk made of puncheon logs. There were two steps that led up to the walkway, and on them were baskets with flowers set in them. Meant as decoration, they looked pretty, but completely out of place in this rough frontier town.

Nevertheless, Effie admired them as she climbed the steps. Then, turning back to the man, she gestured toward an empty space beside her. She said, "Won't you join me?"

With the pipe held firmly in hand, the man paced toward the stairs and stepped one foot up, but the end of his pipe hit the hitching post. It caught on something, a nail perhaps. He tried to extract it from the wood. He pulled on it, but it held fast, and instead of it coming away from the post, the force of his exertion caused him to fall forward against the steps, knocking the baskets off.

He tried to right the baskets, but each time he attempted it, he must not have been looking very clearly at what he was doing, for he set the baskets half on, half off the steps. They, too, fell.

He tried again, replacing the baskets; same results.

Sheepishly, he gazed up at her; he grimaced, and tried to set the flower baskets back into place once more. But it was useless, and when they fell over again, he ignored them, as though he had accomplished the feat perfectly.

He came to stand beside her.

And Effie chose not to comment on his clumsiness.

"You say you understand English? How?"

Pretending that nothing had happened, he said, "I scouted for a black robe who was traveling through this country in his search for the Flathead tribe. It was through him that I learned the language."

"I see," she replied. "No wonder your pronunciation of the language is excellent. You were taught by a monk."

He treated her to a rakish grin and for a moment Effie forgot to breathe.

Collecting herself, she continued, "Do you know the way to the Gates of the Rocky Mountains?"

"*Aa*," he said, as he stood over her, yet next to her. "I do. I am from that country."

"Are you? What tribe are you?" she asked.

"I am from the Southern Pikunis," he replied proudly.

"Oh," she said. "I was hoping you might be from the Blackfeet tribe, since the Gates of the Mountains are in their territory."

"Southern Pikunis are part of the Blackfoot Confederation," he said, standing stiffly, as though afraid to make a move, any move, lest something else tumble down around him. "There are three tribes that make up the Blackfoot Confederation and they are the Blackfoot, the Bloods and the Northern and Southern Piegan or what we refer to as the Pikunis."

"Oh," she said. "This is good. If I were to hire you for a job, would you be able to start in a few days?"

"*Aa*," he said, and again he nodded.

"*Aa*? Does that mean 'yes'?"

"*Aa*."

She frowned. "Hmmm. I suppose that it does."

He didn't answer, merely continued to stand rigidly, uncomfortably.

"I would like to meet with you tomorrow. Where would be a convenient place and time for us to talk? If I am to hire you, I would need to tell you the reason I am here, the project that needs doing and the journey ahead."

He nodded. "You come here to town," he said. "I will find you."

"No matter where I am?"

"I will find you."

She grinned at him. "Thank you, Mister . . . Ah . . . Mister . . . ?"

After a time, he said, as though educating her, "An Indian never speaks his own name unless he has to. It is impolite to do so."

"Oh."

"But you could call me Red Hawk."

"Ah, thank you, Mr. Hawk," she said. "Well, that explains a thing or two." But she didn't elaborate as to what that thing or two was. "Till tomorrow then."

Again, he nodded.

And with a quick smile at him, she turned to walk away. Having rounded the building, however, she peeked at the man from around the corner.

She could see him draw in a deep breath, and then move away from the post, which she supposed had been holding him up and keeping him standing straight. In truth, he looked as bewildered about the entire exchange as she felt.

But heaven help her, he was certainly an interesting character. Clumsy, yet handsome . . . and, if she were to be honest, something about him seemed achingly familiar. If she thought for a moment, maybe she could remember . . .

Frowning, Effie turned away.

"Are we going to abandon the project, then?"

The question came from dark-haired Carl Bell. With mugs and teacups in hand, the group was seated around a rudely cut, wood-hewn table, which sat in a far corner of a smoke-filled, dimly lit tavern. It was the only establishment in town that served food.

"No, we're not going to abandon it." Effie glanced at the young man. "Why would we?"

"Because of the trouble last night, as well as the matter of our guide quitting the project this morning. We can't very well travel into Blackfeet country without a guide. Plus—"

"All excavations have their problems," said Effie, interrupting. "It's part of our duty to overcome them. We all knew that there might be danger connected with this project, by its very nature."

"Yes, but somebody accosted you in your room, Effie. They shot at you. That's never been done before," responded Lesley.

Effie frowned in Lesley's direction. "This isn't the first time we've been threatened. Do you remember that dig in Mexico that our parents were part of? Do you recall the danger of bandits?"

"Yes," said Lesley, "but somehow it seemed more adventurous at the time, not dangerous . . ."

Effie nodded, smiled slightly, then said, "You're right, Lesley, it did seem more adventurous. In fact, if any of you wish to quit the project, please feel free to do so. You are by no means bound to continue."

Effie watched as Carl shifted uneasily in his chair, as did Henry, while both women stared anywhere but at her.

As if to press the point, Effie said, "If you're going to quit, I would prefer it if you did so soon. At least then I will have a better idea of what I must do to get this project going."

Effie waited. A moment passed, then two, the seconds clicking by slowly.

But when no one rose to leave or interrupt the silence, Effie continued. "Then we're all agreed to go on?"

Each one nodded.

"Good," said Effie. "Then I should tell you that I have this day hired another guide. And this one, I think, will do well for us. In fact, I believe he'll even be better than the last, for he is Indian."

"Indian? Really?" gasped Henry Smith.

"Yes. His name is Red Hawk, he is Blackfeet, he knows the country that we must journey to and he is willing to guide us and provide some protection, as well. I will be meeting with him later to finalize the details."

"Miss Rutledge, I don't know about this," uttered Madeline, who was a pretty, slender, ginger-haired woman. "Are you certain you can trust such a one? After all, aren't our people and his at war?"

"Come now, Maddy," censured Carl. "We're here to discover the truth about an Indian tribe. Surely it's our good luck to have an Indian accompanying us. I don't know about the rest of you, but I can think of many things I would like to ask him, if given the chance."

"But I've heard that Indians are not trustworthy."

"I think that might be pure gossip, Madeline," Effie replied. "I have spoken with the gentleman, and I can assure you that he is trustworthy. In fact, I think much more so than the gentleman I had first hired."

But Madeline seemed reluctant, and she stared at the others, as if seeking an appeal. When no one spoke up for her, she uttered, "Am I the only one who objects?"

Silence met this question, and Madeline went on to say, "There will be trouble because of this. I'm certain of it. I can feel it."

"We already have trouble," said Effie. "Perhaps that is

what you feel. Personally, it is my hope that this man will help end any difficulties we've encountered. Later you shall all meet him, and then you can each share your opinions. In the meanwhile, let us review again our plans for the rest of the afternoon. If we work quickly, I believe that we shall be ready to leave as originally scheduled. Mr. Bell, Mr. Smith, have you arranged for a wagon yet?"

"We are negotiating."

"Good, good," said Effie. "And Lesley and Mrs. Bell?"

"You can call me Madeline."

Effie smiled. "Thank you. Have you both arranged for rations?"

"We, too, are negotiating."

"Very well, then," said Effie. "It seems to me as if we already have our day planned. Shall we continue?"

Various nods and agreeable noises met Effie's question. At that very moment, their waitress arrived, bringing with her the delicious aroma of roast beef and cabbage. And as they applied themselves to the meal, it occurred to Effie that for the first time this day, things seemed to be going well.

As was his way, Red Hawk welcomed in the new day with song. Naked, and with burning sage on a rock at his feet, he smudged himself with the sacred herbs, turning slowly in its smoke. After a moment, he knelt by the rock, and, using a feather as well as his hands, passed the herbal smoke over his face, his neck, his entire body. It was a necessary procedure, for sage cleansed.

Looking upward, and raising his arms toward the heavens, he lifted his voice in song:

"Haiya, haiya. *Thank you,* A'pistotooki, *for this new day.*

Haiya, haiya, *I have discovered the water being, and have found her beautiful.*

It is good. And though she has changed greatly, I am happy to see her again.

Haiya, haiya, *I will help her by doing all that I can to find the thing she seeks.*

Haiya, haiya. *Her problems, her troubles will be as mine.*

Haiya, haiya, *but Creator,*

I do not know what she seeks, or why she seeks this thing, that for which I also quest.

And I do not understand the poem you have given me.

Haiya, haiya, *Creator, I would see the sea dog, my protector, again.*

Haiya, haiya, *for I have questions I would ask of my spirit protector.*

I would understand this sign that you have shown me better.

Haiya, haiya, *have pity on me. My needs are simple.*

Haiya, haiya, haiya, *my prayer is done."*

Lowering his arms, Red Hawk stepped out of the sacred smoke and knelt down beside the stone, taking care to smother the fire and ensure that it was out. Carefully, he returned his feather to a pouch, before arising to pace the few necessary steps to the water. At last, inhaling deeply, he dove into the middle of the lagoon. The water was cold and invigorating as it slid over his body. He lingered there, beneath the water. Here, he felt closer to something. In due time, however, he surfaced, and shaking his head, he felt the droplets of water run down his back, watched as they splattered everywhere.

For a moment, he worried that the ever-expanding circles in the water might warn an enemy of his position here. But, though Red Hawk was, indeed, within enemy territory—Crow country—he held little fear.

He had scouted the area thoroughly before engaging in his daily prayers; he had found nothing. He supposed this was due to the fact that the Crow were friendly toward the whites. Further, he conjectured that in order to discourage any incident between the two peoples, the Crows, as a rule, stayed away from the white man's town. In truth, this was a part of the country that held little reputation for shootings or killings.

With these thoughts effectively stifling any fear he might have held, Red Hawk returned his attention to the matter at hand, and plunging further underwater, he awaited contact from his spiritual helper, hoping that the Creator had heard his plea. He waited . . . and he waited.

But of one thing, there was no doubt. Though he had bathed himself again and again, when there was no need, he did not meet the sea dog this day.

CHAPTER 7

The mist was ushering in another fine morning as Effie stepped to her room's only window. Staring off due east, she could see that the sky was still navy blue, a sign that she had awakened long before the others were to arise. Unbidden, her thoughts turned to *him*, the boy from her youth.

Where was he? And why was he etched so deeply in her mind?

Effie had spent a sleepless night. Not due to the boy, but rather because of the previous evening's "guest." Alas, she had barely closed her eyes.

But, tired though she was, sleeplessness wasn't the worst of her troubles. Effie was worried about the turn of events; she could no longer leave the artifacts in her room. Locked or not, this hotel was no longer safe.

Briefly, she considered her options.

"I could carry them in my purse," she whispered under her breath.

But no. A purse is often set down; it could be too easily stolen.

"I could purchase a safety deposit box."

On second thought, no, she couldn't. A bank might be too easily robbed, particularly in an out-of-the-way mining town like Virginia City. Plus, there was an additional difficulty: She would require these artifacts to be at hand as soon as the digging commenced. If their excavation did uncover the other two nuggets, only as a complete set of four could they be presented to the Lost Clan.

But surely, she thought, there was something else she could do to protect the golden valuables.

"I could ask Madeline or Carl to keep them for me," she mumbled to herself. "Or perhaps Lesley might be willing to hold them in trust."

No. In reality, Effie wasn't certain that she could trust Lesley, or even any of the others in her group.

She immediately pulled up on that thought.

What a terrible thing to believe. After all, out of the many different kinds of people in this town, her crew was probably the most trustworthy.

"And yet . . ." She paused.

It was that uncertainty that made Effie hesitate to include the others in her confidence. True, everyone in her party had already seen the artifacts. It had been necessary to show them to her crew so that each would know what the nuggets looked like. Indeed, identification without a good representation of what needed identifying was almost impossible.

But this had taken place while they were back East. And truth be told, it was her understanding that Madeline and Carl Bell thought that Effie still held the valuables there. Only Lesley, and perhaps her husband, knew the entire story of the legend; only they were aware that all four artifacts were required to be present together, otherwise . . .

"You don't suppose . . . ?"

No, that was another rather unpleasant thought.

Still, Effie couldn't shake the rather startling idea, and she wondered: Could Lesley be the one who was trying to steal the artifacts? Had she sent her husband to do her dirty work? Was it he who had broken into her room?

Effie frowned. *It could be.*

It was certainly true that Lesley liked the finer things in life, and the nuggets would fetch a handsome dollar.

"No, it can't be," Effie said to no one in particular.

Hadn't she known Lesley all her life? Though Lesley might be more than a little spoiled, and perhaps a bit frivolous, Effie could not envision the other girl as a thief.

But if not Lesley, then who?

Perhaps Lesley or her husband had let slip to someone that Effie carried the precious nuggets? Had some conversation between the two of them been overheard?

"If that be the case," whispered Effie, "then the thief could be anybody."

It was all rather confusing. And for a moment, Effie wondered if her father had realized what dangers would follow in the wake of the artifacts leaving their secure place back East. Had he realized that if his daughter carried them on her person . . .

Wait! *On her person . . .*

Surely *that* might present a solution. Could *she* not carry them? Hidden in her effects?

After all, the stones themselves weren't terribly heavy, weighing about two pounds apiece. She could place them each into a satchel and hang them from around her waist by a string, perhaps one on either side of her hips. No doubt her very full skirts would hide them.

But was there a drawback to doing so? Briefly Effie tried to envision a scenario where the artifacts, if tied to her person, might be insecure. There was only one possibility that she could foresee.

Once on location, she would be forced to bathe in a river or stream. It would be then, and perhaps only then, that she would be required to set the stones aside.

Or would she? Could she possibly arrange it so that, even then, the artifacts remained with her at all times?

Suddenly it came to her, and gasping aloud, she snapped her fingers. That was it. It would be perfect.

Her bathing suit would be her solution, since it was full enough to hide the valuables. But could she wash those secret places on her body and remain clothed at the same time?

She would have to conduct a test of it, bathe in a stream and see if it were possible. If it were, her problem would be solved.

Effie quickly stepped to her vanity and rummaged through the drawer until she found a needle, thread and some sturdy material. Next she scooted the vanity chair toward the window, where she could gaze outside with ease. Then at last, she sat down, preparing to sew together two satchels, one for each rock.

It wasn't long, however, before the fog swirled in through the open window and into her room. And it surely was a short time after when memories of the past swept to the fore of her mind, prompting her to recall another place and time.

Where was he?

It was odd how much her new guide, Mr. Hawk, reminded her of the boy from her past. Maybe it was because both tended to be clumsy. Was that why the man seemed so familiar?

On that thought, she frowned.

* * *

Virginia City was a gold mining town, having been quickly established at the end of the Bozeman Trail for this specific purpose. It sat in the grasslands of the friendly Crow Indians, thus making raids by the natives few.

On any given day, from a venue on a hill outside the city, one was presented with perhaps the most chaotic sight in all the territory. Men, six thousand or more of them, were crowded into the gulch where gold had been discovered. There these men dug, fought, cursed, drank, pushed and shoved. Teams and wagons stood knee deep in mud, the road was almost impassible. Tents were everywhere, but there was a sawmill here, as well, a little farther downstream, with its smoke and horrible noise adding pollution to the already turbulent nature of the place.

The din was almost unbearable, for the buzz of those saws was continuous. Add to this the clamor from more than six thousand men, and the effect was deafening.

But there was another aspect of the city that few had ever taken the time to discover. Being located in the heart of the Plains, and skirted by grass-covered hills, Virginia City also spawned places where one could sit and think.

On the other side of town, over a few hills, one might discover a quiet stream, one that was rather deep, and babbled its way eastward. Alongside that stream grew a few scarce cottonwood trees, as well as one immense willow whose roots were well embedded in the soil. The rocks in the stream were slick; the water was swift, but cool and refreshing.

Effie had discovered the place soon after arrival, and had promised herself to come back often, if only to get away from the hubbub of the town. But to date, she had not had a chance to return until this morning. Now she came to test her skill in bathing fully clothed.

Certain that she had awakened before anyone else in the town was about, Effie finished her sewing and tied the artifacts to the top of her bloomers. Next, she donned her red-plaid bathing suit and slipped on her cloak. Catching a glimpse of herself in the mirror, she decided to leave her hair down, since she intended to wash it while at the stream. Pushing a heavy part of her bangs out of the way, she was blind to the effect of her mane, which fell in a hue of dark, crimson curls to her waist.

The morning was still wet with dew, she noted, as she stepped away from the hotel and plodded over grass and mud; there was also a chill in the air. But determined as she was to keep the artifacts safe, she barely noticed the discomfort.

The mining hadn't started yet, and the songs of the larks, the thrushes, the sparrows, even the doves, filled an otherwise quiet, early morning atmosphere. There was no well-worn path leading to the spot, and Effie soon became glad that she had decided to wear boots, for once away from the township, the grasses began to grow taller, longer.

At last, the cottonwood trees came into view, and with a few more lumbering steps, she arrived at her destination. Striding right up to the water, she took a moment to listen, and to simply soak up the peace of the place.

The stream gurgled and murmured on its way to some unknown destination, the sound soothing to her troubled nerves. Inhaling deeply of the moist, pure air, she relaxed, and it wasn't long before she threw off her cloak. Instantly, the red flannel of her bathing dress caught in the wind. She hugged her bosom, realizing that the breeze felt good.

Briefly she caught sight of her reflection in the stream. What a spectacle she was. The trousers of her ensemble resembled knickerbockers, over which she had donned a shorter, though full dress, one that reached just below her knees. And though the outfit came complete with belt and matching hat, making Effie the picture of a postwar modern girl, she felt uncomfortable.

Oh, to be able to throw it all off and slip into the pool with nothing between her skin and the water. The urge was almost overbearing. But it could not be. She was an adult now, not a child.

Remaining afoot in her shoes, for if she remembered correctly, the bottom of the stream was rocky, she took a step forward and waded out into the silvery blue water. It was cold, but refreshing; slick, yet the river's bottom was solid. The smell of the fresh water sent her mood soaring.

All at once, she smiled; memory after memory flooded her senses. She recalled again how much she had loved the early morning and her swims all those years ago. Back East she had taken to bathing in either a tub, or a washbasin, since the waters in that part of the country were becoming polluted.

However, she was beginning to realize that a bath was a poor substitute for the real thing. There was no sense of being one with the Earth, with all life. It was as though the water in a bath weren't . . . alive.

A giggle escaped her lips as she plunged under the water; she surfaced, dove, surfaced again. Spreading her arms, she danced within the water like a nymph, diving more deeply, exercising her limbs and lungs.

Feeling more vital than she had only moments earlier, she sensed her troubles lift away, if only momentarily. It induced her to frolic and play within that stream. Winded, she headed for the shallows, where she sat for a moment, using her hands to spray water over herself.

A goldenish sort of light was spreading through the fog

from the east, there against the opposite shoreline. Was it her imagination? Could a person feel the Earth coming alive? Enchanted, she watched as a moose surveyed her from a safe distance across the water.

"Won't you join me?" she asked it.

When it snorted and shook its head, as if in answer, Effie laughed, then plunged out into the current once more. Moments later, she surfaced, executed a few turns beneath the water and tarried yet again. Ah, such pleasure.

But time was wearing on, and she knew she would have to come back to the world as she knew it. She hadn't made this trek for pure enjoyment.

A few well-placed strokes in the stream brought her to a spot where her feet would touch bottom, yet the water would cover her completely, and she stood up. Bending, she grabbed hold of some sand on the river's bottom, and commenced using it to scrub herself.

Glancing around to ensure she was still alone, she opened the front of her dress to wash her chest and underarms. Next, reaching up under her skirt, she bent to cleanse her stomach, thighs and legs.

So far, so good. There was no problem.

However, when she left the water, would there be visible traces of the satchels that were still tied to her waist?

She'd never know by simply standing here contemplating. Carefully, she rose up from the water and waded to the shore. And so intent was she in measuring the fullness of her hips—to ensure that the satchels were not visible—she didn't at first see him.

When he said, " 'Tis good that you are not as round as a bull. Why do you wear clothes that make you appear so?" Effie gasped, her muscles tensing as she glanced to her right, then to her left. But the man was reclining on the shore, directly in front of her.

"You!"

He nodded. "I had feared that, by the way you now dressed, you had grown overly big since we last met. Not that it would matter to me if you had . . ."

"Since we last met?"

"Do you not remember me?" he asked. "And here am I having never forgotten you." He pulled at something around his neck, producing a gold chain for her perusal. She recognized it at once.

"Then it *was* you yesterday . . . and all those years ago. No wonder," she said, as though speaking to herself.

She took one step forward and extracted her necklace, which rarely left its place between her breasts. Holding it up so that he could see it, she said, "Does this look as though I had forgotten you, Mr. Hawk?"

Effie thought she might have witnessed a smile appear upon the man's handsome face, but the light at this time of day was not great, and the shadows concealed much.

They stared at one another for some moments, neither making an effort at conversation. Time and place seemed to distort. There were only the two of them, here together, alone, at last. Her spirits lifted.

Finally, he said, "My heart is happy to see you again. In these many years that have passed since we first met, you have been in my thoughts often."

"Yes." It was the only thing she could think of to say.

"I would ask what it is that you seek."

The question caught her by surprise, perhaps because she wasn't prepared for it. Indeed, so caught up was she in the fact that he was here, now, before her—when she had never expected to see him again—that she felt as though she were jolted back to the present. Her head reeled.

However, by the grace of God, she was alert enough to

respond in a somewhat intelligent fashion, and she said, "And why would you be asking me, Mr. Hawk?"

He veered his head to the left, giving it a slight jerk. "As your guide, I would ensure the safety of your party. Therefore, I would know what trouble awaits us."

"Trouble? You expect trouble?"

"I believe that I might," he put forth. " 'Tis rumored in this town that your—what did you call it?—expedition?—is cursed."

"Cursed? I don't believe this. That is so unfair."

It was her hope that her words might obtain a respectable degree of sympathy from him, but he didn't so much as move a hair in response. After a slight pause, he continued, saying, " 'Tis also said that someone broke into your quarters during the night. This person shot at you. If these things be true, then I would venture to say that you already have trouble. If I am to guide you and protect you I would know what awaits us."

Effie sighed, looked away from him and remained silent. The man had certainly done his homework.

Suddenly, she felt cold, and glancing down, she was dismayed to witness that the entire bottom half of her body was still standing in the water. She'd almost forgotten. Glancing up at him, she said, "Would you mind if I wade to shore? I am getting chilled as I stand here."

He motioned her forward.

But she hesitated. "I don't think you understand. I cannot leave the water so long as you are here."

He frowned. "You wish me to leave?"

"Yes."

"That is to be regretted," he said. "Perhaps I should not have spoken out so readily or so soon. Have my words caused you grief?"

"It's not that."

"Nor do I mean to frighten you." He held up his hands. "I hold no guns, no weapons. I am not threatening you. Would you like my word that I will not—"

She cut him off. "It is for modesty's sake that I ask you to leave, Mr. Hawk, nothing more."

"Modesty?"

"Yes, modesty." She repeated. "Now, do not pretend ignorance of what I speak, if you please. You are a man, I am a woman. We are alone. I must ensure that there is nothing scandalous about my attire or about my demeanor. But I would do so in private."

"*Aa*, now I understand. 'Tis foolish of me not to have realized that before." He turned his head away from her, and, rotating so that his back was turned toward her, he folded his arms over his chest. As soon as he had done so, he continued speaking, saying, "It is good that you bring this to my attention, for I have seen nothing dishonorable about you this entire morning."

"Thank you."

He continued, "Once, long ago, you wore less clothing than this."

"Yes, I did," she agreed. Then sarcastically, she added, "And how kind of you to make mention of it."

She watched as he bowed his head and shook it back and forth; if she hadn't known better, she might have thought that he laughed at her. From what she could see of it, his chest certainly shook.

He said, "'Tis good to behold that there is nothing wrong with your tongue."

"No, there's not, and there's nothing wrong with my voice either should I choose to scream."

"What you say is true." He nodded absentmindedly as

though her words were profound. "If you want me to go so that you have more seclusion, I will leave. But I would be unthinking and unkind if I did not tell you that I think you would be unwise to make me go."

"Unwise? Why?"

"Because as long as a man is in front of you, you can know where his eyes tend. But send him from you, and he may hide and watch you while you are unaware."

She snorted. "Then that man is not honorable."

And he shrugged. "Men are men."

Yes, they are, she thought to herself. Then, aloud, "I believe that you use this as an excuse to remain here, Mr. Hawk."

"Perhaps I do . . . *aa*, it could be true. Surely, I have thought of you often in these many years. And though I know I should go and let you have the privacy that you seek, I must admit that I do not want to leave you. At least not yet."

As she stared at the back of his head, Effie felt a glimmering spark of kinship with the man. Couldn't the same be said of her?

After all, what could it harm if they spent a few more moments in one another's company? Especially since it did appear that they were alone. Glancing around once again, she found herself saying, "Very well. I suppose you're right. We have much to discuss, and perhaps now would be a good time to settle a few matters between us. The only condition I demand is that you remain seated with your back to me until I am ready to receive you properly."

"*Soka'pii*. This I will do," he said, and she relaxed. But he broke the spell by adding, "I wonder if it is a good time to tell you that I have been here for some time, and I have already seen you in your beautiful red dress."

Immediately embarrassed, she said, "But how? I looked carefully around before entering the water, and I saw nothing."

"Then you need to be taught how to look."

"I see just fine."

"And yet I have been here all this time, and I was not hiding."

She raised her eyes in disbelief.

"Do not despair," he went on to say. " 'Tis a trait I have found common amongst the white man. He does not often live in peace with his environment, and so he many times does not see that which is right in front of him."

"And Indians miss nothing, I suppose?"

"Upon a rare occasion, they might. But it is taught to the young Indian lad and maiden that, if a man does not know his environment well, and does not observe the obvious, the error could cost him his life. Wise ones are never at their ease; they are always alert, except perhaps when they are within the safety of their village."

"Maybe so," she retaliated, "but you are lecturing me, and I do not like to argue so much. Besides, we leave the point. You may have spied me in this dress before I entered the water, but it is not the same when the clothing is wet. Water emphasizes . . . curves."

"I understand."

"Thank you, Mr. Hawk. I am glad that you do. However, the arrangements for our talk will remain as I have already stated, at least for the time being."

"As you say."

Slowly, she rose up out of the water and waded to shore. As she had intended all along, she glanced down at her skirts, then breathed in a sigh of relief. It was good. The bathing suit covered not only her, but the artifacts as well.

Very well. One problem solved.

She sat beside the man she knew as Mr. Hawk, who reclined in the grass. She said, "Would you please hand me my towel? It is on the ground beside you." She gestured to where she had left her cloak even though she knew he couldn't see the motion.

He reached for the cloak, but his hand stopped midair. He said, "*Aa*, that I will do—for a price." He glanced at her over his shoulder, and smirked.

"A price? And keep your head turned away from me, Mr. Hawk."

"As you say." He looked forward once again.

"And no peeking," she commanded. "What is it that I must pay, Mr. Hawk? And do hurry to tell me, for I am cold."

"It is simple," he said. "I would like you to tell me what it is that you hide."

Chapter 8

Effie gulped. "Hide?" she asked. "What makes you think that I hide something?"

"I sense it," he said. "Common reasoning would tell me this, also. You must be concealing something. Either that, or you have committed an offense so worthy of another's wrath that they would enter your room and shoot at you."

Ah, she thought as she drew in a deep breath to calm herself. He wasn't inferring that she was hiding something on her person *at this very moment*.

She said, "Well, I think that your 'reasoning' is faulty."

"*Aa*. I believe I understand you. What you are really saying is that you won't tell me."

"Exactly."

"*Haiya*. It would be better if you did, I think."

"Better for whom? You?"

"Perhaps. Better for you, as well, since, if I know what it is that you hide, I can more easily assist you."

"Humph! So you say."

"You do not trust me." It wasn't a question. "And this is wise of you," he continued. "One should not blindly put one's faith in those one does not know well. So do not tell me what it is that you seek to mask. Simply know that I know that you do."

"Humph!" was all she said.

"But if you will not speak of that, perhaps you could at least tell me what it is that you hope to discover by your journey."

Effie smiled. She couldn't help it. "I see what you're doing. You're trying to distract me so that I might tell you what it is you really want to know. You certainly are a persistent man, Mr. Hawk," she said, "I'll give you that. And you are assuming a great deal. What makes you think that I seek something?"

Glimpsing him from over her shoulder, she saw that he lifted his shoulders as though it were obvious. He said, "Why else would you be traveling such a long distance into a territory that is dangerous to a white person?"

"Maybe you have not considered many other possibilities," she said, then she sent him a coy glance, though its effect was lost on him because his back was to her. "Have you contemplated the fact that maybe I travel there to meet a lover? Which would make the hardship all the more worthwhile?"

"Saa," he said. "It cannot be so."

"Why could it not?"

"Because you do not have the look of a woman seeking a man."

"Balderdash."

"And you forget," he continued, "that the country you seek is Blackfeet territory. Therefore, it is doubtful that you will find a white man there peacefully awaiting you. Besides, if that were true, you would not be taking others with you."

Touché. She pouted. "I'm not saying that's why I need

to go there, I'm simply bringing up the point that it could be true."

He nodded. "*Aa*, it could be, but it is not. Are you going to tell me what it is that makes you willing to risk so much?"

"No, I am not."

"*Soka'pii*, it is as I had thought." Leaning forward, he grabbed hold of the cloak she requested. "Is this what you require?"

"Yes," she said. "Well, partially. My towel is in the inner pocket of my mantle. There," she said, as his hand skimmed over the material of her pocket.

"Is this what you wish?" he asked as he grasped hold of the towel and pulled it away from her cloak.

"It is." Snatching the towel away from him, she dried herself as best she could, then pulled it around her shoulders. Instantly warmth spread through her.

After awhile, he said, "May I turn around now?"

"Yes, you may," she said, "but first, could you please hand me my comb, which is in the same pocket?"

He produced the object in short order, then turned toward her. He said, "I would ask you a question."

"Fine. Ask away," she said, beginning to feel at ease with the man.

"What is this archaeology that you mention?"

He surprised her. "Archaeology?"

"*Aa*. Is that not one of the tasks that takes you into Blackfeet country? Turn around."

"Turn around? Why?"

"I will comb your hair."

"But—"

"Turn around." He made a circling motion with his finger.

"I'm not asking you to comb my hair."

"I know," he said. "Do you object to me doing it?"

In truth, the idea of this man touching her anywhere caused her stomach to tighten.

And yet, how many times in a person's life was one offered such a luxury? Though she supposed she shouldn't let him do it, the opportunity to let another person attend to the tangles in her hair—just this once—seemed too appealing to let slip by unheeded. She said, "No, it's not that I object to your combing my hair—not really. It's only that I'm . . . astonished."

"Do not be," he replied, as she scooted around, to place her back toward him. And before he launched himself into the task at hand, he said, "Your hair has many twists and waves, and it would be difficult for you to brush it on your own."

"True. But I am used to doing it."

"Then sit and enjoy. It is, after all, a man's job."

"A man's job?"

"*Aa*, it is so with my people. Is it not true with yours?"

"No, not at all."

"Humph! Your hair is also an unusual color, even amongst the white people, I think."

"Yes," she said. "I have been told that."

He ran the comb gently through a snarled lock. Pausing, he untangled the delicate curl, his fingers inadvertently skimming over the skin at her neck.

Tingles raced along her spine, and she knew she should stop this. It was intimate, too intimate.

But she didn't cease it. In truth, it felt much too wonderful to put a stop to.

Slowly, he ran his fingers from the top of her head, to the very tips of her hair, the delicate graze awakening every nerve ending in her neck and back. A feeling of serenity settled over her. "You do that well," she said.

"*Aa*. I used to comb my grandfather's hair—every day. And I have often done the same for my adopted grandmother."

"Oh? I didn't know you were adopted. Who are your adopted people?"

"The Pikunis."

She spun back toward him, and he dropped his hands to his lap. "Oh? Then you have been adopted by the Blackfoot, and are not a blood member of the tribe?"

"*Saa*, I am not adopted by the Blackfoot."

"But . . ." She frowned. "Didn't you say that the Pikunis are part of the Blackfoot Confederation? And if that is so . . ."

He sighed. "'Tis a complicated story."

. "Oh," she commented, swinging back around so that once again, her back was presented to him. She only hoped he would continue his ministrations.

He did. "Do you wish to hear the story?"

"I believe that I would. Otherwise, I must admit that I am confused."

"*Soka'pii.*"

"What does that word mean?"

"*Soka'pii*? 'Good.' It means, 'good.' " He made a quick hand motion, out, away from his chest.

"Thank you," she said. "Now about that story."

He returned the comb to the tangles in her hair, running it slowly through her locks. In due time, he began, "Once, when I was very young—"

"Before or after we met?" She turned slightly toward him.

"After, and I would be greatly honored if you would let me tell the story . . . perhaps without interruption . . ."

"All right," she agreed, then shot a flirtatious little smile at him from over her shoulder.

She saw him catch his breath, then he dropped the comb. He stared at her for a long moment. Then, as though it took great will, he looked away from her. Clumsily, he picked up the comb, but she could tell that his composure was shaken, for his Adam's apple bounced up and down, if only for a moment.

Still grinning, Effie spun back around, satisfied for the time being that he appeared to be as affected by her as she was by him.

He cleared his throat, and began again. "It is true that I am of the Blackfoot Confederation, but not the Pikunis. My own tribe is the Blood, or as we say it, the *Kainan*. The *Kainan* is also a part of the Blackfoot Confederation. My mother and father were visiting friends when I was a baby . . . I am told I was only weeks old. They were killed."

"I'm so sorry," she murmured. "Is that why you speak of only your grandfather and grandmother?"

"*Aa*, it is partially so. Also, when I was still fairly young, I was lost from those who had raised me—"

"You mean the Blood Indians?"

"No, the Blackfoot."

"But I thought—"

"My mother and father were visiting the Blackfoot, and the man that I call Grandfather is of that tribe. But later I was lost even from them and was eventually found by the Southern Pikunis. Because my father and mother were already gone, the Pikunis adopted me into their tribe."

"I see . . . I think. So you were raised within the Blackfoot Confederation . . . different tribes within it, but basically by the Blackfoot. And by blood you are also of the Blackfoot Confederation?"

"*Soka'pii*, that is correct." He paused as he drew the comb through her hair. Then, quite abruptly, he stopped. He said, "Now it is your turn."

"My turn?"

"I have a question for you."

"I will not tell you what I seek in the mountains, if I am even looking for anything. So do not ask me."

"*Aa*, I have come to understand this. But that is not what I am hoping to learn—at least not at this moment."

"Oh?"

"What I would like to ask is: What is archaeology?"

"Archaeology? Well, let me think of the best way to explain it." Crossing her legs in front of her, Effie leaned forward, placing her arms on her thighs. But it was hard to think when his hands were all over the back of her head.

Perhaps she made too much of a simple thing, however, for his graze was hardly sensual. And his fingertips were rarely touching her delicate skin now, as though he were carefully avoiding doing so.

Sighing, she hugged her knees.

A thought came out of nowhere. Was this what it would be like to be married? To this man?

A flush stole slowly over her face.

Her thoughts seemed to betray her. And, more as an attempt to distance herself from the waywardness of her musings, she began to talk, saying, "Well, I suppose you could say that an archaeologist studies man, or rather things that man has made. As such, we don't really probe into man's social orders or groups or religions. But rather we look at and examine the things that man has created with his own hands, and mostly those things that he made in the past. Once we find these objects, we study them, because from them, we can discover many things about how that man lived."

"Hmmmm . . . ," he said.

"Now most of the items that we investigate," she continued, "must be dug up and found again, since hundreds or even thousands of years have changed the landscape of the land. And so when an archaeologist talks about a dig or an excavation, what he truly means is that he is going to quarry in a particular area. By use of shovels, trowels and brushes, we delve into the earth and into the past, looking for objects. And from those objects we find, we seek to know more about the man of the long ago."

"*Soka'pii,*" he said. "And this is what you wish to do in the country that the white man calls the Gates of the Mountains?"

"Yes."

"And which mountain it is that you seek to find?"

"I wish I knew the name of it, but even my father never learned its exact identity—only its location. It is a mountainous area north of the town of Helena and above the Gates of the Rocky Mountains. It was an area once used by the Indians as a buffalo jump."

"A *piskan*?"

"If that word means a place where the buffalo jump off a cliff to their doom, yes."

"*Aa.*"

"Do you know of it? For if not, I do have a map of the place, and I can show you where it is."

"*Aa,* a map would be good," he said. Simple words, yet something had suddenly changed about him. His voice had lowered or altered in some fashion, or had he simply hesitated ever so slightly? Whatever it was, she sensed that something was wrong, and she couldn't understand exactly why. However, he was continuing to speak, "I think that if you show me a map, I might know of the place, since I am familiar with that part of the country."

"Oh, I wish I'd brought it with me. But I didn't. We must meet again sometime today. I will show you the exact spot."

"Is the place where you are going close to where we first met?"

"Yes, it is."

Again, he hesitated, but the silence was hardly comfortable, and she longed to bring it to an end. Finally, he said, "Then I have no need of a map."

"Nevertheless, I can show you the exact spot," she argued. "Don't you think that I should?"

"Perhaps," he said. "You mention that, as an archaeologist, you dig up things from the past?"

"That's right."

"Is there a specific tribe that you seek to find?"

"Yes," she said. "It is a mythological tribe, I'm afraid, one of legend. It is my hope to discover if the legend be true."

"Perhaps I know of it."

"Maybe," she said. "But I do not believe that its origin is steeped in Blackfoot myths."

"You may be correct," he said. "However, I am aware of many legends—not only those of my people, but of other Indian tribes, as well."

She glanced at him from over her shoulder. "Very well. I will tell you, but only if you promise that if I mention the name of the tribe, and perhaps a bit of the legend that surrounds it, you will repeat this to no one."

"You have my word," he said without hesitation.

She studied his solemn expression warily. Could she

trust him? Instinct said that she could. However, the events of the past few days—including the intruder in the night—caused her to hesitate. At the moment, she trusted no one, not even her fellow companions.

Very well. She would be cautious.

Turning around, so that her back was once again presented to him, she said, "In truth, it might be best that I tell you the particulars of the legend, since you will be involved in the expedition by association. I suspect it will be better that you know."

"*Soka-pii*, I agree."

Once again, glancing at him from over her shoulder, she said, "Have you ever heard of the legend of the Lost Clan?"

His fingers stilled in their work; the comb dangled limply in his right hand. And though no emotion stole over his countenance, it seemed to take him a moment before he could speak. At last, however, he said, "The Lost Clan? *Aa*, I believe that I have heard of this clan . . . and this legend . . . in my youth. In truth, I believe I know a little of it . . ."

CHAPTER 9

"How is it that you have come to learn of this tribe?" Red Hawk asked Effie, once he had recovered enough to speak. He wasn't certain why her knowledge of his clan surprised him. He should have expected it—after all, his spirit protector had led him to this woman. Yet, hearing another person speak the name of his clan in the present—aloud, and in his company—was jolting.

Sitting with her legs folded in front of her, she had turned to face him. And she was glorious.

With her red hair framing her face and spilling out over her shoulders, she looked as though she were the stuff of legend. She was a small thing, at least in comparison to the women in his tribe, who were generally bigger boned and taller. But this woman was delicately framed.

Dainty brown spots—which he had once heard referred to as "freckles"—splattered across her nose. And her eyes, which in color resembled those of a doe, were clear, reflecting a sincerity that he suspected was a part of her inner being.

However, at present, those light brown eyes looked anything but calm. She was on her guard.

Nevertheless, she answered his question, saying, "I know of the legend because an old anthropologist, named Trent Clark, once lived amongst the Indians in that area; he was told this story by a very old native. Before Mr. Clark's death, he related the tale and solicited a promise from my father to search for evidence of the tribe. My father has been looking for signs and information of the tribe ever since."

"Information?" asked Red Hawk. "Was your father looking for anything in particular?"

She sighed and her glance fell to the ground. Absentmindedly, she ran her hand over the lush grass. But she didn't answer.

It was then that he knew: *Her father had been looking for something specific, and it was probably this that she, herself, was seeking.*

He gently said, "What is it that your father hoped to find, that you must now pursue?"

She shrugged. Without looking at him, she said, "Artifacts."

"Artifacts? What are 'artifacts'?"

She stared off into the distance, but went on to explain, "Artifacts may be many things—specifically something that man made. Bits of pottery, arrowheads, paintings on caves or shaped bones—these are artifacts. A simple rock, made by nature, no matter how old, would not be an artifact."

Red Hawk nodded. "And what did your father intend to do with these . . . artifacts? If he found any?"

"Prove that the tribe existed, and learn more about them," she answered.

"And did he?"

She started to rise. "Mr. Hawk, I really must go."

He reached out a hand to detain her. Her eyes grew wide, as though astonished that he might touch her, and she stared straight at him.

His fingertips tingled at the contact. At once, he broke off his hold on her, but he said, "Do not leave yet. Perhaps I go too fast. 'Tis only that I think it best that I know as much as possible about your circumstance. You have trouble, I think. I wish to help."

"Help? Truly? I don't know. It's really a matter of trust, isn't it?" she said. "How do I know I can trust you?"

He said, "Is the article you hope to find so valuable that you cannot tell me anything of it?"

She set her lips into a frown. "Mr. Hawk, you didn't answer my question. How do I know I can trust you?"

He sighed. "You do not," he answered honestly. "You will have to decide that for yourself . . . or not. As the old, wise ones in my country would say, you must trust to your heart."

She hunched over, hands on her forehead, as though her thoughts were heavy. At last, she lifted her head, and stated, "I can't do that. Not only my heart, but my mind must be involved in any decisions I make regarding this project. But I'll tell you what I will do. I will strike a bargain with you."

"A bargain?"

"A trade," she said. "If you'll tell me why you are so interested in what it is that I seek, I will tell you what it is that my father and I hope to find . . . if we are, in fact, trying to find anything . . ."

Silence.

"And don't say again," she said, "that you wish only to protect me." She raised her chin. "My father warned me long ago about people who *have* to proclaim their trustworthiness. Many times he said that if such people were really virtuous, why would they announce it hither and wide? A truly honest man doesn't *have* to tell others about his integrity. He simply is honorable, and others recognize it."

Red Hawk grinned at her. "That is good advice," he said, "and it was not in my mind to repeat myself."

"Good," she said. "See that you don't."

What could he say? He couldn't very well accept her challenge without cost to him, to his clan, to the Above Ones.

How could he detail his vision? For it was this that had led him to her. To tell another about it would be to break with tradition, and to render the vision worthless. Nor could he delineate the history of his life to her. Who would believe him?

After several moments passed, she at last said, "Check."

"Check?"

"It is a phrase from a game, called chess. When one has his opponent cornered, and unable to move, and yet neither one has won the game, the person says, 'check.' It is my belief, Mr. Hawk, that we both hold one another in check."

He nodded. "I understand. You are saying that we neither one trust the other enough to open our hearts."

"Yes."

"*Haiya*, I must have time to think on your words. 'Tis not a small thing that you ask of me."

"Nor is your request of me. How much time do you require?"

"Until tomorrow night. I will give you my answer then."

"Fair enough," she agreed. "Tomorrow night, then. Where shall we meet?"

"I will come to your room."

"My hotel room?"

"*Aa.*"

"But how? I don't think the front desk would allow you up the stairs since you are not a guest."

"I will be there."

"Which means that you know where my room is. How long have you known?"

"Long enough," he answered.

"I see." She cleared her throat. "Well, I thank you for your time."

Again, she made to rise and leave. Again, a simple touch of his fingers on her arm detained her.

"Tell me one last thing," he said. "That first time we met, you were with your father?"

"Yes."

"And was your father there to try to discover clues about the Lost Clan?"

"Yes."

"Did he find anything?"

She paused, frowning. "Let us adjourn this conversation until tomorrow evening, shall we?"

"I am not asking you to tell me what it is that you seek. I am only wondering if your father found something in that long-ago time."

She hesitated, and he watched as a multitude of thoughts were displayed upon her countenance. At some length, she told him, "My father did find something that made him believe that the legend is true. And that is why I am here. I seek to learn the truth of the legend. This is why I am going back to that area—myself and my colleagues will look for . . . things in the hope that we will find a clue about the existence of the Lost Clan."

"These things that your father found, that you are searching for, are they prized much by the white man?"

"They could be. We are being financially supported in our quest by a museum in the East. Most of the things that we find will belong to them."

"But not all? *Aa*, now I understand." He nodded.

"Understand what?" she asked. She straightened her spine and sat forward. "Do you think that I am some fortune hunter? That I am only here to add to my wealth, not to discover the truth?"

"I did not say that."

"Well, let me tell you, Mr. Hawk, that I am an archaeologist, like my father and my mother before me. I do not go on these expeditions to find things, only to collect them. Nor am I a fortune seeker, hoping to locate something that I might sell to the highest bidder. My interest is in the truth."

"I did not accuse you of anything."

"No, but you inferred it."

"I do not know this word, 'inferred.' "

"It means to imply something—to say something is so without directly stating it."

With eyes narrowed, he scrutinized her, from the top of her head to the very tip of her chin, as though looking could probe the secret she carried.

But to her credit she said nothing, nor did she flinch under the heat of his gaze.

At last, he said, "And so your father's work is continued through you?"

"Yes," she agreed, her chin lifting into the air.

Again, he stated nothing, but he was aware that his staring at her was hardly comforting. At some length, he finally said, "*Soka'pii*, it is good."

"I'm so glad you approve," she said, though her voice stated the exact opposite.

He wanted to laugh at her, for she looked so stubborn,

and yet so forlorn. Indeed, at this moment, he thought she resembled a rabbit, staring up into the eyes of a wolf. Unfortunately for him, he was that wolf.

He said, "You are frightened, especially after what happened a few nights ago. And because you do not understand why I am here, asking you these questions, you fear for your safety, even with me. I only hope you will give me a chance to prove myself to you."

"I hope so, too," she said, then she rose up to her knees. "And now if you will excuse me, I must get back to my hotel. The others will wonder about me."

When she made to rise this time, he did not stop her. Instead, he gave her one quick nod.

"Thank you for combing my hair." She smiled, to ease the tension in the situation between them. She continued, "I could all too easily become accustomed to such things."

It was that smile that was his undoing. Was she some sort of enchantress that she could ensnare him with an action so simple?

He wanted to get lost in that grin, to bask in it. Moreover he longed to spend more time with her, wanted the rest of the world to go away when he was with her. He swallowed, hard, then said, "You are most beautiful when you smile."

She opened her mouth to speak. But even she seemed at a loss for words, and her lips, now parted, looked inviting.

He cleared his throat, started to say something, but had second thoughts.

She mumbled, "I never forgot you."

"Nor I, you," he said. "I waited for you that day."

"And I came back to that pool day after day," she confessed. "You never returned."

"I was gone from that country by then."

"Gone? But I thought you lived there."

His dark eyes met the question in hers. What could he say that she might understand? Certainly not the truth.

Not knowing what to utter, or what not to, he simply gazed at her. At long last, however, he uttered, "I, too, have my secrets. Perhaps tomorrow evening we will unburden ourselves . . ."

"Perhaps."

He said, "I would touch you, if you would let me."

Shyly, her glance met his. "Would you? How?"

What was she suggesting? He closed his eyes briefly. Swamped by a craving to know every little thing about her, he tried to speak. Nothing happened.

At last, for lack of knowing what else to do, he brought up his hand to her cheek, smoothing the backs of his fingers downward toward her neck. With the action, desire, hot and urgent, raced through him. Her skin was soft, delicate, fragrant with femininity. He swallowed. "It's not enough," he said.

"What?"

"I thought a simple touch would be plenty—that it would last me . . . several days. I was wrong. It's not enough."

She shut her eyes, then slowly she drew in toward him. Her lips parted, she swallowed and she whispered, "Then how else would you touch me? That is, if you could?"

Did she, too, want more? The thought sent him quietly out of his mind. He replied, "Perhaps I might stroke you like this." Bending, he brought his cheek to hers. "Or maybe like this," he mumbled, as he wrapped his arm around her and drew her closer. *Haiya*, he needed to feel her flesh against his.

But it was not to be. It could never be.

He should let her go. He *would* let her go.

And then, from out of nowhere, came her words, "Do you kiss?"

"Of course I kiss." Hardly able to believe he was having this conversation with her, he tried to gulp down the lump that had formed in his throat. "Are you going to let me kiss you?"

She murmured, "You might try it and see . . ."

He lowered his head; she lifted hers. Gently, his lips sought the silky texture of her mouth, and he thought that pleasure might surely burst within him.

Everything about her was right—the way her lips fit against his, the clean taste of her breath. He hungered to know more of her.

She groaned. The sound excited him, and in reaction to it, he thought he would surely burst.

He nipped at her lips once, again, his tongue darting in and out of her mouth, teasing her, testing her. How much more of this could he take before he demanded more?

She leaned in toward him, and he caught her, pulling her closer yet. But he didn't continue his foray of her, instead he brought her body in as near as he possibly could—given the fullness of her swimming attire—and hugged her. He said, "I have dreamed of doing this from the moment I first saw you."

It was her turn to gasp, as though she couldn't quite breathe in sufficient oxygen. "Now or back then?"

"Both," he said. "But neither time has been a good time for us. Back then, we were too young, and now, we have secrets from one another."

He set her away from him, but he couldn't let her go completely, and the backs of his fingers came up to smooth over her cheek. Downward he caressed, toward her neck.

He knew what he should do, what he should suggest. He only hoped he had the courage to do it, to say it.

"Do not be lured by matters of the flesh . . ."

White Claw's words echoed in Red Hawk's mind. But was this a simple matter of the flesh? Red Hawk argued with himself. Or was this more?

Deep within himself, he knew the answer, as surely as he knew his heart. And, after a few moments, he gulped down air, summonsed his nerve and said, "We should marry."

CHAPTER 10

"What?" She backed away from him.

He knew he had surprised her. Yet it was the only thing that made sense, the only thing they could do if they were to be in each other's constant company. Otherwise, how could they keep a firm hold on their integrity?

He tried to explain further, and said, "I want more than a kiss or a hug from you. I am not permitted more than this unless we marry. Please, marry me, spend your life with me."

She moved even farther away. "I . . . I . . . am flabbergasted."

"I do not know this word."

"It means that you have taken me off my guard. We have only kissed."

"So far," he elaborated. "But I know that if I am around you—and I will be in the near future—I will find reasons to be with you, hold you, and before long, I will try to make you mine. I know that I will. *You* know that I will."

"Mr. Hawk, I do believe that I might have something to say about whether or not I will respond to you."

"*Aa*, I am sure that you would. But look at us, here, now. You know it would take little on my part to convince you to lay with me."

"Whoa. You go too far."

"That is what I fear," he said, "and so I think we must do the honorable thing. We must marry."

"I . . . I . . ."

He knew there were many reasons why what he proposed was not wise. Possibly, it was the most impossible thing he had ever considered—for himself, for her. Yet, he would not take it back. He meant it.

"No one else need ever know," he said, as though to solve a problem as yet unspoken, "unless you wish to tell. For, as I understand it, the white world might frown upon such a union. Even my people would do so. You and I already have many secrets from one another—but let us now share one between us, instead."

She backed away still farther. She said, "You move too fast, Mr. Hawk."

"But I must. Soon we will be spending a good deal of time with one another. Let us look to that time now, and do what we can to make it honorable. For I believe that we will be together, married or not."

"You don't understand," she said. "I cannot marry you. I have come into this country for one reason alone, and that is to excavate the site of this dig, and I . . ."

All at once, she broke off. Her eyes opened wide, and as he stared at her, there came a tormented look about her.

And he knew: *What she had said wasn't true . . . not entirely . . .*

He said, as though to ease her situation, "I will help you to do that which you are here to do."

"No," she replied at once, "you can't. It is something that I have to do on my own."

He nodded gently. "I, too, have a great task set before me, and it is one I cannot share with you," he said. "But we should do something to keep the honor between us. As I have already said, we are soon to be in one another's company, and if your feelings are similar to mine, there could be a problem."

She didn't answer.

"My heart tells me that you might care for me. Do you?"

She remained mute, and her gaze fell to the ground.

Still, he continued speaking as though she had answered him, and in the positive. "Knowing that you are not immune to me, I can only foresee that I will press it, even if I try not to."

"But . . . marriage?" she asked, glancing up at him, her eyes still wide. "What do we really know of each other?"

His fingers grazed down her cheek, trailing over her neck. "That we share a passion. Many who have married on short acquaintance have married for less."

"Well, that's not me," she countered, and looked away from him. "If I do find that which I seek, I will need to return to the East, for I have obligations there. I doubt if you would like to go there."

He nodded. "Perhaps, then, we could marry, but make it easy for you to leave, if you chose to go."

"You mean to marry for the moment only?"

"*Saa*, no," he said. "When you would again return to this country, we would still be married."

"And you think that would work?"

He shrugged.

"What would *you* do in the time between when I was here and when I returned? It might be several years."

He didn't answer.

"Don't Indian men take more than one wife?"

"Sometimes, they do," he said, "but not always."

"And are you already married, Mr. Hawk?"

"*Saa*, I am not," he stated, and then, although he was fairly certain he knew the answer, he asked, "Are you?"

"No," she said. "But what if you were to marry while I was gone? I would not be able to stay with you, for in my culture, a man may take only one wife at a time."

"That would be difficult, I agree. Would you rather we separate altogether, if you go back East?"

"I *will* go back East."

"And I cannot come with you?"

"You could, but I do not think you would like it there. Besides, isn't it the woman's place to stay wherever her man is?"

The comment struck him as odd, and he countered, saying, "Why should she?"

"Don't Indian men demand this?"

"Of course not. A woman is the heart of our Nation. If she is not happy in one place, perhaps another might be better. The Blackfeet have a saying, "*Mat'-ah-kwi tam-ap-i-ni-o-ke-mi-o-sin.* 'Not found is happiness without woman.' ""

Lips open, she stared at him.

"We could agree," he advised, "that if you wish it, when you leave, our marriage will dissolve."

"Then the marriage wouldn't be real, would it? Since we both know that I will return East?"

"It will be real. I will simply not require you to stay if you wish to leave. That is, so long as you are not with child."

She swallowed, her throat muscles constricting before she said, "And what if you don't wish to remain with me?"

"That will not happen."

"But let's say that it does. In my world when people marry, they stay married. It is a life sentence, so to speak."

"I understand. In my village, people usually stay married also, but it is not frowned upon if both people find this hard to do. Sometimes these things happen. And so no one will look down on you, if you decided to marry me, but then leave me."

She shook her head, and he decided to take another tack. He said, "If you cannot answer me now, consider it, think on it and give me your decision tomorrow night. As you have allowed me time to consider the good and the bad of these things, so, too, must I grant the same to you."

She moaned. "I don't need time," she said. "I know what my answer must be. But very well," she capitulated, "tomorrow night we will discuss it again. And now I really must go. Already the sky is turning pink in the east. I have other duties."

She rose to her feet, and this time he didn't stop her. Gazing down on him, she said, "Till tomorrow night," and departed.

Yawning and rubbing her eyes, Effie sat up and came slowly awake. What was this? Had she actually fallen asleep in the chair where she'd been working?

Where was he?

It was her first thought. Hadn't Red Hawk agreed to be here tonight?

Her second concern was that she felt . . . odd, as though she had been drugged. Perhaps it was the wine she had shared with her colleagues before retiring. Certainly, she was unused to strong drink.

Effie glanced around the tiny room as if to get her bearings. After retiring to her room, she had positioned herself next to the window, intending to work while she awaited Red Hawk's arrival. Beside her, on a small table, was a candle, the room's only lighting.

Effie stretched up her arms, and ran a hand over her forehead. It must be late, she decided—much too late to be awake and sitting in a chair. Why, she wondered, had she ever agreed to this secret rendezvous with a man she barely knew?

Intending to rise and dress for bed, Effie leaned over and blew out the candle. Immediately, two things happened. Her legs felt strange, as though she couldn't move them, and on the far side of the room, there was an unmistakable sound of material scrapping across the wooden floor. Looking up, Effie witnessed a dark shadow glide to the other side of the room.

"Mr. Hawk?" she called out.

There was no answer. She frowned. Shouldn't he have said something?

All at once, adrenaline pumped through her body. He *would* have answered, were it he who had slithered just now into the shadows.

She tried again. "Who is it?"

Silence.

She attempted to come up to her feet. She couldn't. It was as though she had been tied.

Tied?

Then she heard it, the quiet motion of a shadow as it drew closer to where she sat.

With her heart beating so swiftly that she could hear it in her ears, she called out again, "Who are you?" though her voice was no more than a whisper.

Silence was her response.

It couldn't be Red Hawk, for he would make himself known. She was certain of that.

With this knowledge came a barrage of thoughts each

more frightening than the last. If not Red Hawk, then who was it? Her assailant of a few nights past? Was she to be assaulted yet again?

Instinctively, Effie knew she must get to her feet, but she couldn't. Twisting slightly, silently, she found her answer quickly. She had indeed been tied. Not only were her feet bound, but the lower part of her body was lashed to the chair.

Terror washed through her, and involuntarily, she screamed. Straightaway, a hand covered her mouth, replaced momentarily by a hanky, while her hands were jerked in front of her and tied.

A knife was shoved against her ribs. Effie shut her eyes, certain that this was truly the end.

A gravelly, low-pitched voice said, "Where are they?"

Effie endeavored to say something, but it was a difficult thing to do when gagged. Again that odd voice said, "I will remove this hanky, but you are not to cry out. Just tell me where they are."

He took the hanky away, and although Effie had not intended it, instinct took over. She screamed, and she screamed and she kept on screaming, her voice high-pitched and deafening. Acting on impulse, to avoid being butchered, she forced the chair sideways, away from her aggressor, bracing herself for the fall.

She heard the knife drop.

Effie screamed again, and this time added, "Help!"

At last, running footsteps sounded in the corridor outside her door.

"We will meet again," said that horrible voice before her assailant turned and ran toward the window. Moonbeams caught and held his slender image, even as he disappeared into the night.

At that same moment, someone pushed the door open.

And as an assortment of flickering candles met Effie's vision, she called out, "Over here. I'm on the floor, tied to this chair."

It was Carl Bell who rushed toward her.

"Are you all right?" Carl asked as he knelt down beside her. Righting the chair first, he then reached down to untie her. It took several moments, allowing Effie a chance to gain her composure.

Still, she didn't know what to say. She was unharmed, but was she all right?

After several moments, Lesley and Henry Smith came into the room, along with Carl's wife, Madeline.

"What happened?" asked Lesley.

Effie wasn't certain she could tell the story. Luckily, she was saved the effort when Madeline rushed to her side and took her in her arms.

She said, "Don't bother her with questions right now. Can't you see that she's terrified?"

Lesley retreated to a corner of the room, while Madeline resorted to cooing, as though she comforted a baby.

Oddly enough, it worked. Within moments, Effie felt able to speak, and she said, "Someone threatened me with a knife. I think he dropped it here in this room, on the floor."

Immediately everyone's attention went to the floor.

"Is this it?" It was Madeline who found the thing and held it up for Effie's inspection.

Effie nodded. At that same moment, Red Hawk entered the room, but no one acknowledged his appearance. He didn't come forward, but rather took station at the door.

Effie briefly inspected the object that Madeline showed her. Nodding, Effie said, "I think that is it. It was dark. I didn't see the thing—I only felt it."

"Look at it. What's this?" asked Henry Smith, as he

strode forward to get a clearer look at the object. Taking
hold of it and turning it over and over in his palm, he said,
"If I'm correct in my assumption, this looks like the sort
of knife that the savages use."

"Savages?" said Effie.

"The Indians. Do you see its blade?" He pointed it at
her, and Effie retreated. "See, its end is sharp, as well as its
blade, and on both sides. And look at its black handle—
gutta-percha, I believe. It's a scalping knife, made by J.
Russell & Co. of Green River Works; traders have brought
this sort of item into this country by the hundreds to trade
with the savages."

Effie glanced toward the door, the others following her
lead. Five pairs of eyes scrutinized the man.

"Is that our new guide?" whispered Madeline.

"Yes," said Effie. Then in a louder voice, "Mr. Hawk,
if you will come closer, I will introduce you to my colleagues."

But Red Hawk didn't move away from the door. He
didn't say a word, either. With arms folded over his chest,
he glared back at them.

"You don't suppose it was he . . ." Madeline's voice
trailed away.

"It's mere coincidence, that's all," said Effie to fill the
silence in the room. "Anyone here could have access to
the same knives. To think it was an Indian who attacked
me makes no sense. Why in the good Lord's name would
an Indian wish to invade my private room and threaten
my life? Wouldn't they simply kill me?"

The two men nodded, but no one spoke a word.

Effie extended her hand toward Henry. "You will leave
the knife with me, won't you?" she asked. "Though I don't
expect the sheriff to do much, I will still have to report the
incident to him."

"Of course you do, and of course he will," said Madeline. "Do you want one of us to stay with you through the rest of the night, Effie? Both Lesley and myself would be happy to be with you tonight."

"No, no," murmured Effie. From out of the corner of her eye, she caught Lesley's stifled frown. Ignoring it, she continued, "I think I'll be fine."

"Are you certain?" asked Madeline.

Effie nodded. "I . . . I don't plan to go back to sleep anyway. I don't believe I would be capable of it right now. So, thank you, but—"

"We will post a watch by your door, nonetheless, Miss Rutledge," said Carl. "Both Henry and I will take turns."

"That is kind of you."

"In fact," said Henry, stepping forward, "we will stand guard at your door every night we are here in this town. Once we are on our way, the danger may pass. I fear that perhaps it is the town itself that is at fault. Maybe someone here believes you to be on a treasure hunt, and so concludes that you would be carrying something of value."

"Yes," said Effie, "perhaps. Let us hope that you are right. Carl," she added, "you and the others haven't by chance been talking about our project where the townspeople could hear, have you?"

Carl hesitated, and despite his tanned complexion, his face turned a deep shade of red. He said, "I'm sorry, Miss Rutledge. We have been so enthusiastic that we have discussed the project openly."

"Do you know of anyone who has overheard you?"

Carl grimaced. "To tell you the truth, we have spoken of the project to many people—the shop owners, the men in the livery, several tradesmen. We should have been more discreet, Miss Rutledge," he continued, "but these people ask so many questions . . ."

"I see."

He hung his head. Again, he apologized. "I'm sorry. We had no idea it would come to this."

"No need to ask pardon," Effie offered politely. "However, if that be the case, and several people know what the project entails, then it could be anyone who is doing this."

No one in the room seemed to have a reply to that, although Carl again muttered, "I'm sorry."

"That's all right," said Effie. "It is better to know what one might expect than to continue to speculate."

"I'm sorry, too," said Madeline, who was still kneeling at Effie's side. She squeezed Effie's hand.

"As I am, too," muttered Henry. Only Lesley remained silent.

"Well, the women had best be seeking their beds yet again this night," Carl suggested, "thus allowing you a chance to recover. I hope you will excuse us. Have no fear, Miss Rutledge. Henry and I will take turns standing guard by your door."

"Yes," said Effie, "that would be good of you."

So it was that on this note they all said their "good nights," each one of her friends squeezing her hand before leaving. Madeline hugged her as well.

Effie smiled at the other woman, thinking that it was indeed a stroke of luck that Carl and Madeline had consented to join her on this excavation. Perhaps by the end of their journey, she and Madeline would be fast friends.

Red Hawk was the last to leave, and his gaze was stern, though strangely, something in his look tugged at her heart. But then, even he turned to leave.

Effie, however, was having none of that, and she said, "Where are *you* going, Mr. Hawk? I believe we have things to discuss."

He directed a questioning gaze at her.

"And where have you been, I might add?" said Effie. "As memory serves me, didn't we have an appointment tonight?"

She rose up from where she had been seated, and with her arms crossed in front of her chest, she fixed the man with a heated glare. She said, "I waited for you tonight for a time that seemed without end. In truth, so long was it, I fell asleep. Or had you forgotten that we had an appointment?"

He remained mute.

She continued, "I can't help feeling that if you had been here, as you were supposed to be, that, well . . . the whole incident would not have happened."

Red Hawk stood still, staring at her. After a while, however, a half smile pulled at the corners of his lips.

"How can you smile?" she complained.

"Perhaps it is not good that I find amusement in this, a serious moment," he said. "But I am thinking that it is well that we have earlier spoken of marriage."

She frowned. "I do not follow your reasoning."

"Do you not?" he asked. "Can you not see that already you treat me as a wife might a wayward husband?"

The statement silenced Effie, at least for a moment. In due time, however, she sighed. "Come in, Mr. Hawk," she said, "and please close the door behind you. There are some matters we must discuss."

This time, with a quick nod, Red Hawk took a step into the room.

Chapter 11

Red Hawk quietly shut the door. He understood the reason for her upset; he had not been with her at a time of urgency. But that didn't mean it was easier on him. Pivoting, he took another step forward without looking where he was going. It was a mistake. His guard was down, and he hadn't sensed that she had crossed the room. He fell into her, knocking them both to the floor.

He landed on top of her. At once, the scent of her delicate skin filled his nostrils and the soft touch of her body beneath his caused his own to respond to her, quite out of his control. Feeling much more like a young boy than a seasoned warrior, Red Hawk gulped.

"You are heavy," she said, and her breath, sweet and intoxicating, sent his thoughts on to other, much more pleasurable things. She was so close, so very, very close, and he had only to move his lips a short distance.

He did it. He kissed her. In truth, given their circumstances, he wondered if any man would have been able to resist the temptation.

His lips lingered over hers, his tongue dipping into the

sweet recess of her mouth. And for a delicate, wonderful moment, she responded in kind.

Then, as though coming to her senses, she pushed against him. "Mr. Hawk, you are heavy."

He fell to her side, but he didn't release her . . . not yet. Passion still raged within his heart, and although unlikely, there was always the hope that she might be persuaded.

With one arm thrown over her, and one leg atop hers, he said, "I am sorry that I was not here to help you. I feel bad that you, alone, had to confront your attacker."

Reaching up, he ran the backs of his fingers down over her cheek. He knew he played with fire, for he could sense her wrath, but the prospect of touching, of feeling her soft skin beneath his fingers . . .

She slapped his hand away. "You are still on me, and I am not overly pleased with you."

He nodded. "*Aa*, that I am, and I know."

"Well, remove yourself at once."

He withdrew his leg from across her, though his arm still held her tightly.

"Mr. Hawk?"

Rolling onto his back, he released her completely. He said, by way of explanation, "I was not here because I have been following the man that I thought might be your attacker."

"You have?" she queried as she sat up. She raised an eyebrow at him. "If that be the case, then you should have been here, shouldn't you?"

"*Aa*, I should have. But the man I was following was not your attacker."

Red Hawk sat up, crossed his legs in front of him and looked at her.

She was adjusting her clothing, he noted with interest. The action was curious, for the waist of her dress was very tight against her tiny stomach. Still, she made herself as comfortable as possible, then stared back at him with as defiant a countenance as any warrior he had ever fought. All she said was, "Yes? As you were saying?"

"I was wrong to follow this man," he responded, "I admit now that this is so. Know, however, that I did not realize this at the time."

"Hmmm . . . That could be true," she conceded.

"I have discovered, nonetheless, that whoever is doing this to you is clever."

"Indeed," she said. "But you still have not answered my original question, Mr. Hawk. Whether or not you were following this person, you forget that we had made arrangements to meet. I . . . expected you."

He frowned. Had her voice quivered?

Omaniit, had he disappointed her that greatly? He inhaled deeply, but the simple action didn't ease his spirits. Instead the erotic scent of her filled his lungs, distracting him.

"I am sorry that I kept you waiting. Perhaps I might be excused when I tell you that the man I followed was one whom I saw enter your room earlier today. I waited until he let himself out, and then I trailed him. This person, however, was not your attacker tonight, for I have had him well in my sights all evening."

"Oh?" she said. "And who was it that you followed?"

"The sheriff of this town."

"The sheriff?" she repeated. "That's the most puzzling piece of news that I've heard tonight. Why would the sheriff come to my room?" She scowled. "Unless . . . He must have been searching for something."

"I believe that he was."

"Yet I saw no evidence that someone went through my things."

Red Hawk smiled at her. "Remind me once we have embarked on our journey to teach you how to look and observe things properly."

Effie blew out a breath in disgust.

Red Hawk, however, continued to smirk at her. Then without another word, he rose up, and took a few steps toward the window. He said, "I must leave you now."

"Where are you going?" she asked crossly, as she, too, stood up.

He glanced at her from over his shoulder, and said, "Your assailant will have left a trail. He will have no choice but to do so, for our Mother, the Earth, will have recorded each step that he took. I would find his tracks now before others in this town awaken and take away the evidence."

"Yes, yes," she said. "Of course you must, but please, we have other things to discuss, don't we?"

"We did," he agreed, "but perhaps we should leave that talk until tomorrow." He took several more steps toward the window.

"Yes," she repeated, and he glanced at her again from over his shoulder. What he saw, however, puzzled him, for her gaze at him was odd. . . . Was it shy?

She said, "Please don't leave me yet."

He pivoted back toward her. "I must."

"But I . . ." She hesitated. "I need your advice . . . on something . . . You see, I . . . I'm not certain that I can trust anyone else in my party . . . at least not at this moment. In truth, I'm not so certain I can trust you, either— it *was* a trading knife that was found here, one that has been brought into this country specifically to trade with the Indians."

"Easily obtained by anyone," he pointed out, "not simply by an Indian."

"I know that," she said. "It's why I'm dismissing the information as insignificant. Yet, I need advice."

He drew back into the room. Taking a few steps toward the bed, he pulled off one of the blankets, which he spread over the floor. Then, gesturing toward the blanket, he said, "Let us sit and talk."

She nodded. "That is good. Yes." They sat; she, with her legs to the side, he, cross-legged.

At first, she seemed reluctant to say anything, but as he remained silent, waiting, at last she began, saying, "My father isn't here to guide me, and . . . I do not know what to do. Therefore, I must turn to someone to hear out my thoughts . . . someone who might be able to counsel me . . ."

He was flattered. "My heart is happy that you have chosen me to assist you. I will listen to you and help you as best I can."

"All right." She hesitated once again, then, "The truth is, I am doubtful of what I must do from this point forward. It is evident that there is someone—possibly someone close to me—who does not have my best interest at heart. I have already been assaulted by this person twice since arriving in this town. This last time was the worst. If I continue on toward the Gates of the Mountains, do I invite more harm?"

Red Hawk might have answered forthwith, but before he could utter a word, she continued, "And what happens if I do reach that country, find the things for which I search, and another in my party takes them from me by force? All my plans, all my work, will be for nothing. I would have failed my father . . . and another people in more need . . ."

Another people in more need? Red Hawk sat up straighter, focusing on her words. However, she didn't take heed of the change in him and went on talking. "Would it be better if I disband the entire project, cut my losses and return here later, having picked another crew?" Solemnly, she looked up to him.

Weighing his words carefully, Red Hawk didn't respond at once. Though it was important to him, and to the welfare of his tribe, that she continue on exactly as she was, he couldn't very well tell her this. And so he said, "You could do that."

"Then you believe that would be advisable? To return back East?"

He shook his head. "*Saa*, no, I do not. I merely said that you could do that if you decide it is right. But I am uncertain that your returning to the East—without discovering who it is that is doing this to you—will solve your problem. You might well find that you could be bothered by the same dilemma."

"What do you mean? I would be back home. Things there would be different."

"Would they?"

She frowned. "Wouldn't they? Before I left, there were none of these occurrences. Nor did I encounter anything unusual on the way here."

Red Hawk shrugged. "I understand what you say. However, without discovering who this thief is," he said, "the man remains free to do the same thing to you in the East, as well as here, or wherever you are."

After a short space of time, she said, "I'm not certain I agree with you. I think that things would be different there. In the East, my father would take great precaution, and he would lock up the valuables that I carry."

"Then you *do* bear something valuable?"

She gasped aloud. Clearly, she had not intended to give that away.

At last, she must have decided on a course of action, for she set back her shoulders, and said, "I guess I might as well admit it, since it is evident that someone else knows that I carry something. In truth, simple deduction would prove that I must have a thing of worth in my possession, otherwise . . ."

"May I see what this thing is?" asked Red Hawk carefully.

Effie tilted her head to the left, her glance piercing into his, as though she would read his thoughts. But after awhile, she seemed to give up the attempt, and said, "I don't think so."

He had expected nothing less. Still he was disappointed, and nodding, he said, "I can only tell you this: Sometimes it is wise to go elsewhere if one's life is in danger. But this is not always advisable. There are times when it is better to hold to one's position and confront what danger exists—especially if the trouble might follow a person wherever she may go. Tell me," he continued, "would you be as vulnerable on your trip back East, as you are here? Before you reach the safety of your father's lodge?"

"I could be," she replied, "but I could also travel alone, away from my colleagues, since I am beginning to distrust them."

"And do you think traveling by yourself would help you?" he asked, startled at the idea that she might think this would be secure. "Is not one alone easier for an enemy to conquer than one of many?"

She drew her brows together. "Of course you are right," she said. "But I don't think I could stay here in this town until the culprit is caught. Why this hotel, as dull and dirty as it is, is costing me a fortune. I'm afraid my finances will not permit a long stay. Besides, now that I have a guide, I only have need to stay here until the rest of our party joins us. Yet if I continue on with this journey, don't I risk putting the entire project in danger?"

"Is it not already in danger?"

Her eyes met his, and there, within her glance, he could see clearly that she at last understood her situation.

He pressed onward. "Why not continue your trek to where you originally intended going?" he suggested. "*Haiya*, it is the best way, for you are right. You cannot stay here. There is trouble here for you. If you leave immediately, it is true that you might bring the danger with you. But it is also true that, if this person means to take something from you, no matter where you go, the threat will go with you. At least here, you have several people to defend you. *Annisa*, I am afraid that until you complete the task set before you, there will be much difficulty for you."

"You may be right."

"*Aa*, I believe that I am." He continued, "I think that your best course is to go onward, as you have already planned. At least once you have finished the task set before you, everything will be out, for it is my belief that your attacker will have no choice but to present himself. Then, and only then, can you once more live your life without fear of assault."

She stared at him as though she could see him clearly for the first time. She said, "You present quite a persuasive argument, Mr. Hawk. But at the same time, I wonder why you champion so greatly going forward?" She hesitated. "Tell me, I know why I am here—and at this moment, so do you. I have told you this plainly. It is your turn to share now. Tell me, what draws you here?"

Truth be told, Red Hawk had prepared for their meeting tonight, and had braced himself for this very question, deciding that his best defense was to impart at least a portion of the truth. However, he quickly revised his plan.

True, he might be tempted to tell her the truth of his plight, for he had discovered he had feelings for her. And this alone carried with it a tendency to trust her.

But he hesitated. Too much depended on his ability to discover what she sought, why she sought it and what she stood to gain from it. Besides, if he were completely honest, it was doubtful she would believe him.

And so he evaded her question. Hoping to draw her attention on to something else besides him, and he said, "It is true that I desire you to continue to the Gates of the Rocky Mountains, and that I wish you to succeed in your quest. 'Tis also true that there are reasons why I am here and why I am giving you aid.

"But I do not think that you have been completely open with me," he continued. "Let me retell a few of the facts as I understand them. *Aa*, you seek something, but your very profession proclaims this. This thing which you desire to find is valuable. But the fact that someone else is attempting to steal it from you would show me that what you seek, and what you have, is valuable. So do not think you have deceived me."

"I am not trying to deceive you."

"Are you not? And yet you have not told me what this thing is."

"True, but we made a pact, and I still know nothing about why *you* are here," she countered, "and are so interested in this thing that I carry. Is it not unusual for an Indian to have concern for such things?"

"Perhaps."

She paused. "Check," she said. "Once again we are at an impasse."

He nodded.

"Mr. Hawk," she began after a short while, "I . . . actually . . . well, if you must know, I am caught. I am afraid to go onward. I'm also afraid to go back. And I cannot, nor do I want to stay here. What am I to do?"

He reached out to touch her, his fingers clasping hers. He said, "I am here, and I will remain with you, no matter your decision. And though I think it wise to continue onward, I cannot tell you what to do—you must make that choice yourself. Know that whatever you decide, I will lend you assistance."

"I . . . thank you."

Again, he nodded. "Perhaps," he said, "once on the road, others will come to your defense, as well."

"Others?"

"*Aa.* Besides myself, our Mother, the Earth, will protect you."

"Mother Earth?" She stared at him. "We're not talking about a live being, are we?"

"All things are alive, even the air that we breathe."

Effie gave him a wide-eyed gawk. But he ignored the look, and went on to explain, "Does the air not nourish us? Can we live without it? Does it not impart life to us?"

"But it's not . . . really . . . alive. I can't talk to it, and it certainly can't speak back—"

"Because you do not know how to listen. It is in contact with you every day. 'Tis all a matter of perception. *Haiya*, all things are alive, or were once alive, and all living creatures are a part of life's circle and are able to receive and give communication."

She frowned at him. "You are speaking of things, which I do not believe, and I—"

"Just as you have intuition, so, too, can every living creature sense whether or not another intends harm or good."

"Maybe, but—"

"As an example, it has been told to me by my elders that there was once a tree that saved the lives of seven helpless people."

She said, "But could that not be a myth? We have many such tales in my culture, as well, but they are stories that we relate to the very young, in order to entertain them."

"Are you certain that this is all?" he countered. "Do not discount those things that you have not seen, merely because you have not yet experienced them. Many myths are based on fact."

"That's probably true," she conceded.

"*Aa,*" he continued, "I do think that our Mother, the Earth, is your best protection. In the open spaces, whoever this is will have to show himself or herself."

"Herself?" Effie became immediately distracted, and said further, "Do you think that the guilty party might be one of the women . . . perhaps Lesley?"

Red Hawk shrugged. "I do not know. The important thing to remember is that no matter where you go, I fear that your attacker will follow you."

Effie nodded. After a few minutes, she said, "I will consider all you have said, and I thank you for your advice. But now, since it is late, and before it gets any later," she said, "perhaps we should discuss the sheriff and what you discovered today. Why would he break into my room? And why would he rummage through my things?"

Red Hawk breathed out deeply, then said, "All of the men in this town are loco, I believe. These men talk of nothing but gold and silver. They argue amongst themselves over who owns what piece of ground, and they work endlessly, digging into our Mother, the Earth, scarring her. They ignore her cries, because they have no ears with which to hear, and because their machines drown out her voice."

"But they are miners and seek their fortune. That is what miners do."

"So I have been told. But there is more. Have you observed that there are few women here?"

"There are some."

"But they are not the kind of women that a man will most often marry."

Effie lifted her brow.

"Therefore," he said, "one can only wonder what purpose these men serve. How can a man build a town without women? Do they forget that without a woman, there is little happiness?"

"An excellent point," she said, "but what does this have to do with the sheriff?"

" 'Tis simple, I think. The only conclusion I can draw from the manner of madness that I see all around me is that these men hope to easily obtain something that does not belong to them, but rather belongs to our Mother, the Earth. Gold and silver hold these men's hearts for ransom, and perhaps the sheriff suffers the same ailment as the rest and hopes to attain something easily, even though it does not belong to him. Perhaps that is all. I do not know. All I can tell you is that the man came to your room, he searched it and left. He did not return here, but spent the remainder of the day over the hills where the young men are digging."

Effie nodded. "It is curious, Mr. Hawk. Very curious. But maybe you are right and he was hoping to obtain something more easily than the rest." She yawned.

Red Hawk watched her for the space of a moment, then said, "Are you going to tell me or show me what this thing is? So many people are searching for it . . . your life is in danger because of it . . . Do you not think I should see it?"

"No," she said flatly, no explanation given. "Now if

you will excuse me, I believe that it is time that I get some sleep."

He ignored her words. "I could readily find out what this thing is from the others. You realize this, don't you?"

She didn't utter a word. Instead, she gazed away from him.

Without taking his glance from her, he said, "I would rather you show it to me."

"They won't tell you."

"Your friends won't *have* to tell me," he stated. "I know how to listen."

Effie gave a deep sigh and, resigned, said, "Oh, very well. If you turn your back and blow out the candle, I will show it to you."

He nodded and did as she directed, listening. She must have adjusted her clothing once again, for he could hear the rustling of her garments.

She commanded him to turn around, and when he did so, he saw it.

She held out both hands to him. In the center of her palms were two pieces of white, glittering rock, beautiful, even in this lighting, which was only a mere streak of moonlight. But it wasn't only the rock that caught and held his attention. Imbued into the niche of each piece of quartz was the golden image of . . .

She said, "I don't know if you can see the engravings well, for we have little light by which to see them. But they are figures, half bird, half human. They are supposed to represent the—"

"Children of the Thunderer," he finished for her.

Her curious eyes caught his. She asked, "You must have heard about that part of the legend, then?"

He didn't answer her right away. He couldn't, for

without warning, a memory had pressed itself into his consciousness:

> *"Four golden images,*
> *When all in a row,*
> *Slaves, your people will be,*
> *No more."*

It was the song, the poem of his protector, the sea dog. He hadn't understood it, then. He did so now.

"Mr. Hawk," she was saying. "Is something wrong?"

"Saa," he replied after a long hesitation, "nothing is wrong. In truth, something is very right. And now," he added, "it is time that I tell you the truth about me, because we are united in cause."

"I don't understand. . . ."

" 'Tis simple. I am of the Lost Clan."

Chapter 12

"Did you find them?" the voice was deep, baritone and masculine.

"No, I didn't," the second person, in a tone that was higher-pitched, as well as sweet and feminine, said. "And I almost got caught. She screamed so much, even I became scared."

A masculine finger reached out to lift the woman's dainty chin. He smiled. "You have no reason to ever be scared. I am here for you. I will always be here for you, as you are for me." He kissed her.

"Oh, hold me, darling, just hold me. It was awful, just awful."

The man took the woman in his arms and pressed her lithe form against the hard contours of his. "I picked up something for you today," he said. And reaching into a pocket, he pulled out a pair of golden earrings.

"Oh!" she exclaimed. "They're beautiful."

"But you can't wear them . . . not yet. When our job here is finished, there will be more where these came from."

"Really?" She giggled.

"Yes," said the man, his voice deep and resonant. "Really. And now to the more pleasant aspects of life. My darling, come lie down with me. I must admit that I am weary."

"As I am, too," she said. "How I would like to sleep away these next few days instead of . . . Oh, well. There is work to be done, I suppose."

"It's one of the things I've always loved about you most."

"What?"

"Your dedication. All this would be for nothing, if not for you."

The woman smiled widely. "Hmmm, I like the sound of that."

"Yes? What is it?"

She grinned. "Help me out of my things."

"Ah . . . with great pleasure, my dear. By the by, where did you find such a charming little black outfit?"

"I have my means," she replied with a slight giggle. "I have my means."

"You're a minx. Come here," he coaxed, and very soon, one black silk shirt hit the floor, followed by a pair of men's black trousers.

"Ah," said the man. "You are beautiful."

She giggled.

Given a choice, this was not the manner in which Red Hawk would have chosen to travel. He was a scout, and scouts commonly traversed enemy territory at night; they also used various means to blend into their environment. So much was this the case that only the well-trained eye could detect the presence of a scout, if at all.

Unfortunately, there was no plan Red Hawk could

employ to hide the horses and wagons of Effie's group, no manner by which to disguise the noise of the wagons, the neighing of the animals nor the dust kicked up by their procession. Moreover because of these wagons—and there were two of them—their party was restricted to using the sunlight hours in which to travel. Thus, the chance of meeting a war party was great.

Luckily for them, because the Crow Indians were friendly toward the whites, Effie's company would not likely encounter hostilities on this leg of their journey, even though *he*—a traditional enemy of the Crow—traveled with them. He only hoped the same would hold true once they reached Blackfeet country.

However, scouting was the least of his duties. In addition, there was the trail to blaze, meat to procure, protection and lookouts to be kept. One more experienced man would have been preferable.

Red Hawk had tried to find such a person. In the few days before setting out on the trail, he had considered seeking out the Crow to determine if there might be a few warriors among them who would be willing to aid the whites.

But he had rejected the idea almost immediately. Since the Blackfeet and the Crow were enemies, he figured he would never be able to trust a Crow warrior with his scalp.

In addition, he had also sought out several of the young men who had flocked to Virginia City. But that, too, had been to no avail.

Unfortunately, there was no one else; this had left him with many tasks to perform, and required a rigorous schedule: to bed early, after posting one of the white men to stand watch. Arising in the middle of the night and setting out on the trail to explore the territory ahead, he watched for signs of enemies—in this way Red Hawk secured safe passage for the next day's journey.

Then in the very early morning, Red Hawk would return to camp, there to awaken the others, and set them into preparation for their continued trip. Add to this that Red Hawk's main duty was to provide fresh meat, as well as to lead Effie's group on the shortest and safest path through Crow country, and one might realize the extent of his responsibilities.

That this cut his hours of sleep to less than a few a night was something he did without thought or complaint. Perhaps when they attained his own country, he could let down his guard.

There had been one change, however. While still in Virginia City, two more people had joined their party—a man by the name of John Owens, and his butler, Fieldman. Owens's wife was to have accompanied him, originally, it seemed, but had not felt up to the challenge of travel.

Owens was an elder to the rest of the group, by perhaps twenty-five years. He was also the father of one of the other women in the group, the one known as Lesley.

John Owens was also Effie's father's best friend, her father's *naapi*, as the men of the Blackfeet would say. A middle-aged man, with short, graying, dark hair—at least what was left of it—he sported a mustache that was predominately gray. In height, he stood a little shorter than Red Hawk, and he carried a great deal of fat around the middle of his belly.

At first Red Hawk hadn't known what to think of the elder man, for Red Hawk had sensed an air of antagonism about him. Upon further acquaintance, however, Owens had seemed amicable enough, and any doubts Red Hawk had harbored at first unwarranted.

Still Red Hawk frowned. It was puzzling, for he tended to trust his instincts, as well as first impressions.

And then there was Owens's butler, Fieldman. Though

Fieldman seemed devoted to Owens, Red Hawk little trusted a man whose living depended on the leave and "goodwill" of another.

But enough.

The weather on this fine day in *Niipiaato's*, or June, the summer month, was pleasant, warm and sunny. It was a condition he had expected, since it had been foretold by the red sun at sunset on the previous day.

"The sun will not lie to you," he could almost hear his grandfather say, "and if it is red at sunset, the next day will be fair."

At present, Red Hawk was riding his mustang, a mare, a little distance ahead of the others; his senses were alert for signs of enemies, but not blind to the splendor all around him. The countryside was as fine an example of Mother Earth at her best as he could remember.

Here was a meadow of newly growing green grass. To his right was another sea of green, which was littered with a profusion of flowering dogwood, pink twin flowers and *a-sat-chiot-ake* or purple loco weed. He took careful note of this latter, for it had a medicinal purpose.

Swinging his left leg over his pony's neck, he jumped down and walked the short distance to the other meadow, where he proceeded to gather up parts of the plant. They might prove useful later, he decided, for their medicine was often good for sore throats or swellings.

The scent as the wind blew its fragrance around him was clean, balmy and full of the perfume of the grasses and flowers, and he relished it as he drew in a deep breath. Even the smell of balsam wafted through the air, for this part of the prairie was flanked by stands of pine trees.

In the distance from these meadows, and due north, were snow-capped mountains, majestic looking, steep and rugged, though from this angle, they appeared deceptively serene. These would be the mountains that Effie's party would either skirt or cross, depending on the safety of the various trails. It was his hope to escape the dangerous mountain passes, however, and bypass them entirely.

"It's like a fairyland, isn't it?" He recognized Effie's voice at once. On foot, she stood above him, since he was still hunched over the ground.

"Fairyland?" he queried, gazing up at her.

"A place of mystical beauty. That's what a fairyland is," she said. "I think that when I was younger I fell in love with this country."

This he could understand. He said, "I, too, love this land . . . almost as much as I love and respect my . . . people, my grandfather."

"Yes," she agreed. "What is it that you are collecting?"

"A plant. We call it *a-sat-chiot-ake* or purple loco weed. It is used as a medicine for sore throats. We may have need of it later."

She nodded. "How many days' journey are left before us, do you suppose?"

"It will depend on the weather and the trails, and if we are bothered by the Crow tribes or not."

"Bothered?"

"We are in Crow country, and though they are friendly to whites, they are my traditional enemy. Many of their warriors would covet my scalp, if they see I am here. It would not be a good thing, since we are vulnerable to attack."

"We are?"

"*Aa*, we are. Though there are four other men with us, I have not observed that any of them are good shots. Perhaps they fight well hand to hand. I do not know. I can only hope that the fear of the whites and fear of their retaliation will keep the Crow from attacking us."

"But we never had trouble when I was here with my father, many years ago."

"As you have already told me."

"I guess we were lucky back then."

"Perhaps you were," he said. "And I pray that luck is with you as much today as in the past."

"As do I," she said. After a moment, she dropped to her knees beside him. "May I help you with that?"

"I would welcome it," he said. "You must pick the flower up stem and all. Do not bother with the roots, for it is the flower and stem that I require."

"All right," she acknowledged. Then she fell into silence as she worked, but after a moment, she said, "Mr. Hawk, I wish to speak of a delicate matter between us."

"You may say whatever you please to me."

Her look was guarded at first, but then, with a shake of her head, she said, "Very well. I have many questions I might ask about you, your life and the Lost Clan, as you well might understand. But first there is another matter that sits heavily on my mind."

He raised an eyebrow at her.

"Truth be told," she continued, "I never did answer your question as to marriage, and you have never inquired after it. Have you changed your mind?"

Her question, as well as the subject itself, was indeed "delicate." It also had the effect of knocking the breath from him, but he kept the reaction to himself.

"I do not change my mind," he said, dismayed to hear that his voice was unsteady, "I simply try to give you space to consider it, as well as some time away from me so as to decide the matter for yourself." He paused. "Did you think I might have changed? That I would take back my offer?"

"Yes." Her glance skimmed off of his. "You have been . . . distant from me since we started this journey."

"I have much on my mind—it is my duty to lead and to protect us." Again, he hesitated, then, "Did you have an answer for me?"

He didn't look at her. He dared not.

"Yes," she said, and she reached out to touch his hand. "I . . . I am afraid . . . that I cannot marry you."

He nodded without looking at her. It was as he had expected.

But then she added, "Now . . ."

"Now?"

"I need to find out more about you, about what you said about the Lost Clan, before I can . . . I was so startled by what you said," she continued hurriedly, "and you left so quickly after, that I haven't known what to think. So as you see, I have many questions."

"*Aa*, I have had much to consider. But I am here now. If you have other things that trouble your thoughts, feel free to question me."

She didn't respond right away. In truth, she seemed to be carefully choosing her words, as now and again she sent him a tentative look.

Gazing at her now, with her fiery hair, as well as her dress blowing softly about her, she presented such a beautiful picture, it was almost more than he could do to keep himself from staring at her like a lovesick calf. Though she was on her knees picking several flowers, she now and again frowned at him, and he felt urged to smooth out those two wrinkles between her brows.

"Very well," she acknowledged, sitting back. "My first question is about the Lost Clan."

He nodded. "I thought that you might have questions for me about that."

"Yes. Well, what I've been trying to understand, and what I can't quite comprehend is this: You said that you are of the Lost Clan?"

"*Aa.*"

"But how can this be so? They are a clan of legend, are they not?"

" 'Tis so."

Her frown grew deeper. "I still don't understand," she muttered. "I am here to dig for evidence that they did at one time exist . . . but in the past. To say that you are of that tribe would infer that they are in the present, and not in the past . . ." Her voice trailed away.

He hesitated and considered her question solemnly. In due time, he said, "I understand your confusion, and you are correct, the Lost Clan is a clan of legend. But it is also a clan that the Creator blessed with a chance to end the curse."

"Yes. That's right. I had almost forgotten that part of the legend. Once a generation, a boy is chosen—"

"To take on real form," he continued for her, "and to go out into the world in an attempt to end the curse for the Clan."

"Real form? Then what you're saying is that you were once entrapped in the mist?"

"*Aa.*"

"Excuse me, but I find that a bit hard to believe."

He shrugged, looking away from her, and glanced back toward the ground. It was as he had thought. The truth was too bizarre to be accepted.

She continued to speak, however. "And so what you are saying is that you are one of those boys who was chosen to try to end the curse?"

He grimaced. "*Aa*, it is so."

"Hmmm . . ."

"And yet, no, I am not truly a chosen one."

She shook her head. "Now I'm really confused."

"Let me explain. The elders did not wish to choose me. It is as uncomplicated as that."

"But if they didn't want to—"

"They had no one else from whom to pick; the rest of the boys from my tribal band were injured."

"Oh."

"That day when we met, I was coming from the council that named me as champion."

"Were you? How exciting . . . you must have been delighted."

"No," he said flatly. "Though I had long wished to be champion, knowing that I was picked only because there was no one else was not the way in which I had dreamed of becoming our tribe's defender . . ."

He noted that whether she believed him or not, she at least bestowed upon him a sympathetic look, and said, "I'm sorry."

"You do not need to be. Regardless of how it was done, I am still the one who must break the curse for my people or live with the knowledge of my failure. I take that obligation seriously, if for no other reason than to make my grandfather proud."

"And so you should," she said. "That is very commendable. I notice that you speak of your grandfather often. You must love him dearly."

"*Aa*, it is so. He adopted me when I was so young that I do not remember it."

"Adopted?"

"*Aa*, though I am of Blackfoot descent, the Lost Clan is not my tribe of birth. My parents, who were visiting the Clan at the time when the trouble began, were killed by the Thunderer. I would have been left homeless, were it not for Grandfather."

"Your parents were killed by the Thunderer?"

"*Aa, aa.* In my youth, I often dreamed of revenging myself on the Thunder Being or the Thunderbird, as he is sometimes known, because I blamed him for all my troubles. But I have since grown up, and I have put those desires of vengeance away from me . . . or at least I have tried to. Now I only seek to free my people, my grandfather."

"I see," she said. She drew her hand over the ground, as though trying to decide which flower to pick next. She continued, "But tell me, if all you say is so, why are you here with me now? Why aren't you out somewhere trying to break the curse?"

"Because," he said without even hesitating, "I *am* 'out somewhere' trying to break the curse."

"I don't understand."

"You are somehow connected with the Clan."

"Oh, am I?" she said, then she brightened suddenly. "I'm think I'm beginning to understand what this is all about," she uttered slowly. "It's the artifacts, isn't it? Somehow, these artifacts that I carry, and those that I search for, are important to you. Am I right?" She looked to him hopefully.

He didn't respond. He couldn't, and remain true to his vision, for a vision, if told to anyone other than a medicine man, was to render the prophecy powerless.

At length she gazed away from him, and all the while, the reddish strands of hair that framed her face fluttered prettily in the wind. He wished he could take her in his arms, if only to make her believe him. But he knew that if he wanted her to trust him, to really trust him, he dare not.

At last, she said, "I don't know what to think, Mr. Hawk. Your story is fantastic. Nevertheless, my father certainly believes in the legend, which is the only reason why I am here. However, I have to admit that not only you, but this entire trip, is incredible, more like fantasy than real life. Perhaps if we lived in a more mystical place and time, I might be more inclined to believe these stories. At present it is difficult."

" 'Mystical'? What do you mean by this word?"

She arched a brow at him. " 'Mystical' means something to do with those things that are not necessarily of the flesh—those things of mystery, of magic perhaps."

"*Haiya*, but there is mystery all around us."

"Is there, now?"

" 'Tis so." Sitting back on his haunches, he motioned all around him. "Have you never wished for something, and it came true? Never seen the birth of a colt? Never witnessed the Creator's hand in every blade of grass that grows? Is it so unusual that the Clan is cursed? After all, there is a price to pay for all one's ill deeds. Grandfather told me before I left the Clan, no one can escape the consequences of his own acts, for life is an endless circle, and what one forces another to experience, one will, himself, be made to endure.

"The Clan killed the children of the Thunder god," he continued, "and now they pay the price for having done so."

She exhaled. "I think that whether I believe you or not, your grandfather was a wise man."

"*Aa*, he was, he is. I have tried to remember those words, for the urge for revenge still festers within my heart."

"Truly?"

"*Aa*. I am a warrior. I would risk a warrior's death to

avenge my parents. But I cannot. I must not. I am on a quest—I can never lose sight of that. Grandfather, my entire Clan, depends on me."

"It is indeed a hefty responsibility that you carry," she said. Again, she paused, then sitting forward, that she might look behind her, she said, "Mr. Hawk, listen. Do you hear them? The wagons? They are not far behind me, and I would like more time to speak with you earnestly about . . . one or two other things. . . ."

"Other things?"

"Yes. More about the Lost Clan—I still have questions—also, I feel I should tell you that I think someone could be following us. I'm not certain, for I have seen only shadows, but I fear that we might indeed have a straggler in out midst."

"Humph!" Red Hawk considered her words somberly, then said, "I have not been scouting to our rear. Perhaps that has been an error."

"Perhaps. I will leave it to you to determine. But again, I would like a moment more of your time—away from the others."

"*Aa,*" he said, then suggested, "we could talk again while the others take their noonday nap."

"We could," she said, "or maybe we might have our conversation tonight? Once the others are asleep?"

"It could be arranged."

"Very well, then. I look forward to seeing you tonight. Thank you for your time."

They both stood then; she turned toward him and dazzled him with a radiant smile. He took hold of her hand at once, and as awareness of her swept through him, he wished to never let her go, to never let this moment slip away.

But time has a way of plodding forward, and no man

can hold it back. Eventually, she pulled her hand away. However, before she left, she brought forward, from a hand she'd been hiding behind her back, the bouquet of flowers she had picked. She said, "My gift to you."

It was a simple overture. Still, he hardly knew how to react. As he watched the sun dance off the unusual color of her hair, it came to him how utterly beautiful she was. The freckles on her face had become more pronounced under the steady influence of the sun, and raising his fingers toward her, he touched each golden fleck on her face, one by one.

It was almost as an afterthought that he accepted her gift, though as he grasped hold of the flowers, his fingers caressed her palm, stroking her sensitive skin.

Tentatively, she raised her gaze to his. Her lips parted, their wetness engaging, inviting. Unable to help himself, he accepted what he hoped was an invitation, and he bent to press his lips to hers, gently, adoringly.

At once, desire shot through him. Raising his head only slightly, he brought up a hand to stroke her cheek, moving down to her neck, her shoulders, pulling her in closer to him.

He said, "*Kitsikakomimmo,*" then he kissed her again.

"What does that mean?" she whispered, her breath coming in short gasps.

"I will tell you tonight."

"Do you promise?"

"*Aa,*" he murmured. "I promise."

Her eyes were closed, and bending, he smoothed his cheek against hers, confiding in her ear, "I have something for you, too."

"Oh?"

"Keep your eyes closed, and give me your hand."

She complied.

Reaching up to the back of his head, he unfastened an eagle feather suspended from his hair, drew it off and urged it into her hand.

"Open your eyes."

She did so, and seeing the gift, she smiled up at him.

"'Tis from a golden eagle," he said. "For you are like that bird to me. Proud, protective, majestic. *Kitsikakomimmo*."

"*Kitsikakomimmo*," she repeated after him, and, listening to her speak the words, even though he knew she did not grasp their meaning, had his insides tied in knots.

He swallowed hard, then said, "I, too, hear the sounds of the wagons and they are close. Soon they will be in view, as we will be to them. We will finish our talk tonight."

"Yes," she agree. "Tonight." She stepped back, out of his arms, and he immediately felt bereft. She said, "Thank you for the feather."

He nodded, then watched as she turned and walked away. Soon, as she stepped toward the wagons, she faded from sight. And though he knew he shouldn't, he couldn't help but think, *Oh, that she had said "yes."*

CHAPTER 13

It was evening. In the distance, Effie could barely discern the figures of Red Hawk and Henry Smith as they sat at the edge of their encampment, huddled together. That Red Hawk was initiating Henry into the finer points of standing the evening watch was without doubt, for now and again Red Hawk would add gestures that were all too recognizable.

Carl was watching the two of them as well, and after awhile, he said, "I suppose it will be my turn to stand watch tomorrow evening . . . yet again."

"I think you're right," said Effie.

Carl paused, then, "Do you know if Mr. Owens or his butler will eventually be taking their turns at this?"

"I don't believe that they will," said Effie, laying aside her soup bowl and spoon. "Though at first Red Hawk did expect them both to take their turns, they have refused."

"Refused? Is it possible to refuse?"

"When you're as old as they are, it is. Though I must admit that Red Hawk does not understand why I'm acting so leniently with them. Apparently in Red Hawk's tribe, an elder considers such duty a compliment."

"Well, if you want my opinion," Lesley spoke up, "I agree with Red Hawk. It seems to me that father and his man, Fieldman, should take their turns with the watch. We are a small group, and it would certainly relieve Henry and Carl of this constant every-other-night vigil."

"I understand, Lesley," said Effie. "And you make a good point, but I also sympathize with your father. He's worked hard all his life so that he can enjoy his later years with a little more leisure. We are actually lucky that he has agreed to this excavation. There is no better field supervisor to be found than he."

"I'm not so bad at it," said Lesley.

"That's true," agreed Effie. "I'll keep that in mind."

"Oh, that reminds me," said Lesley, getting to her feet. "I have some other things I need to speak to Father about. Please do excuse me."

"Certainly," said Effie, while the others murmured similar agreeable noises.

As Lesley stepped toward her father's tent, which sat farther apart than the others, Effie noted that Madeline seemed to watch the other woman's progress closely. But then, as though realizing that she was staring, Madeline rose up to her knees, and scooted closer to Carl.

"I'm cold," said Madeline.

"Then come even closer," urged Carl, as he opened his arms wide to his wife, wrapping her in the warmth of his blanket.

Wistfully, Effie watched the two of them. They looked so happy together. What would it be like to be married?

Shaking her head, as though the action might rid her of the thought, she rose to her feet. "Well," she said. "I'm tired, I've eaten until I'm full and since we need to get an early start tomorrow, I'd best be off to bed."

Carl nodded. "Good night, Miss Rutledge. I think we will follow your lead very soon."

"That's good," murmured Effie. "Good night then, Carl, Madeline. Sleep tight."

Effie rose up and padded to her tent. With an admiring glance thrown upward toward a star-ladened sky, Effie pulled back the entrance flap of her tent, and slipped into its cold, moldy interior, wishing herself back next to the warmth of the fire. Sitting down on her blankets to warm herself, she listened to the sounds of the nearby stream as it rushed past. Locusts and crickets added to the general noise of the evening, as well as the whirling calls of the ever-present nighthawk.

What should she do first? she wondered, as she waited not only for her colleagues to retire to their beds, but Red Hawk's presence. Straightening her shoulders, she rolled them back to loosen the muscles of her neck and back. Tentatively, she rubbed them, then sighed.

She wouldn't remain long in the tent, she decided. She couldn't.

She was simply too excited to stay put, although the exact reason for such enthusiasm continued to confuse her. True, the rendezvous with Red Hawk was part of the cause, but was he the only reason? Yes, she was thrilled because she would have the opportunity to see him tonight, alone and without the others.

Or was there more to it than that? Was her excitement due to the opportunity she would have to put more questions to him? If he really *were* from the Lost Clan, then the chance to learn more about her own craft was endless.

"Think for a moment of the opportunity if it were true . . . if we could meet these people in the present. Think of the questions we might ask those people, the knowledge we might acquire . . ."

So had her father spoken, long ago.

She exhaled deeply. Certainly, she was not immune to the possibilities that such a thing might present: No long sessions studying artifacts, no guesses, no conjectures to make about the way man lived long ago; she could find out about the past firsthand. As an added bonus, her reputation would be secure.

As one thought after another chased through her mind, she sat up onto her knees, and reached for her comb. Grabbing hold of it, she leaned back and began the process of removing the pins from her hair, as well as the lone eagle feather that adorned it. The feather she placed in a box, along with the gun that she always carried. Carefully, she set the box aside.

She shook her head, allowing the natural curls of her mane to cascade down her back. Picking up the comb, she ran it through her tangled locks.

"You wear too many clothes."

She gasped.

"Do not cry out. It is I, Red Hawk."

"I know," she said, "I recognized your voice. It's only that you startled me."

"You did not see me here?"

"No, I did not."

She could hear him sigh. "Don't say it," she said. "Don't tell me again that you will teach me how to look."

"I will do as you say," he conceded.

He sat behind her, and she scooted around to face him, nudging him with her hand in the process. He made no comment, though for her part, a feeling of awareness darted from her fingertips, up her arm, all the way to her midsection.

She said, "Are we to meet here, inside my tent, then?"

At her question, the excitement from his touch ebbed a little, while a feeling not unlike disappointment came over her, causing her to realize that she had been very much looking forward to a stroll beneath a starlit sky.

"We could stay here," he said, "if you wish it."

Her eyes met his in the darkness of the tent. With no light, it was difficult to discern much about him, she thought. But his presence, as well as the scent of mint, all mixed up with the clean, musky aroma of masculinity, filled the air. And she wondered how it could be that she had been so unaware of this man.

"I had not intended that we stay here," he said. "As well as speaking to you, I have to be about my night duties."

"Night duties? I didn't know you had night duties, beyond taking your turn at standing watch."

She could sense his frown, as he said, "Are you truly unaware of them?"

"Of course I am. When we made the arrangements for this trip, you said nothing about night duties."

"*Annisa*, that is my mistake. I assumed that you would understand that protecting you would demand that I use the evening to scout, seeking the best trail to follow. If there is an enemy about, I will find him in the evening, thus allowing me to avoid any trail that would intersect with his."

Effie sat silently for a moment. Then, "I had no idea," she said, frowning. "I am not that familiar with scouting. In truth, I assumed that you knew the trails so well that—"

"I do know them. What I do not know is where the enemy is. This I determine by looking for him at night."

"When do you sleep?"

"In the early morning."

"But that would only allow you a few hours of sleep a night. That's not enough."

"It is enough . . . for now. When we reach my country, I will rest."

"I see. And I'm sorry. Had I not been so unfamiliar with scouting—"

"Perhaps you would like to accompany me this night so you can better determine how scouting is done."

"Yes," she said at once. "Yes, I think that best."

Perhaps she should have hesitated before agreeing so readily—it would have been the proper, ladylike thing to do. After all, any such excursion would necessitate her being alone with this man—a man to whom she was not immune. However, as the director of this project, was it not also her duty to accompany him?

She sighed, and said again, as though to convince herself, "Yes, that would be good."

"Soka'pii," he acknowledged huskily. "I will require a promise, however."

"What sort of promise?"

"Once we leave camp, you will come under my influence. You will have to pledge that you will do exactly as I say, when I say it."

"That seems fair enough," she said, "as long as your demands are reasonable—"

"Saa. You do not understand. You must obey me in all things, if you come with me. We are in enemy country."

"I think I can agree to that." She hesitated, trying to discern his features in the dark. After awhile, she said, "I guess I have been naive, haven't I? When my father and mother were in this country before, I was unaware that anything like scouting was done. But perhaps we were better armed then, and didn't need scouting. I know that besides my father and Mr. Owens, there were several other men working for us, and they all carried guns."

He nodded.

"Tell me, Mr. Hawk, on these nightly jaunts, have you found evidence of any enemies?"

"*Saa*, I have not. As I have said, the Crows are friendly to whites. But there are other tribes that use this country, as well. All it would take is one mistake to kill us all."

"Oh, dear." Effie shuddered, then paused. "What you're really saying," she continued, "is that I should have hired more people to help you."

"*Saa*, I do not say that. Tell me, were there more people for you to hire?"

Again, she hesitated. "No. You know there were not."

"Then we make do with what we have. We will hope, also, that your luck from the days of your parents continues to hold for us now in the present."

"Yes," she said. "Tell me, what would you do if you did find signs of an enemy?"

"I would leave a diversion for them to discover, then set our course toward another direction."

She looked away from him. "I realize now that my ignorance has put you through much, and will continue to do so. I am truly sorry."

"I know this. 'Tis not important. When we reach my country, I will relax, and perhaps find another to help with scouting."

"Yes," she said, "that would be good. But what of the other men, can they help you with the scouting?"

"They would not know what to do, or how to do it. Even if I taught them, they could easily make mistakes that would give us away, and they might get themselves killed. Besides, I would not trust their judgment."

"Then all I can say is that I hope that we find ourselves in your country very soon."

"I, too, wish to visit my country soon," he said, and there was a smile in his voice. "But until this time comes, I will continue to ensure that the trails we take during the day are free of enemies." He paused. "Now if you are to accompany me this night, the first thing we must do is prepare you."

"Prepare me?"

"You will need to look . . . Indian. Do you have other clothes that are not as full as this dress?"

"I have the thing I was wearing when you saw me in the water."

"*Saa*, that will not do. It, too, is full, and it is red. It could be easily seen, even at night. Have you not something less . . . big, and perhaps of a material that does not tear easily?"

She frowned.

"I think I have a solution. Wait here. I will get something for you."

And before she could open her mouth to speak, he had disappeared. But he was soon back, pulling up the bottom edge of her shelter and scooting in beneath it.

Ah, so that was how he came to be in my tent, she thought.

Silently, he drew in close to her and handed over a stack of what felt to be soft leather, scented very much like him. He murmured, "There are leggings here, and a shirt, as well as moccasins. They will be a little big for you, but I think we can make them fit. We can tie the shirt securely, and if you bind the moccasins tightly, they should adapt to your feet well enough. I will leave you now that you might change your clothes privately."

"Yes," she said, though oddly, mild dissatisfaction washed through her. Why was this?

She said, "That would be most proper. But Mr. Hawk," she paused, reaching out a hand to keep him by her side. "If we are to hurry, I might need your aid. There are many buttons on my dress that take a great deal of time to unfasten. Will you help me?"

She could sense—no, she could practically *hear*—the silence of his hesitation. At some length, however, he said, "I will help."

Secretly, she smiled, surprising herself. For all her effort at presenting a professional image, it appeared that down deep, *this* was what she wanted. She offered him her back.

Endearingly, his fingers shook at their task; she could feel them, there at her back. She marveled at the effect of his touch on her, for the tingling along her spine was seducing her into a sort of lethargy. However, it wasn't long before he cleared his throat, and said, "They are most difficult . . . these buttons."

"Yes," she said. "I know. That is why I often require assistance." Her voice was raised no more than a whisper, and she went on to say, "Mr. Hawk, might I ask you something that has been on my mind since we last spoke?"

"*Aa.*" His voice, too, was low.

"The Clan—the Lost Clan—how old is the tribe?"

She felt him shrug. "I do not know," he said. "How would I measure the time?"

"I don't understand. How can you not know this?"

"Because when I was with the Clan, and I laid down to sleep at night, when I would awaken in the morning, it would seem to me as though a mere night had passed. But the elders told me and the other boys that many winters had passed while we slept, sometimes as many as fifty."

"Then you didn't notice any difference between being part of a clan that slept for fifty years, and your life now?"

"*Saa.*" He shook his head. "Until I came out into this world, I had known nothing but the Clan. But I can tell you, having lived here now, that there is little difference, except that being part of the Clan, one rarely ventured out away from it. In this world, one has greater freedom of movement."

"Yes, yes. And what of your traditions?" she asked, as she swallowed—hard—then, deciding to plunge in, she said, "For instance, what would it be like if I were . . . your wife, for instance?"

One of the buttons on her dress slipped beneath his grasp. The material tore.

She heard him gulp, but she had come too far to back down, and she asked, "Do husbands and wives live together?"

"*Aa*, it is so."

"Good, good," she said. "Do not be too surprised by my questions. There are some cultures where husbands and wives do not live together."

"Then I am glad that I am not from those societies, for I would very much like to keep my wife close to me."

"Would you?"

"*Aa.*"

"How . . . close?" She turned slightly toward him.

"Would you like me to show you?"

"I . . . well, I think . . . yes . . ."

She felt him shift position. "Perhaps," he began, "if we were married, it would be like this," and he kissed her neck, her shoulders, the path that the chain around her neck made, her back; his breath, his lips were hot and moist over her skin.

Fire, rapture, excitement swept through her so swiftly,

she rocked back and forth. Indeed, so much emotion swelled up inside her, she shut her eyes, for it felt overpowering.

Leaning back, she moaned, then whispered, "What are you doing to me?"

He didn't answer, but her words seemed to give him determination, for he went on to confide, "Or maybe if we were married, I would want you closer, and perhaps our married life would be like this . . ."

He drew the top of her dress down over her shoulders. Rising up to his knees, he brought his hands around to feel her neck and the top of her chest through the material of her dress and chemise. That his hands shook was hardly noticeable.

"I am pleased," he said, "that you wear this necklace that holds the white shell earrings that I gave you. It brings me great honor that you wear it here . . ." His fingers trailed down the path between her breasts.

By mutual consent, they pushed against each other, she leaning back, he holding her and showering her neck, her cheek, her ear with kisses.

"You smell so good," he said, as he nuzzled his face against her hair. "I could get lost in the scent of your hair, in the fragrance of your skin. But come, though I wish to linger here forever, I must finish my task and undo the rest of these buttons, or I fear we will never leave this tent. And unfortunately for me, there is much yet to do this night."

"Red Hawk," she said, her voice soft, not more than a murmur, "I feel vulnerable, and I so desire you to—"

Rip-p-p.

Another button tumbled to the ground. She could feel his fingers trembling, there at her back.

"Excuse me," he proffered by way of explanation.

She simply smiled dreamily, enchanted with him, with

his clumsiness, with the entire process. The dress could be fixed, but this moment was forever.

He inhaled deeply, exhaled harshly, and she felt the last of her buttons come loose. He said, " 'Tis done."

"Yes," she agreed, "thank you." And she tugged on the dress, pulling her arms out of the sleeves. It exposed the top of her chemise.

"You wear many clothes."

"Yes, I do," she agreed, inhaling with a gulp, as his fingertips trailed down over each of her arms.

"You will have to remove them all if you hope to journey with me this night. For they, too, are full and will catch on many things, giving away our passage through this country. Do you require my assistance any further?"

He followed the statement with a kiss against the back of her neck, while one of his hands massaged a sensitive spot there.

A soft sigh escaped her throat.

"If we were married, I could do this every night." And he kissed every bit of bare skin, there at her neck, her shoulders, her back.

"But what else would we do?"

She felt him swallow, hard.

"Much more," he said. "However, I remind you that the others, who camp close to us, are not yet asleep. Do you wish me to show you more of what we might do? Here, now?"

"I . . . I . . ." Why couldn't she speak? "I don't . . . I suppose not . . . but . . ."

"Do not worry," he said, "once we are away from here, and it is determined that we are in safe country, you might ask me again. And if you do, we might be able to more deeply indulge." His lips teased a trail of kisses along her shoulders.

"Red Hawk." She turned her face toward him. "What's happening to me? To us?"

"Do you seek the truth?"

"Yes," she said. "I think so."

"I can only tell you what is true for me. Perhaps you feel the same way I do, I do not know."

"Yes?"

"Love," he said simply.

"Love?"

He nodded. "I am falling in love with you."

Such simple words, and yet so stunned was she by his honest confession, she was speechless. She wondered, was she falling in love with him?

Involuntarily, one image after another filled her mind: a young boy playing with her in the water, teasing her, yet keeping her lonely being company; a soulful wish from the bottom of her heart to see that same boy again. That this man had recently come to her aid when no one else would endeared him to her.

Interrupting her thoughts, he said, "And now you must dress. I will not be able to help you with your clothes any further, however. I must prepare for our journey. Do you think you can manage it on your own?"

"Yes," she whispered. "But I would like you to stay."

He sighed. "I cannot. You know I cannot. If I stay, it is natural that I will try to urge more passion from you, and I fear, because we both are aware of our desire for each other, you might let me succeed."

"Is that so bad? I have some friends who often indulge—"

"Without marriage, I would disgrace you. As it is, I fear I may have already pushed you too far."

"Too far?"

"It is well known that a woman, when she desires a

man, can lose concept of where she is and who she is
with, if a man takes her too far into passion. 'Tis why a
girl, after a certain age, is guarded so greatly by her parents and her aunts. When a man truly loves a woman, it is
up to him to stop these things and keep his woman's honor
intact. Sometimes, though, he, too, goes too far and cannot pull back."

For the second time that evening, Effie was astonished
by this man's wisdom. Not knowing what to say or how
to respond, she remained silent.

"I will meet you at the river as soon as you are dressed
in my clothes."

She dipped her head in agreement, then whispered,
"Very well."

No sooner had the words been uttered than he was gone.

CHAPTER 14

Red Hawk took pains to make her invisible to the environment. Even at night, a scout took no risks. So to this end, he had applied mud to her face, her clothes and every inch of her skin.

"It stings," she complained softly, as she followed Red Hawk in an unchartered path across the prairie. That they traveled beneath shrubs, crawling through and over prairie grass, using it, when it was long enough, as a cover, she would never have expected. Had she thought about it, she would have reckoned that they would have ridden horses. How wrong she was.

Apparently, scouts did not do their work mounted. Nor did they keep to well-known and useable trails.

"You will become accustomed to the sting of the mud." His voice was low, barely audible.

"Will I? Somehow that seems almost impossible."

"I cannot wash it off you. 'Tis your defense when you are entering a country that you do not know well. You must blend into your environment."

"Oh, very well. How much farther have we to go?"

He turned to face her. He, too, was a sight to behold. He wore nothing more than breechcloth, leggings and moccasins; every other inch of his skin was covered in mud, with grass and twigs sticking out at random places. His ever-present quiver full of arrows was strung over his back, and his bow was at present flung over his arm. There was a bag hanging around his neck and shoulder, as well.

Despite the mud, his breast was wide, his arms were strong and those leggings fit him quite tightly. His hair was in braids; two at the side of his face and one braided lock of hair straight down his back. Though most Indian men of her acquaintance commonly wore an incredible amount of jewelry, there was little to be seen on this man, except for her chain around his neck and a string of blue and white beads dangling from a lock of his hair. Yet, odd or not, mud or not, the man exuded a provocative quality that was as stimulating as it was endearing.

Grinning at her, he said, "You remind me of a young child. Know that a good scout does not complain, for we have an entire night ahead of us."

"Have you considered the fact that I am not a scout?"

"*Saa*, so you are not. Do you wish to rest here for a little while?"

"Yes." She jumped on the chance. "I don't think my knees will ever be the same again. I am glad that the leather of these leggings is tough, for I fear that were I dressed in any of my own clothes, they would have given out long ago."

Again, he grinned at her. "I am glad that you appreciate them. Come," he said, assuming once again a hands and knees position. "There is a stand of bushes next to that stream." He pointed. "Do you see them?"

"Yes."

"We will go there. So far, I have not detected a sign of an enemy, but we must be certain. I will take you there—you may relax, and I will scout the area around the place, to ensure that it is safe enough to stay there."

"Very well."

It took only a few minutes to crawl to the bushes, which grew in a thick patch adjacent to the narrow shoreline of the stream. And the two of them did literally crawl there, on arms and belly.

She said, "I don't think I will ever take your duties for granted again, Mr. Hawk."

He didn't acknowledge this. Instead, he said, "Wait here. Do not move, do not say anything, do nothing at all until I return. Do you understand?"

"May I breathe?"

He shot her a alluring grin, and then he was gone.

She scratched a particular itchy part of her skin, wondering what she would look like on the morrow. Would she be red from the mud caked all over her? Would she have welts where the dry and unruly grasses had scratched her?

At least the mud acted as a sort of protection, she thought, which went a long way to shield her against many cuts and scrapes. But dear Lord, her feminine persona was certainly taking a beating tonight. With gook covering every inch of her, she probably looked more like a monster than a woman. So much for her vision of strolling leisurely across the prairie, with Red Hawk admiring her beauty beneath a full moon.

There wasn't even a full moon. In fact, there was no moon at all this night. At first she fretted over this condition—certain it would be too dark to go anywhere—Red Hawk had calmed her, telling her that the lack of a moon was to their advantage.

"Old Woman, or the moon, as you call her," he had explained, "casts shadows, and a scout must always be wary of his silhouette beneath her beams, for its reflection can be seen even when he cannot be."

Settling down beneath the bushes and glancing above her, she looked at the millions of stars winking at her.

She was startled by a sound. *What was that?*

Her heart beat a cadence against her chest. There it was again. A snapping sound, like someone moving. She looked in the direction from whence it came, and saw that a doe had wandered to the stream, just ahead of her.

She hadn't sensed its presence, and she felt a little silly for starting at the least sound. Inhaling deeply, if only to calm herself, she was at once struck by the fragrances of the night. Here in the bushes was a leafy scent, quite different from the earthy odor of the grasses and mud to which she had become quite accustomed this evening.

"I believe this place is secure enough."

Effie jumped. She hadn't heard Red Hawk return.

"Don't do that," she gasped. "Don't sneak up on me like that. There is enough to be frightened of in the night, without you giving me a start."

"But I made much noise."

"Perhaps you did. However, I am not accustomed to this, and do not know what sounds are dangerous and what are not."

"You are right, of course. But I disagree that there is much to be frightened of at night. It is the safest time in which to travel."

"Perhaps," she said, not willing to give quarter.

But he seemed to have dismissed the subject, and he sat down beside her, and held out his hand. "I have brought some dry meat with me," he offered. "Would you like some?"

"Yes, please," she said, taking the proffered jerky from him. "I hadn't even thought of food, or getting hungry on the trail—I guess maybe I didn't think we would be gone very long."

"We will be traveling through most of the night. It is to be regretted that it is taking longer for me to scout the trail ahead of us. But it is necessary to go slower."

"Because of me."

"Because I would be more careful and keep you safe."

"Thank you, I think." She stretched. "I surely need the rest. I am so tired and sore that I believe I will sleep well tomorrow night."

He grinned at her. " 'Tis to be expected that you are, and that you will." He handed her another piece of jerky, which she took from him eagerly. "Your fingers are very small," he commented, as he held up his hand in comparison.

She grinned. "Yes, they are. I believe that nature has intended it to be this way."

"*Aa.*"

"Mr. Hawk?"

"Yes?"

"Tell me, what was it like living in a mist?"

He shrugged. "Much the same as I live here from day to day. Except perhaps that the mornings were always filled with fog. Always. But it was not as different as you might think."

"Really?"

"I would simply go to sleep and arise with what seemed to me to be the next day. I was unaware that as many as fifty winters had passed between laying my head down and arising, or that the elders of our tribe were awake and aware all through those years. Until I learned of it, I did not realize that our tribe was cursed."

She nodded. "Did you notice changes to the land?"

"Aa," he said. "In this way, one could discern that many years had passed."

"But it didn't occur to you that this was unusual?"

"It did not," he responded. "Not until I was older."

"And what about the language? You tell me that the Lost Clan is a band of the Blackfoot people? And when you left, you came to live with a tribe that is also part of the Blackfoot Confederacy?"

"Aa."

"Is the language now much different than the language of the Clan?"

"It has changed somewhat, but not enough that I do not speak or understand it well."

"I see," she said. "It does remind me that you promised to tell me what *kitsikakomimmo* means. Did you forget?"

He paused. "I have not forgotten. But before I tell you what it means, let me hear you say it again."

"What? *Kitsikakomimmo?"*

"Aa. One more time."

"Kitsikakomimmo. What does it mean?"

He winked at her. "It means 'I love you,' and 'thank you.'"

She laughed softly. "You tricked me."

"So I did. But it was good to hear it from your lips." If he had expected her to say the phrase again, or to comment on his teasing, he certainly didn't give any indication of it. Instead, he lay on his back, and after awhile, she did the same. Pointing toward the heavens, he said, "Do you see that group of stars that the white man names the Big Dipper?"

"Yes."

"In my country, we call those stars the Seven Brothers," he commented. As the legend goes, there were once seven brothers who escaped into the sky to prevent certain death. *Hannia*, once they were taken up there, next to the heavens, they remained safe and unharmed. It was a good place for them, and so there they linger, to this day.

"And that," he pointed out the beautiful Pleiades constellation, "we call the Lost Children."

"We call it the—"

"Pleiades," he finished. "Yes, I know. Perhaps you might remember that I did once escort a black robe into Flathead country, and it was from him that I learned your language."

"Yes. And what do you call that?" She indicated the planet Mars.

"The Blackfeet have named that the Big Fire Star."

"How appropriate," she said, and sighed. "It's quite beautiful, here on the Plains at night isn't it? It's one of the things I remember most from my childhood. When we were here before, we often slept out under the stars. I think it's one of the main reasons why I have continued the career that my father loves so much. I, too, share the adoration of antiquity, plus I love the open spaces."

"As do I," he said. "As do I."

After a time, she asked, "Have you seen any signs of an enemy?"

"*Saa,*" he answered. "And it is good that I have not. I think our journey tomorrow will be safe enough, unless a war party comes upon us unexpected, and stops us."

"And how likely is that to happen?"

"It could occur."

"Yes, I suppose you're right. In truth, we'll face that most every day of this journey, won't we?"

"*Aa,*" he said, "we will. But I will do all I can to keep us safe. And now, tell me, what else weighs on your mind?"

"I do have one question, and it is this: Is the only reason

you want to marry me because you feel that I will lead you
to the other artifacts? I am assuming that these treasures
are in some way tied to your hope of ending the curse for
your people."

When he remained silent, she went on, "Is that why
you are eager for marriage?"

His first answer was a smile, as he slowly shook his
head. Then he said, "Have you never seen yourself in one
of the white man's mirrors?"

"Of course I have, but—"

"*Haiya*, then you should understand why I want to
marry you. 'Tis the honorable thing to do, for I mean to
have you."

"Have me?"

He picked up her hand, and said, "I want to make love
to you."

No sooner had the words been spoken than excitement
shot through her. She caught her breath.

"But you have said," he added, "that you do not want
to marry me, and so I must not—"

"It's not a matter of 'want,' or 'not wanting,' " she asserted, interrupting him. "It's a concern of . . . of . . ." *Of
what?* she wondered. "Of trust," she added, groping. "How
do I know that you're not proposing marriage in order to
get at the artifacts that I carry? Marriage would certainly
make it easier, and I know that you want them."

"I do want them, as do you."

"You see? There. You said it." She folded her arms
over her chest.

At last he sat up, and turning to face her, he took her
hand in his again, his fingers entwining with hers. He said,
"Long is the time I have thought of you. Long is the time I
have wondered about you. Long is the time I have awaited

your return to this country. That you carry something that could help me, my people, is important, but it is not important to how I feel. I would love you despite this."

She stared straight into his eyes, wishing that she could read his mind. But it was a pointless activity, and after awhile, she said, "How do I know that's true? That you're not just repeating words that you know will get you what you want?"

"You don't know that . . . not yet . . ."

Something splashed in the stream next to them. She jumped.

"Do not fret," he soothed, taking her in his arms. " 'Tis probably a fish or a beaver. Stay here while I investigate."

And as quickly as that, he was gone.

Not more than a few minutes passed before he was back at her side, however. He said, "*Poohsapoot*, come. I wish to show you something."

"What? What is it?"

"Come." Taking her hand, he urged her to follow him. Belly crawling, they scooted toward the water.

"There," he said, "look."

At first she didn't see it, so caught up was she in admiring the delightful scene unfolding before her. The smooth-standing water, which was laid out over the prairie like a gigantic mirror, magnified the sky overhead. It was as though she gazed onto a dark, star-laden canvass, and the stars twinkled not only above them, but below them, as well. Thus, it took awhile before she noted the pony, which had stopped by the water's edge to drink.

"He is wild," Red Hawk said in a low voice, pointing to the animal. "There are no marks on him to show his master, so I do not believe there is someone close by who owns him. And he is young. Probably he has feuded with the leader of his herd, and has been cast out as a result. He will have to fend for himself, get his own mares and create his own herd."

"Is he all on his own, then?"

"Perhaps."

"Isn't that dangerous at this time of night?"

Red Hawk looked at her and smiled. "You sound like a mother," he said, "but you are right. He should not be alone, and there are probably a few other young males with him, as they tend to herd together when they are this young."

What a magical moment it was, for such was the peace and tranquility of this place that she found a part of herself reaching out into the environment. Was man really meant to live in cities? Apart from the Earth? she wondered. And was it really necessary to tame the wilderness, as well as the individuals who lived in it? Especially when it seemed perfect, just as it was?

How long they sat as such, taking in the perfect harmony of the land, the sky, the water, she would never be able to estimate, nor did it cross her mind to do so.

At last, however, the young stud must have drunk his fill, for he lifted his head, turned around and calmly trotted back the way he had come. Within moments, he was followed by a few more ponies.

She whispered, "I hadn't seen those two."

"*Aa*, it is to be expected," he said. " 'Tis difficult sometimes for the eyes to see that far away, at least in this light. Come, let us drink as well."

But she held him back when he would have moved forward. "Won't we run the risk of washing off this mud? After all, didn't you say it was our 'cover'?" she asked.

"It is so," he said, "but there is the same sort of mud here that I used to paint our bodies. We can repaint ourselves, if we must."

"Very well," she declared, and she followed him as they crept toward the stream.

The water was not deep, at least here at its shoreline.

Coming down, onto their bellies, they reached out around the grasses to drink of the cool, liquid refreshment.

"Oh, it's cold," she said, as soon as her hands cupped the water.

"It is fed by mountain streams, so yes, it will be cold."

"Oh," she said, glancing toward him. It was then that she realized that he was not more than a hand's breadth away from her. Not far at all. A rather easy target, actually.

All at once, a naughty urge took hold of her. No, she shouldn't do it. She mustn't, for she felt in all likelihood that he might retaliate in kind.

The urge proved to be more than she could resist, however. Cupping her hands full of water, she splashed him, face-first, and he jerked back.

She giggled. Indeed, he looked so odd with mud running down his face that it was all she could do to keep from laughing outright.

Of course, as she had predicted, he gave her back as good as she gave, making it her turn to show a clownish face to him. Still she giggled.

And he *did* laugh outright.

"Sh-h-h," she said. "We don't want the enemy to find us."

"If there are enemies about, they will surely have found us out by now."

"Then you think it is safe?"

"As safe as can be expected when in enemy territory," he said, before he grabbed hold of her, and, pulling her into his arms, with her full form against his, he rolled them both over and over until they fell with a splash into the water.

Then he let go of her, and they both came up laughing.

Getting up to their knees, they faced each other, and he took her hand in his. Looking up at her mischievously, he asked, "Have you ever stripped off all your clothes, and swam naked in the water?" Her mouth fell open.

"Why, I . . . I . . ."

He didn't wait to hear more. Taking full advantage of her, while she was still gaping at him, he kissed her quite soundly.

CHAPTER 15

She ended the kiss at once, pushed him away from her and said, "Why, Mr. Hawk. That was unfair."

"Was it?" he asked. "But you might agree that it was pleasurable. And you have not answered my question."

"Haven't I?"

He shook his head at her.

"Very well. If you must know, then no, I have never swum naked. No well-brought-up girl would have. Have you?"

"Most usually," he affirmed with a cheeky smirk. "And I disagree. Many girls I know are well brought up, and swim naked. Come," he said, "I think you should try it."

"What? With you here?"

"*Aa.*"

"Well, this is quite a change, isn't it? I thought you were the one who had to make sure you didn't 'push me too far into passion.' Aren't you afraid that I might lure you into doing something—"

"Please," he broke in to say.

"Please? Please what?"

"Please would you lure me?"

Her stomach seemed to be having trouble digesting its earlier snack of jerky, for something in the center of her abdomen turned over and over. She said, "Why, Mr. Hawk, I do believe you might have changed your mind."

"It is possible."

"Well, so it's skinny-dipping that you want, is it?"

"If swimming naked means 'skinny-dipping,' then *aa*, it is so."

"Hmmm . . . I might need some mighty good convincing."

"I can be convincing."

"I'm sure you can be," came her response, as she stood to her feet and waded toward him. "But . . . Stop that."

He had reached up to untie the belt that she'd used to make his shirt "fit" her. He, too, came up along with her, and with as slick a motion as possible, he removed the articles of war from around his neck and shoulder and threw them to the shore.

His action took her by surprise, for the sight of his nude torso with all the mud gone was playing havoc with her mind.

He reached around behind her, and as he did so, he said, "You have asked what it would be like being married to me, and I think it time to show you more thoroughly what a married couple might do." Taking her in his arms, he fell backward in the water, cushioning her as she tumbled along with him.

With intents of retaliation, she reached toward him and pulled on the strings that held up his leggings.

"Thank you," he said, smiling at her as he pulled the clothing off, and threw them also to the shore. "But I think, Miss Effie," he said, "that you again wear too many clothes."

Perhaps she should have thought her actions through more thoroughly. But alas, witnessing the man's almost nude form, for he was standing before her in no more than a breechcloth and her necklace—and there was no longer any mud to cover him—was so disconcerting that when he extended his arm out to grab hold of her shirt and pulled it up and over her head, she acquiesced a little too easily.

The end result was perhaps something he'd not reckoned, for he stopped suddenly, and stared at her as though he could hardly believe his eyes. Eventually he laughed.

"What?" she asked. "Did you honestly think I would go anywhere without this?" She had worn her corset beneath his shirt.

"But the thing must be uncomfortable."

"Of course it is. However, that doesn't mean that I shouldn't wear it."

He shook his head at her. "White women dress strangely," he said. "How does it come off?"

"And why should it come off?"

"Do you not wish to feel the pleasure of swimming without the burden of clothing? To experience the cool water running over every part of your skin?"

When he put it like that, it *did* sound wonderful. With a teasing note, she said, "Is that the only reason you wish to remove my clothes?"

"I did have something else in mind, but only if you agree that it is something you might like. In the meanwhile, why do we not undress and swim, like we have done in the past?"

"You mean that time about seventeen years ago? But we were fully clothed then."

"Not fully," he said. "If I remember correctly, you were covered from the waist down only."

"But I was also eight years old at the time."

"*Aa,*" he said. "We were, the two of us, much too young to understand what was happening between us. We are not that young now. But come, if it bothers you, leave that thing on. I do not wish to make you feel uncomfortable. Do you object to taking off the leggings you wear?"

"Not at all."

"Then let us do so now. Come here."

She did as instructed, uncertain why she was so easily going along with his suggestions. True, she wasn't nude, but standing before him in nothing more than her corset was producing an effect similar to that of a fire being lit beneath her. And it occurred to her that it was strange that she should be standing in waist-deep cold water with her temperature rising.

Reaching forward, he pulled on the strings that kept up the leggings she wore, and they fell off into his hands. With a quick flick of his arm and wrist, he sent these, too, flying toward the shoreline.

This time, he didn't seem as surprised to see that she wore her own "leggings" beneath his leather ones, her pantalettes. He said, "You are beautiful," and with a finger, he tipped her face up to his. Gently, he brought his lips to hers, and her body responded to him as though she had lived all her life for this single moment.

As a steady rush of elation filled her, she pressed her body against his. And he seemed only too willing to welcome her.

"*Poohsapoot,*" he said, "come. Let us swim." Shifting her in his grasp, he propelled himself through the water sideways, his arm still firmly wrapped around her, his feet paddling. He said, "If we . . . marry . . . perhaps we will swim like this often."

It would be heaven, she thought, as she did nothing but relax, and let herself be led through the water.

He executed a smooth turn in the water, taking her with him and pulling her on top of him, until he was holding her from his other side. Still paddling in the water, he brought her up closer, and stole a wet, lingering kiss.

Then he spun over in the water again, calmly, naturally, bringing her back to his original side. It was like being caught up in a dance, as they slid through a liquid paradise. Kissing her once more, he repeated the process.

At last he stopped, and standing, he brought her in close in his arms. He said, *"Kitsikakomimmo.* I have dreamed of this. I have waited for this. Since that first time we met, I have wished for you to be in my arms, like this. There is no one else like you, there will never be anyone else like you."

"You turn my head," she said. "But tell me, in all this time, there has been no one else?"

"None like you."

"I find that hard to believe, especially because you are a handsome man. Surely there has been a girl here or there who has caught your eye."

"Saa," he said. "It is not so. Of course, a young boy in a village like ours does not go without experience, for there are widows who are more than anxious to show a youngster what to do. And often a girl is thought of as a conquest, much like one might conquer an enemy. But boys who take advantage of a girl are not well thought of, for it is known that they rarely make good husbands. But if you ask if I have ever loved another as I love you, then you have my answer. I have never considered marrying another, nor have I longed for another. I think, Miss Effie, that I have waited for you since that first day we met."

"In truth, Mr. Hawk, I, too, believe that I have been waiting for you." Then in a voice barely over a whisper, she said, "The corset comes off here in the front." Briefly, she showed him. "There are hooks and eyes. Do you see them?"

He moaned, and swayed back and forth with her still in his arms. It was some moments before he reached up a hand to begin the lengthy process of removing her corset.

It was an impossible task, even at the best of times. He was using both his hands, but his fingers were also unsteady. Watching him struggle with the project, she moved his hands out of the way, and slowly undid each and every hook herself.

When it was done, he slowly peeled the thing away from her, and as he had done with their other clothing, he threw it to the shore.

"Are your leggings also difficult to remove?" he asked.

She shook her head. "But let us leave them on for now—you still have your breechcloth on."

"That is easily remedied."

"No," she said. "It is too soon."

"*Aa*, I think I understand. Let us swim underwater."

Securing her hand in his, he said, "Are you ready?"

"I am."

"Then take a deep breath, and come with me."

Inhaling, she followed him in a dive.

It was an experience unlike any other. The cool liquid rushed over her like a lingering caress, gently massaging every part of her body. Her nipples were taunt, aching, as though they awaited a master's touch. It felt naughty, yet heavenly, to be here like this with him.

Their movements through the dark liquid were slow, sensual, their legs and arms entwining as though they danced, there beneath the water. She had never swum in the water at night, and in truth, so many shadows filled the stream, from the trees, the shrubs and the clouds overhead, that she might have found the experience more than a little frightening, were it not for Red Hawk's hand, which still held hers tightly.

Forging through the water, Red Hawk pulled her into his arms, his form stretched out in full, and hers up tight against his. Over and over he rolled with her, there under the water's surface, executing a slow rhythmic performance, bringing her ever and ever closer to him.

Their legs entangled, and they held each other tightly. The feel of her bare chest touching against the naked expanse of his sent her blood boiling. All at once the water, once so cold, felt much too warm.

But she needed breath. Pointing her index finger upward, she signaled that she required air. Both of them gasped as they broke the surface. When he reached down to pull off her drawers, throwing them toward the shoreline, she only knew relief that at last she could feel the water against her there, as well.

"What are these?" he asked, as he glanced down and fingered the satchels tied to her waist.

Effie grimaced. How could she have forgotten about the artifacts so easily? She said, "These tiny sacks contain valuables that I carry with me always."

He nodded. "This is where you keep the artifacts."

She didn't answer.

"You are a very smart woman to keep these so close to you. Your clothes protect them, and no one can see them or get to them easily. It is a good place. Do not worry, your secret is safe with me."

She nodded, but buried within her heart, she worried; was it true? Was her secret really safe with him? Didn't he desire to gain the artifacts as much as anyone else?

However, she had no time in which to debate the question. For now, she trusted him, and he was close, so very, very close, and she wanted him closer yet. She could feel the evidence of his sex, there at the apex of her legs. And the knowledge quietly sent her pulse into convulsions.

"Poohsapoot," he whispered against her ear, and he half led, half carried her to the shore, where he lay her back against the soft grasses that lined the stream.

"Are there snakes here?" she asked, shivering slightly.

"We are too far north for snakes to inhabit these waters. A little farther south and you might find a few. The danger of snakes in this country is on the land, not here in the water."

"Good," she said.

In a voice most teasing, he stated, "We married folks have many ways of showing each other our love. One of them is like this." And he came up over her, taking one of her breasts into his mouth.

She groaned.

"Oh," he murmured against her, and then so softly, she barely heard him, he added, "to see you with my child, suckling on your breast. How proud I would be."

He shifted to her other breast, and she twisted beneath him, as though she might squirm her way to some unknown pinnacle. And deep within her, at the junction of her legs, an excitement roused. She wanted more . . . more . . . but of what?

Momentarily, he left her breasts and moved upward until he was raining wet kisses over her neck, her chest, her ear, her cheeks, her lips, her eyes. In truth, no part of her face escaped his notice.

He repeated, *"Kitsikakomimmo."*

And she murmured back, *"Kitsikakomimmo,"* which had the immediate response of eliciting a groan from him.

He asked, "Do you mean it?"

"I think so."

"Then we will marry," he said.

So lost was she to the moment, it was beyond her to respond back to him, whether in the positive or the negative. She only wanted him to continue what he was doing . . . now . . . Then she found herself saying, "Red Hawk?"

"Yes?"

"I believe you have on too many clothes."

He looked down at himself, then grinned sheepishly up at her. "I think you are right." He remedied the situation at once, untying his breechcloth and tossing it aside. "I fear," he said, "that we have left a scattering of our garments up and down this shoreline."

"Yes."

"But we will find them easily enough."

"Good, good," she said. "But Red Hawk, you stopped."

He smiled down at her, kissed her gently on the lips, then said, "How foolish of me," and his mouth immediately found a most sensitive spot on her neck.

Downward he roamed again, following the path of her necklace, his lips suckling on her breasts, until she thought she might cry out with sheer pleasure.

So this was what lovemaking was about, she thought. No wonder men and women everywhere yearned for it.

But was this all? Did a man simply make a woman dizzy with kisses? Carnally, she understood that there had to be more to it than this—that a part of her which was most private—and a part of him—would need to align in some fashion or the other. But the exact extent of what this entailed was beyond her.

He made a foray downward over her body, his lips on her stomach, her belly button, down farther, until she feared he went too far . . .

She sat up suddenly. "What are you doing?"

He gazed up at her with no apology, and said, "I am making love to you."

"But you are way down there. Shouldn't you be up here?" She placed her hand on her chest.

"*Aa,*" he agreed. "Sometimes."

"I thought—"

"But not now." His voice was low, but firm. "Lie back. I would kiss you here, and I would have you enjoy this, your first time."

"But . . ."

Come, I am showing you what it would be like to be married to me. Lie down."

She laid down as he commanded.

"You must spread your legs around me," he said. Then before she could deny him, he parted her legs and came down between them. Then he kissed her there on her most feminine spot—and those kisses were quite warm and wet.

She sighed. Had she ever felt anything more wonderful?

His tongue slid all over her, his fingers helping stimulate her. As passion took hold of her, she opened her legs wider to give him further access.

And then it began within her, a pressure, a desire, a need to move, to squirm beneath his ministrations. Her breathing quickened, and her pulse beat staccato in her ears.

A crescendo was building up inside her, and she was pushing toward some peak. In truth, she felt much like a volcano, ready to blast at any time.

Over and over she twisted her hips against him, until she thought she might explode, and then all at once, she did. She slid over the edge of a precipice; waves of ecstasy washed over her, feelings of love and admiration swamping her. She pressed upward to enhance the pleasure, until at last the sensation of fulfillment possessed her.

Coming down from that emotional pinnacle, she lay still for a moment, letting her breathing return to normal. Her first thought, however, was of him. Had he, too, reached the same sort of peak she had?

"That was wonderful," she muttered. "Did you, too, attain your pleasure?"

"Not yet," he whispered, his voice as soft as hers. "But soon."

She nodded and then fell into silence.

Dear Lord, she thought, was this what married people experienced with one another? No wonder people aspired to marriage.

Indeed, before this moment, marriage had seemed to her to be a dream that lacked reality. Now she understood the attraction.

Meanwhile, he had brought himself up onto his elbows, and gazing up at her, smiled. When he brought his body up over hers, she soaked up the sight of him. It was also the first time she had glimpsed that essentially male part of him.

Naively, if she had thought about it at all, she had not considered how a man could be so smooth, and slick and . . . large . . .

As he positioned himself over her, his face was only a fraction of an inch away from hers, and he must have read her thoughts, for he said, "You do realize that a man grows in size when aroused?"

"I . . . of course. I have studied biology, and I know that blood flows there and so . . . of course . . . it would . . . But I suppose I didn't realize that it would be so . . . big . . ."

He laughed slightly, then whispered, "Do you mean to compliment me?"

"I . . . why, yes . . ."

"Then I thank you. Now hear me, for this is important.

You should know—you may already know—that it is not always easy for a woman her first time. The first experience a woman has with love may find her sore after. I will be gentle, but it may not be easy for you, and it may hurt. Know that lovemaking will eventually bring to you a thrill similar to what you just experienced. Do you understand?"

She nodded.

"Are you ready to continue?"

She repeated that nod.

And he kissed her. *"Kitsikakomimmo."*

"Kitsikakomimmo," she echoed after him. "Oh, Red Hawk, love me."

"I mean to, sweet Effie. I mean to."

Coming onto his knees, he took hold of her legs, and brought them over his shoulders. And then, with no more than a soft sigh, he joined his body with hers.

It *did* hurt.

Up and down her legs, his fingers massaged her. He didn't move at first, but held back, and she was grateful that he seemed to know exactly what to do.

He waited, and waited, kissing her legs, holding her gently in place.

And then, she could stand the delay no more, and she cried out, "Please, Red Hawk, I need all of you."

He groaned, and began to move within her, and against her. His eyes were closed, and his body thrust into her over and over again, until he crossed what appeared to be a threshold. His action became more intense, his face contorted with effort.

And then with a groan, he rose up and emptied his seed within her. Over and over he pushed against her, as a look of utmost pleasure stole over his face.

Clearly spent, he came up over her, and after kissing her heartily, he rested his body against hers. Before he drifted off to a brief bit of slumber, he said, "At last we are together. And I love you more than life, itself, my wife . . ."

CHAPTER 16

It took a moment for the word to register.

"Wife?" She pushed against him, waking him up. "Don't you dare go to sleep on me now. You had better explain yourself, Red Hawk."

Lifting up slightly, he shifted his weight, though he kept a leg and an arm strategically placed over her. Bending at his elbow, he rested his head against his hand, and raised sleepy eyes to meet hers.

Somewhat guiltily, she recalled that this man had obtained little sleep these past few days. Still, she needed answers, and she said, "What do you mean by calling me your 'wife'?"

"Did we not just commit the act of marriage? You did consent, did you not?"

"Consent?"

"Do you recall that I said that we would marry?"

It was true. He had. She said, "But I didn't respond in the positive."

"*Ho!* Did you not? We committed the act of marriage. Does that not speak for itself?"

She frowned. "No, it does not. We have taken no vows, made no pledges."

"Is the act of love not a pledge?"

Her frown deepened. "Red Hawk," she said, "tell me, do men and women of your tribe marry by means of a wedding ceremony?"

"Of course," he responded, "a ceremony of the heart."

"No," she said, "I mean are your people married by a ceremony run by someone else . . . a holy man, like a black robe?"

"Ho!" he said. "I think I understand what concerns you. Do not worry. Although there are sometimes ceremonies to marry a couple, know that in my country, after what has happened between us, a man and a woman *are* married. For if the man does not marry her, the woman is ruined. I do not wish to ruin you. I would marry you."

"Thank you for that consideration. But it is not my understanding that the act of love makes us married. Where I come from, a couple are only united in marriage if they take vows to be faithful to each other—and if those vows are said in front of someone like a black robe or a holy man. It is an act made sacred because they pledge themselves to one another in the presence of God."

"I have heard of your God," he said. "The black robe spoke of him often. But do you think that your God was with us this night?"

"Of course I believe that He was."

"Then you must realize that He knows of our love, and our fidelity."

"I suppose you're right. But you miss the point I'm trying to make. In my society, even if a person makes love to another, this does not make them married. Only oaths of fidelity said in front of a holy man make a union that will be recognized by others."

He looked somewhat taken aback. "Do you mean to tell me that you made love with me tonight, without the intention of marrying me?"

"Ah . . ." Had she? Dear Lord, seen from his viewpoint, it might appear as though she had. She said, "In truth, I would admit to some confusion about that. When you said that we would marry, I didn't realize that you spoke of the act of love as being a deciding factor. I thought I would have more time in which to consider the suggestion."

He nodded. "*Aa. Ikksisitsi'tsi*, I understand. But what of your reputation? The others will know that you have been with me. What will they think, if they discover that we are not married?"

She said, "They would be more shocked to learn that we *are* married."

"They will not think badly of you?"

"Yes, they might think badly of me . . . either way," she said. "Not that I care what other people think."

But was that really true? Though she might not be the best of friends with any of her colleagues, was she really careless enough to ignore their opinions? And what about her family? Certainly she *did* care what her mother and her father might have to say.

Still, were she and Red Hawk the only two people in the world . . . no artifacts to worry about . . . no project to finish . . . no one back East expecting her reports, she wouldn't hesitate to accept his proposal, and to heck with any critics.

But she was no longer a child of eight, weaving fantasies around a man from a completely different culture. She was a responsible adult, and out of that accountability came the knowledge that being in love wasn't enough. Regardless of the prejudices of others, she, and he, too, could not live in a world devoid of other human beings.

Sooner or later, one or the other of their societies would see that they paid the price for their passion . . .

But Red Hawk was continuing to talk to her, interrupting her thoughts, and he said, "I think I understand. You wanted a moment of passion with me, and then you wished to walk away with little consequence."

"Perhaps," she said. "But in reality, in the moment about which you speak, I was not thinking at all, much less considering walking away. Besides, when you proposed to me originally, didn't you suggest this very thing? To marry, and if it didn't work out, to be free to walk away?"

"*Aa*," he said, "that I did. However, when I suggested that, I had hoped to have more married life than one night."

"Yes, well . . ."

"If this is truly your desire," he continued, "and you wish to put the marriage behind you, that is your right . . . unless you are with child, then you will remain married to me. If that were to happen, we would seek out a black robe, so that you would be satisfied in your own mind that we are married. Otherwise . . . if you wish it, then I am willing to agree that we did not make a marriage this night, even though I think doing so is a mistake."

Why did he have to make her feel as though her actions were so . . . cheap? She said, "Perhaps we could reach a compromise."

"A compromise?"

"Yes, a 'compromise' means that—"

"I know what it means."

She drew a deep breath. "There is one other possibility. In my society, two people who are deeply in love, yet are not ready to marry, become engaged."

" 'Engaged'? This word I do not know."

"To be engaged," she explained, "means that two people announce their intention to marry, and make it known to their family and friends that they expect to marry soon, and that they will remain faithful to one another until such a time as they are ready to take their vows."

"How long do these engagements last?"

"Sometimes many years. Often several months."

"And do these two people make love to one another during this time?"

"It has been known to happen." She smiled.

"And have these 'engagements' ever been known to fall apart?"

"Upon occasion."

Red Hawk shook his head. "The white man is truly cunning," he said.

"Cunning?"

"Only a white man could think up a way to have a woman, without the responsibility of *having* that woman."

"I'm not sure I understand."

"An engagement is irresponsible. *Saa*, in my mind, because of what we have done this night, we are married, nothing less. I have taken what you offered in the heat of passion. It is not something I did lightly, to have it, and then to discard you so easily, by as simple a method as a change of heart. *Saa*, for what you have given me, I will give you back my loyalty and my heart. It will not change."

She was silent. Truly, what could a woman say? Were these not the very words every feminine heart longed to hear?

"Red Hawk," she said at last, reaching out to place her hand on his. "Think for a moment. In what society would we live? Yours? Your people are entrapped in a mist. I don't think I could go there.

"Mine?" she continued. "There is prejudice in mine. That way could be hard for you. In either of our cultures one or the other would be required to give up something."

"It is true that you cannot come with me into the mist. But I cannot go back there, either," he argued. "Whether I break the curse or not, I am here, in this time and in this place, until I die.

"Besides," he continued, "is this not the way of all marriage? By the act of marrying, hasn't one already decided to give up what has gone on before?"

She paused. She turned her head away from him, and said, "Perhaps old prejudices tear at me, or maybe I am frightened by the unknown. Whether it is right or wrong, I only know that I must complete the project. I cannot allow myself to be distracted . . . by anything. After this dig is done, perhaps we could evaluate this again, if you wish to wait."

He nodded, then shrugged. "Perhaps I will. Maybe."

"Then you agree that we are not yet husband and wife?"

"I agree that you have the right to say 'no,' and you have done so. I also agree that if I ever wish to have you acknowledge me as your husband, I have much work to do." He smiled at her.

She grinned back.

"Know, however," he said, "that to my mind, you are my wife. But I understand that our cultures are different, and regardless of what I think, unless you wish it, there is no marriage, except in the depths of this heart." He pointed to his chest. "And so it is done. You are free."

Reaching out toward her, he pressed a kiss to her lips, following it with the words, "*Kitsikakomimmo.* For the moment, nothing changes that."

Effie didn't know what to say. On one hand, she was glad. On the other, she was . . . confused.

He sat up, then looked down on her. "*Poohsapoot,*" he said, "let us leave this bad talk behind us, and take another swim, this time to awaken us, that we might finish our scouting this night. We still have much to do."

"All right," she said. "You are not angry at me?"

"*Saa*, disappointed, perhaps, but not angry. You have the right to say 'yes' or 'no.' 'Tis my mistake that I thought you had said 'yes.' "

He held out a hand to help her up, then scooting his arm around her waist, he brought her right up against him. He sighed deeply, then said, "Let us spend the remainder of this night as a married couple. If this is all we are to have, then let us indulge ourselves. Do you agree?"

"Yes," she whispered, "I don't see any harm in that."

"And much pleasure," he said.

She smiled. "All right, then."

"*Soka'pii*. I am glad that is settled."

The scent of fired guns lingered in the air, there in the meadow where they had left Effie's wagons. Worse, though dawn fast approached, no birds sang here.

Something was wrong.

It was still dark, but the eastern sky was taking on the dull color of silver—a sign that the sun was starting to rise into the early morning sky. Soon, Red Hawk and Effie would be more than visible to the well-trained eye of the scout, if one were about.

Turning back toward Effie, Red Hawk said, "I must investigate. You stay here. Hear me, you are not to move, no matter what cause is given you, nor are you to cry out, not even in warning. Do you understand?"

"Yes, but what's wrong?"

"I do not know. I only know that something is. Do not disobey me. Stay here. Hide well."

She nodded.

Bending toward her, he pressed a kiss to the top of her head. He said, "Know that I love you."

She lay her hand atop his. "I, too."

He nodded solemnly, pressed her hand in acknowledgment and then set off, crawling through the growth and bushes that occasioned the open spaces of the prairie.

Stealthily, Red Hawk approached the meadow where they had left the wagons. He smelled no smoke there; he heard no voices. And yet, the evidence that something had happened here was unmistakable.

He crept up to the spot where Henry Smith should have been standing lookout.

No one was there.

This was a bad sign. A very bad sign.

And then he saw them: Both wagons were turned onto their sides. Wheels were broken, the white canvas coverings were torn; shovels, trowels, papers, clothes and other equipment were scattered over the ground. But he could see no signs of the people.

Stealing carefully around the camp, he looked in vain for signs of an enemy, a scout, renegade whites, anything. There was none to be found. There should have been something.

Slowly, he stole into their former camp. It was a mess. Papers were everywhere, some blowing haphazardly in the wind, others caught on bushes. Indiscriminately, he picked up one, but since there was nothing to be found there, he studied what tracks and prints were left, instead.

He could make no sense of this. Bending down, he fingered a particular imprint on the ground. It was a track made by one of the men. Because of its deep indentation, as well as the fact that the feet were turned out, he recognized the footprint as belonging to the older man, John Owens. Due to the erratic nature of the print, he knew that the man had been frightened. He had also run away.

Looking up, Red Hawk took note of the direction taken, then studied more of the clues left. Here were the tracks of the two women, their two husbands' out in front of them, clearly protecting them.

But from what?

There were no foreign prints here, no enemy that he could find in evidence.

In vain, he searched the camp more thoroughly for signs of a foe. There was nothing.

Nothing, except for a boulder that was cracked, as well as one impression in the ground where the earth had been torn apart, as though the dirt had been pulled up by a white man's plow. But that was all. There was nothing more to show the story of what had happened.

Rising, Red Hawk knew it was useless to try to find more clues in the camp; he had best find the others. Perhaps they could make better sense of this.

Their trail headed toward the water, which was almost a half a mile away. Slowly, carefully, he followed their path through the short prairie grasses.

Soon, arriving at the stream, he saw that none had lingered here, but had set off downstream. Much harder to track, but not completely impossible. Luckily for Red Hawk, one of the women had remained close to the shore, leaving an occasional footprint.

About a half mile downstream was evidence that they had paused. Further along, they had continued, until at last, off in the distance, Red Hawk saw them. Camped for the moment beneath a large cottonwood, they looked a decidedly disheveled, disgruntled bunch. Quietly, he approached them.

One of the women screamed, and a shot was fired directly at him. It missed.

Haiya! This was discouraging. Not because someone had fired at him, rather because whoever it was had missed. The white men were terrible shots.

He called out, "It is I, Red Hawk. I have come in search of you. I have only returned from scouting. What has happened here? I can make no sense of what I have seen back at your camp."

"Scouting, huh?" This came from John Owens. "A likely story."

Red Hawk didn't respond. It was not in his nature to defend his honesty, one way or the other.

"Maybe you can tell us where our 'esteemed' leader Miss Effie is," growled John Owens.

"Miss Effie is safe," Red Hawk responded. "I left her in a place where she would not be harmed." Then, because hunger can often cause a person to be antagonistic, he asked, "Has anyone eaten their morning meal?"

This elicited more response from them. Even the women spoke up, with a hearty "no."

"Before we talk about the night that has passed, perhaps it would be well to eat. I have some dried meat that I will share with you," said Red Hawk. "It is not as robust a breakfast as to what you may be accustomed, but it will give you enough strength to think clearly. Then we might discuss what happened before returning to camp."

"I'm not going back there." This comment came from Madeline.

Red Hawk chose not to respond. *Let them gain strength from nourishment first.* Then he would question them.

Stepping into their midst, Red Hawk removed his bag from around his shoulder, withdrew the jerky from it and handed the bag to Lesley. He said, "Do you think you could fill this with water from the stream?"

She nodded, and set off to do as bidden.

Offering the food around, Red Hawk waited. When at last they each one appeared to be more nourished, and in perhaps a better frame of mind, Red Hawk queried, "What happened here?"

"We were attacked," spat out Carl. "Where were you?"

It was a fair question, and Red Hawk answered at once. "Since we have started on this trail," he said, "I use the night to scout. Because we are not well armed, it is important that I look for signs of enemies, and if I see something that might harm us, to set a path around it. Last night Miss Effie decided to accompany me so that she might more easily understand my duties."

Both Henry Smith and Carl Bell nodded, neither adding a comment.

John Owens was not to be so easily swayed, and he said, "What good would that do? What need does the manager of this expedition have of learning the duties of a scout? If she is the director, then she should have been here to 'go down with the ship.'"

"Father!" cried Lesley. "Please."

Red Hawk eyed John Owens severely. Gone was the elder's congenial veneer. In its place was the hostility Red Hawk had glimpsed upon first acquaintance. At length, Red Hawk said, "Miss Effie had every right to accompany me last night. Since we must first reach the excavation site before any work can be done, it is her duty to ensure that we get there safely. This group is not well manned, and any wandering war party could take advantage of us. It would be irresponsible to remain uninformed of what lies before us."

Again, Carl Bell and Henry Smith seemed to comprehend this without question. But once more, John Owens had a differing viewpoint, and he said, "Tell me, if what you say is true, and you scout through the night, when do you sleep?"

"Whenever I can—usually that is a few hours each morning."

"Humph!"

Red Hawk didn't respond. Instead, he paused, hoping that the former subject might die. In due time, he said, "Who attacked you?"

"We don't know," said Lesley. "It happened in the middle of the night. At first we thought it was no more than a thunderstorm. But the noise came closer and closer, and my father felt the first shot."

"*Soka'pii*. May I see the injury?" Red Hawk directed the question to Owens, who was still glowering.

At first it appeared as if Owens would not cooperate, but then with a shrug, he said, "Don't see why not," and he offered up his arm up for inspection. Definitely, there was an angry, red welt running all along his forearm. "The shot grazed me."

Red Hawk nodded.

"We panicked," Henry interjected. "Carl and I kept up a defense, while the women and Mr. Owens and his man, Fieldman, escaped. We followed them, keeping up a round of shots, until we ran out of ammunition."

"You have no more bullets for your guns?"

"I think I used all that I had left with me when I fired on you," said Carl.

"You did not bring *all* of the weapons and bullets with you?"

"No."

Again, Red Hawk nodded. But he was puzzled. He had not seen any signs of ammunition scattered about the camp, and if they did not have it here, it should have been there. But these facts he kept to himself. He said, "And then what happened?"

"Something we couldn't see kept chasing us," said

Henry. "And though we fired and fired on it, it was as though our shots made little impression—as though bullets couldn't kill it . . ."

Red Hawk frowned. "How did you get away?"

"As soon as we reached the water," Carl continued, "it retreated. We don't know why. We could only thank God that it did. But then all we could think of was putting distance between ourselves and the camp. We ran and ran until we stopped here. And here we have remained . . . until you found us."

Again Red Hawk nodded. "Are you ready to return to your camp now?" Red Hawk said after a pause. "I believe that whatever the danger was, it is now gone."

"Are you sure?" asked Madeline.

"I have been to the camp, and I did not see anything that would have attacked you or me. So yes, I believe the camp is safe now."

"Do you have any idea who it was that attacked us?" queried Lesley.

Red Hawk shook his head.

"Was it Indians?" asked John Owens.

"Were it Indians," said Red Hawk, "you would not be here, able to tell me about it."

"Then who?" Henry asked the question.

"I do not know. But come, it is daylight. I do think the danger has passed. Let us go back to the wagons. There we can strike a fire, and you can further nourish yourselves before we look through the camp for clues. There is much to repair and to do, as well, I fear."

Luckily, there was not a single rejoinder or objection. And as they all seemed ready to return, Red Hawk led them back to camp.

CHAPTER 17

Evening was drawing near. Both Carl Bell and Henry Smith were huddled together at the outskirts of their camp, rifles held ready. Red Hawk stood directly behind them.

Said Red Hawk, "You both hold your weapons well, and standing still, you are both good shots. But it is rare that one can remain in one spot in the midst of a battle. Therefore, you must practice becoming more proficient while moving, even while running. I have set up two posts in the middle of the field. You must practice hitting those posts while at a full run."

Carl shook his head. "But that's impossible," he said skeptically. "How can a man aim and get in a good shot when on the run?"

Instead of explaining, Red Hawk let out a war cry, startling the other two. He jumped forward, around the two of them, and, sprinting toward the targets, Red Hawk pulled his bow and arrows from around his back, took what appeared to be casual aim and hit both targets within seconds, one right after the other.

When he returned to the two men, Henry asked, "How did you do that? And so quickly?"

"With intention," said Red Hawk. "That is how you fight a battle. You take aim, yes, but a man must never fail to intend to hit his target. It is this that makes the difference between a good shot, one who brings home meat to his family, and one who returns home empty-handed."

"But," said Henry, "at least you were able to see the target. That night when we were attacked, we couldn't."

"It does not matter," said Red Hawk with a shrug. "Under such conditions, a man might use instinct, he might call upon his spirit helpers to give aid, but one thing he would never fail to do is to *intend* to hit the target for which is aiming."

Henry nodded. "All right," he said. "I'll try it. I'll practice it. What can it hurt?"

Carl was more reluctant to agree, but eventually, he, too, nodded.

And so it came about that each evening, the three of them set up practice. That a camaraderie of sorts sprang up between them was only to be expected.

What wasn't expected, however—at least by Henry and Carl—was that within only a matter of days, both of them were making those shots, too.

"Who do you think attacked us?"

"I do not know."

Another cool, moonlit evening was spread out before them. As Effie and Red Hawk stood in the shadow of one of the wagons, the cool breeze of evening blew the scents of balsam, pine and prairie grass upon them. It also brought with it the delicious smell of roast duckling.

In the center of their camp a fire was blazing, throwing

out indiscriminate warmth and sparks, on this refreshing Montana night. The two married couples, as well as Mr. Owens and Fieldman, were sitting around the fireside, looking as though they might sleep right where they sat.

It was the first time that Effie and Red Hawk had been alone since the night of their attack, almost five days ago. The camp had been cleaned, the wagon wheels repaired, their equipment and papers restored and their defenses strengthened by finding the missing ammunition.

"Isn't it strange that whoever attacked us," said Effie, "didn't take anything, not even our weapons? Certainly, we had to search to locate many of the valuables, since our ammunition and a few other items had been hauled almost a mile from camp. But everything was left intact. What do you make of it, Mr. Hawk?"

"I do not know what to think of it. 'Tis strange behavior indeed. Stranger still that I have found no clues of an enemy. There were no tracks for me to discover, not even the downturn of a blade of grass to show the direction the enemy came from, or took in retreat."

She nodded. "Did you scout to our rear, then?"

"*Aa*, 'tis so. I can make no sense of the clues left me. Except perhaps one. I hesitate to mention it, however, because I think it unlikely to serve any purpose."

"But there is a clue? What is it?"

He pointed toward the north side of their camp. "A boulder was split in two over there," he said. "And in that direction," he pointed to the east, "Mother Earth was overturned as though a white man's plow had been taken to her. It required great force to do these things, and yet again, there are no tracks."

"Hmmm. What do you suspect?"

"Maybe there are good scouts who are helping the person who seeks these . . ." Gently, he reached out to

touch her waist, there, where he knew she kept the artifacts hidden.

The graze was innocent, yet he was pleased to note
that despite this, she scooted in closer to him. She said,
"Could it be that the sheriff is following us? That maybe
he's hired a few scouts?"

"It could be," said Red Hawk. "But if this is so, he has
hired some very good guides. Do you think many were for
hire in Virginia City?"

She paused for a second, then, "I didn't find any."

He nodded.

"Where do we go from here?"

"We move on," said Red Hawk. "Whoever it is, or whatever it is, will either give up and leave us alone, or will try
the same thing again. Next time we will be more prepared."

"Yes," she said. "I have been thrilled to see how expert
both Henry and Carl have become on their watches—and
in only a matter of days."

"*Aa,*" he said, "it is true. The next time, we will be
more prepared. And if this thing be human, we will stand
a better chance of besting it."

"What do you mean, *if* this thing is human?"

He didn't answer; he merely frowned.

"Mr. Hawk?"

"I hesitate to put my thoughts into words, until I learn
more."

"Learn more of what?"

But Red Hawk wasn't ready to answer any further questions on the subject, and he just shook his head. "And now,
it is time for you to retire."

"Humph!" she uttered. "I suppose you want me to
sleep while you go on ahead, and scout out the trail for tomorrow?"

"*Aa,* such things must be done."

"And may I go with you this time?"

"Not tonight," he said. "I would finish my work as quickly as I might. But do not fret. There are many more evenings ahead of us."

"Yes, Mr. Hawk, there certainly are."

Perhaps, he thought, it was the way in which he had expressed himself. Maybe not. But seeming to realize that his mind was set on the subject, and there was nothing more to discuss about it, she simply said good night, and started to leave.

Reaching out, he grabbed hold of her arm, keeping her back. He said, "You forgot something."

"Oh? Did I?"

"*Aa*," he said, "'tis so." And bending toward her, he kissed her soundly on the lips, and hugged her close to him. "Sleep well," he said, giving her rump a little pat.

"Sir?" she questioned, backing up from him. But she accompanied the word with a smile, and, turning away from him, she stepped to her tent. However, before she pulled the flap back and ducked into the interior of the flimsy structure, she looked back over her shoulder. Shyly, she waved at him.

Red Hawk didn't return the gesture. Instead, he sighed.

The land over which they rode was as awe-inspiring as if they traveled through one natural-made cathedral after another. The countryside was big, massive, spacious, and it was brilliant with luxuriant greenery. From lakes as blue as the deep, azure color of the sky, and valleys where patches of green were emblazoned with winding, meadow streams to craggy, snow-topped mountains and pine-covered hills, each day brought a new splendor that seemed even more spectacular than the last.

The meadows abounded in wildlife, as well. Buffalo were everywhere, as were moose, dear, elk and antelope. Once, a few days back, as she and the other women had been gathering wild berries, Red Hawk had instructed them on the proper manner in which to greet a bear, should they come across one.

"Look him in the eye," he had said, "do not challenge him, and do not smile. Simply look at him, and do not avert your gaze. Since it is the height of summer, and the bears are not starved from their winter sleep, they should not attack."

Because she preferred to walk instead of ride in the wagons, Effie still remembered one day when they had crossed a stream that was hot at its very bottom and cool on top. She had at once reckoned that the riverbed must be a place where some hot spring emptied. Briefly, she had wondered about the stream's medicinal powers, but when their party had forged on ahead, she had forgotten to ask Red Hawk about it.

There were birds everywhere, as well, and she was getting accustomed to being awakened by the magic of their songs, and lulled to sleep at night by their calls. Eagles and hawks flocked the skies during the day, their majestic presence always inspiring wonder. Even Red Hawk paid them tribute, stopping whatever he was doing to gaze up at them. Often, he would sing to them.

When she had queried him about such unusual behavior, wondering why he would sing, when the creatures obviously could not hear him, he had told her, "We honor the eagle, for he will often alert you to an enemy. If they will not fly over a particular area, you can know that there lies an enemy. And," he added, "do you know as a fact that they cannot hear me or know of my admiration?"

"Well . . . no."

He hadn't spoken another word on the subject, but had rather gone on about his duties.

He had educated her about many other birds, as well: "The *nepe-e*, or as you call it, the white-throated sparrow, speaks Blackfeet," he had said. "We all understand his song, and the black breast—or longspur—sings a melody that means, 'Spread out your blanket and I will light upon it.' But the bird that we think is wisest of all is the raven. We look to him to tell us the future. If he lights upon your trail, and he puts his head together with another raven, an enemy is close by. You should seek cover."

"Truly?"

"*Aa.*"

At present, they had come to a stream, home to several beavers.

"Look there." Red Hawk had reined in his pony and had dropped back to her, since she accompanied the last wagon. She was on foot, and was holding on to their horse, as though to guide it. Carl Bell, with reins in hand, was driving the wagon, while John Owens sat next to him. They were awaiting their turn at crossing the river.

Pointing to a particular beaver, Red Hawk said, "Watch *ksis-atukki* closely."

"*Ksis-atukki?*"

"It means Cuts Trees with His Teeth, or, as you call it, *beaver*. But notice this one. He is unusual."

She looked where he indicated. The beaver in question was industriously attempting to fell a tree. But the tree wasn't going anywhere.

After quite a bit of work, the animal moved to another side of the tree, and began chipping away. All to no result.

In a moment, the creature stepped back away from the tree and scratched his head, just like a person might do. Once again, he tried to gash away at the tree from another position—still the tree stood, firmly planted. Again, the beaver backed up and repeated the entire process.

"Oh, my dear Lord," said Effie. "He acts like a human being."

"He does," said Red Hawk. "It is one of the reasons we Blackfeet consider the beaver to be a sacred being."

"Do you?"

"Aa, ohkiimaan," he said.

Gazing up at him, she asked, "What does that word mean?"

"Ohkiimaan?"

"Yes."

Leaning down, he whispered to her, "It means '*my wife.*'" And without awaiting her reaction, he winked at her, set his pony away from her and trotted to the lead wagon and horse, where he took hold of the animal and began leading it toward the other shoreline.

Effie watched Red Hawk for quite some time. His was a proud, majestic figure, she decided, as he disappeared out in front of her. And she feared that she was growing more and more attached to him.

How could she not? The man was gentle and kind in word and deed, but he was also rough when he had to be, wise when others were demonstrating their stupidity and never did a word of complaint cross his lips.

She shook her head. Was she out of her mind, not accepting his proposal?

At last Red Hawk signaled that it was their turn to cross the river, and while he turned around, reining his horse back across the water toward them, Effie guided their horse out into the deep stream.

Crash!

A tree fell behind her, and she wondered if the beaver had at last won his prize.

But then, *crash!* Down came another tree. Then a shot blasted through the air, sounding much like a lightning strike. At that same moment, something whizzed past her. Had it been a bullet?

Meanwhile Red Hawk was whipping his pony across the water toward them, his arms waving in the air. He was yelling at her, and she could barely hear him, but she thought he was saying, "Hold on to the horse, Effie, and get across this river now."

"Yah! Yah!" He fought with his pony to increase her speed, even though the animal was bounding through the creek's current as quickly as she could.

But Red Hawk was still too far away from her. The horse she was leading was frightened, and in reaction it reared. Though the water cushioned the animal's strength, Effie had no choice but to lunge away from it.

Carl tried to rein in the horse. He was on his feet, and Effie could see that every muscle in his body was strained. Owens sat helplessly, his hands white from clutching his seat.

Another blast sounded behind her, causing the horse to panic more and Effie to dive even farther away from it. Another something flew past her, but this time, Effie wasn't certain it had been a bullet. It seemed bigger.

Luckily she was unharmed by both the horse and the shot. But then, perhaps she had thought too soon.

Screams from the other women told her that something terrible had happened. Looking forward, she was in time to watch Red Hawk's pony go down. With horror, she saw him sink along with it.

"Red Hawk!" she added her screams to the others'. She tried to run, but only managed to struggle uselessly through the rushing stream. "Red Hawk!" she shrieked again.

Flailing her arms, she fought through the water until she reached his side. Luckily, Henry Smith had braved the stream from the other side and helped drag Red Hawk toward the shore.

Struggling with him through the river, panic turned to terror, and some barrier broke free within her. As one thought after another rushed through her mind, she knew she had been foolish. She *loved* this man. Certainly, she had always been enchanted by him; no doubt she had loved him when she had given herself to him so freely.

But adoration seemed to come wrapped in many different layers. And what had once appeared as a mild infatuation was in reality as hot and wild as an exploding volcano. She *loved* him. Nothing, not even this all-consuming dig, was more important than *he* was.

Meanwhile, Red Hawk's pony had come to her feet, and had drifted back to the shore. Red Hawk, however, appeared to be unconscious.

"Red Hawk!" she cried out his name, then in a little softer voice, "Red Hawk."

No answer.

"Henry," she said, "in your wagon is a medicine kit. Go fetch it for me, please."

Immediately, he did as bid. Meanwhile, Effie smoothed her hands over every part of Red Hawk's body, seeking evidence of an injury. She found none.

But his eyes were closed, and he wasn't uttering a word. Was he merely unconscious?

Or was it worse?

Frantically, she unfastened his blue and white choker, pushing it out of the way, as she pressed her hands against his neck. The pulse was weak, if there were one, and she couldn't be sure. She practically tore off his shirt, feeling for a heartbeat, her fingers entangling with the necklace she had once given him. She pushed the necklace to the side and fumbled again over his chest, hunting for a heartbeat.

At last, she found it. She exhaled deeply.

Next, she rubbed her hands over his head, her fingers searching for an injury. In falling had his head hit against something? A rock? Wouldn't the water have cushioned the fall enough to render him little harm?

"Red Hawk, can you hear me?" She picked up his hand, holding it in both of hers. "Don't you dare frighten me so. And don't you dare leave me."

But there was no response.

She had to determine if he had hit his head, and as gently as possible, she felt behind and discovered a rather large lump, there on the back side. But it wasn't from the fall. Something had grazed him, had come dangerously close to killing him.

What was she to do? He was still not responding to her.

Still holding his hand, she said, "Red Hawk, if you can hear me, squeeze my hand."

For several moments, nothing happened, but then, she felt a light pressure from his fingers.

He groaned, and Effie almost cried. And it wasn't long before he opened his eyes. Looking straight up at her, he took a deep breath, and said, "Are you all right?"

What a question. She almost laughed. "I'm fine," she said, half crying. "But I fear that you have fallen from your horse."

"*Aa*, I think I am aware of that."

Tentatively, she asked, "Can you move your legs?"

She saw him lift his feet into the air, then he bent his knees. "I can," he said.

"And how about your arms? Can you lift both of them?"

He brought up first one, and then the other into the air,

bringing her hands right along with him. He said, "I can do that also. Should I try to sit up?"

She didn't answer because he did so at once, though he did grab hold of his head in the process.

"Did someone hit me?" he asked. "It feels like I have been in a battle."

"Apparently, something grazed you a little too closely." She indicated the spot without touching it. "I will need to clean the wound. Look at me, for I must stare deeply into your pupils. Oh, dear," she complained, after a moment, "I'm afraid it's almost impossible to see the pupils of your eyes, the iris is so dark."

At that moment, the sky rumbled, and looking up, she was amazed to discover that clouds had gathered above them. Where had those storm clouds come from? And so quickly?

Gradually, Red Hawk rose to his feet, and as Henry rushed to her with the medicine kit, Red Hawk asked, "Where is my pony?"

Espying the animal, she pointed, and said, "She is over there, grazing."

Red Hawk stood. Even though Effie tried to hold him back, he was already striding away from her.

"Red Hawk," she called, coming to her feet and rushing after him. "Don't walk away from me. I need to sterilize that wound."

"It will hold," he said, not even looking at her.

"But what are you doing? Only moments ago, you were unconscious. I need to make sure that you are fine."

"I am fine."

"But *I* need to make sure."

He said, "When I have finished with what I must do, you can then attend to me. In the meanwhile, I think that

I know who is following us, and if I am right—and I believe that I am—it is only I who can handle him."

"But—"

"You must become the leader of these wagons, Miss Effie," he said, gazing at her with concern. "Please lead the wagons in a northerly direction until you find a good place to camp. Ensure it is near water. You are still in Crow country, and they are friendly. You will be fine."

"But—"

"If I do not return in a few days' time, keep heading straight north. Keep to the trails. You will soon find your way to the Gates of the Rocky Mountains."

"But—"

"Do not try to stop me. If I am right, this is something that only I can do."

"Then you know who is doing this to us?"

"I think that I do."

"Well, who is it? And don't you want to take Henry or Carl with you as protection?"

"I need no one else. Besides, you will require them more than I, in case I do not return."

"Do not say that. And I'm not so certain that we cannot do without them."

"They stay."

"All right," she said. "Then take me. I would help you, as you have helped me."

"*Saa.* 'Tis one battle that I must fight on my own."

"Then before you go, I think you should be aware, that I have decided something."

"*Ho!*"

"I have decided that I will marry you. We will need to find a preacher in order to make it legal. We will have to find a place to live where people are not horribly prejudiced. But Red Hawk, I'm in love with you. I cannot live without you."

For one entire heartbeat, Red Hawk looked as though he had found heaven. But then, glancing away from her, he said, "I love you, too. But I cannot stay here now. I must go."

"Take me."

"I cannot."

"Why? Who is it that is doing this?"

" 'Tis my own enemy," he said solemnly. " 'Tis the one I have waited all my life to battle."

"Yes?"

" 'Tis the Thunderer."

CHAPTER 18

It was as an afterthought that Red Hawk bent down and washed the blood off his face. Tenderly, he felt his head with the tips of his fingers, satisfying himself that it was merely a flesh wound. It would hold.

Taking his pony's reins in hand, he leapt upon her back. He checked his gear. His shield, with his medicine pouch, was tied to his blanket, which he used as a saddle. His lance hung by his side, ready to grip. Over his shoulder was his bow, and upon his back, a quiver full of arrows.

He was ready.

Glancing back only once at Effie, he urged his pony into a run, putting as much distance between himself and the wagon train as possible. His spirits soared as he burst out over the prairie, for at last, he could place a cause to the mysterious happenings.

In truth, he felt grounded. Here was something solid for him to hold on to, something tangible to fight. Indeed, he looked forward to the battle ahead of him, had been boldly hoping for such a moment, since before he could remember.

As he rushed his pony across the short, lush prairie grass, he relished the feeling of being one with Mother Earth. The wind raced across his face, seeming to speak to him, and he inhaled the life-giving force of pure air.

Clouds, which had touched down to earth, rolled toward him; off in the distance, lightning struck the ground as the storm, much like a cyclone, sped toward him. His pony danced uneasily beneath him, but Red Hawk soothed her and gave her full berth. For this moment, he was prepared.

"Come and do your worst!" he shouted at the top of his lungs, as his pony reared. "Meet me, man to man!"

From a lone tree to his left, an enormous bird suddenly burst into flame, its ashes falling to the ground. But only moments later, another bird came into view, this one larger than a monster, half black, half blue, and as it flapped its wings, thunder spread all about it.

It was the Thunderbird, and with its breath, it roused the clouds, causing them to spin toward him. With its eyes, it spat lightning. The ground, in reaction, was set afire. But as quickly as it had come, the bird now disappeared into the rolling clouds of thunder.

"Are you afraid?" shouted Red Hawk. "Afraid to do battle with one who hates you?"

Perhaps he had spoken too soon. Clouds had settled upon the earth, and from out of their dust stepped a man, half black, half blue, with long, black blue hair, and lightning stripes branded over his face and torso. Thunder rolled across his chest as though it were part of his breathing. And from his fingertips shot strikes of lightning.

He was the Thunder Being.

Red Hawk's pony raised up onto her hind legs. Still, Red Hawk held her in check. In preparation for battle, he drew his bow, lifted his lance, but then, unexpectedly from those same clouds came a voice.

But it wasn't the Thunderer's call. It was a voice from Red Hawk's past:

"Remember, Poor Orphan, that you are your band's champion. You are not on an errand of revenge. Show your enemies mercy, give aid, but most importantly, do not engage in battle with the Thunderer, even if you are able."

The Thunderer laughed, and said, "I will do battle with you, if you choose, Poor Orphan. Come." With his hand, he urged Red Hawk forward.

"Haiya!" shouted Red Hawk, dismounting, and striding forward. "You, who have ruined my life, I will battle with you."

"Do not engage in battle with the Thunderer, even if you are able."

So came the voice from the clouds one more time.

"Haiya! Saa!" Were his hands to be so tied? Was Red Hawk expected to do nothing, when at last his chance was here, when at last the Thunderer stood before him?

"Haiya!" Red Hawk uttered the word, as though it were a curse.

It took every bit of his strength, his cunning, his integrity. But, at length, though everything within him rebelled, he turned his back on the Thunder Being.

Grabbing hold of his pony's reins, Red Hawk jumped up on her back. Lifting his spear high into the air, he said, "As soon as I have freed my people, *I will do battle with you*. But, alas, that time is not now."

The Thunderer laughed again, the clouds boomed, lightning struck the ground. Looking back, the last thing Red Hawk saw was the Thunder Being becoming a bird again, which set off across the prairie. Black clouds rolled with him, and lightning struck the ground. But he didn't turn back.

Frustration tore at Red Hawk. How could this be? At last, he was justified in doing battle with his nemesis; at last, the evil villain was within reach, had acknowledged Red Hawk by trying to kill him . . .

Or had the Thunderer tried to kill him?

The thought was disturbing. For indeed, if the Thunder Being had truly wished to end Red Hawk's life, there would be little he, Red Hawk, could do. *Aa*, to be certain, he would go down fighting, but make no mistake, he would go down.

"Ha!" Red Hawk cried out in futility, raising his shield high into the air, as if in challenge. "I have had to walk away this time, but there will be a next. This I promise you."

But even as the words left him, Red Hawk knew he could not do it until his people were freed, if that were to ever happen.

Trying to calm himself, Red Hawk allowed his pony to slow down to a trot. If not battle, then what was he to do? To do nothing was wrong, for he could not allow the Thunderer to terrorize Effie and the others.

Glancing up into the sky, he let out another groan, opened his arms wide and shouted, *"Omaopaat!"*

And then it came to him, an idea. Perhaps the awareness was a gift from the Creator. Mayhap the realization occurred because, in his frustration, he could suddenly think clearly. Whatever was the cause, he knew what he must do.

When in doubt, cleanse yourself in the right way, and seek out your spirit protector.

So had spoken his old, wise grandfather.

And in this moment, Red Hawk needed guidance. He would have to seek out and find the sea dog again.

To this end, he rushed off across the prairie.

"Indians. You can't trust them," complained John Owens.

"The man is obviously irresponsible, leaving us alone when he was hired to guide us," added Fieldman. "But he's not to blame, I dare say. Can't help what's in his blood." The man raised his nose in the air.

"That's unfair." Henry spoke up. "We all felt the brunt of the attack—Red Hawk most of all. He was injured, and yet he went off to fight the enemy alone, saving us."

"A likely story," said Owens. "He has left us on the prairie to rot."

"He has not," said Effie.

"Father, really! That was unnecessary," admonished Lesley.

"Be thankful he didn't require you to go with him, Mr. Owens," said Carl. "But I swear if you keep this up, *we* might leave you here—to rot."

Piqued, Owens blew out on a breath. Yet, the threat seemed to quiet him—at least temporarily.

"Well, good, I'm glad that's settled," Effie continued. "Now, we will wait here for him to return, as I assure you, he will. There is plenty of water, we have enough food and we are in the friendly country of the Crow. We can afford to wait . . . at least for a few days."

"I don't like it," said Owens.

"Father! Hush!"

"You're in the minority here," said Carl.

"We *will* wait for Red Hawk here," said Effie in a voice that allowed no debate. "And unless you and Fieldman would like to lead us out of here, and defend us on the trail as well, I suggest you both keep your opinions to yourself."

"Hear, hear!" came the hearty response of Carl, followed by similar approval from Henry.

Owens and Fieldman, however, were not to be persuaded. With a round of disgruntled mumbling, Owens turned away, followed by Fieldman.

"Well done, Miss Rutledge," said Carl.

"Yes," Henry joined in. "Couldn't have expressed it better myself. Though he is my father-in-law, I heartily disagree with him, don't you, Lesley?"

Lesley nodded.

And while Madeline placed a sympathetic hand on Effie's arm, Lesley said, "Please excuse me, Effie. I need to talk to Father."

"Yes," said Effie. "That would be good."

At length, Effie heaved a sigh of relief, then said, "Thank you for your defense. It is much appreciated. But now, if you would excuse me, I am so behind in my work . . ."

"Of course," said Madeline, while the two men nodded.

Effie smiled her thanks at them all, stepped toward her tent, and pulling back its flap, she settled down onto her blanket cross-legged. With another deep breath, she picked up her journal and pen, and without hesitation, began to scribble down her notes.

The lake before him was a deep blue, surrounded by stands of willows, cottonwoods and balsam. It was a beautiful spot, a beautiful water.

It was also a treacherous loch, legended to be haunted by water creatures who could lure man to his death.

Many an Indian soul had been lost to this body of water, and to this very day, no Blackfeet warrior dared enter into its realm without penalty.

But Red Hawk was desperate. If any body of water might house the sea dog, this would be the one.

Having purified himself in the sacred smoke of sweetgrass and sage, he stood at the edge of the lake. Perhaps he would find the sea dog here in this pool, perhaps not. There was a good chance he might lose his life.

All he knew was that he had to try.

Summonsing his courage, for fear of the unknown held sway over him, he prepared to take the plunge into the water. But first Red Hawk lifted his voice to the heavens, offering a prayer to the Above Ones:

> "Haiya, haiya, *"Thank you,* A'pistotooki, *for guiding me this day.*
> Haiya, haiya, *thank you for allowing me to understand that the Thunderer now follows me.*
> Haiya, haiya, *I would ask for your help again,* A'pistotooki, *for the Thunderer is a worthy opponent.*
> Haiya, haiya. A'pistotooki, *I know you cannot take sides.*
> Haiya, haiya, *but Creator, I must find my spirit protector, though I am far from my home.*
> Haiya, haiya, A'pistotooki, *I seek your guidance that I might find the sea dog.*
> Haiya, haiya, *I am following my vision that I might help my people, and I have discovered that the one I love also needs help. She is the one you know as the water being, Effie.*
> Haiya, haiya, *know,* A'pistotooki, *that I think both can be done without one harming the other.*

> Haiya, haiya, *Creator,* A'pistotook*i, have pity on me.*
> *My needs are simple. Help me to help my people and*
>   *the water being.*
> Haiya, haiya, haiya, *my prayer is done."*

With this said, Red Hawk swallowed hard, and plunged into the water. Nothing immediately happened. Heartened by this, he swam from one end of the lake to the other. But though he searched on and on, he found nothing but fish, and certainly not large fish.

His mood sank, and he began to think that he would have to search for the sea dog in the north country, which did his cause of defending Effie little good. For, with his hands tied morally against battle with the Thunder Being, he was of little use to anybody.

Disappointed, Red Hawk surfaced, noting that the sun had long since left the sky. Day was turning to evening. Shadows were already shooting across the water.

Setting his feet on the muddy bottom, Red Hawk walked to shore. So many shadows were there that he could not tell the real thing from a reflection. He saw it, there in the water, but turned his back on it.

"Otahkohsoa' tsis!"

Red Hawk spun around. Something had called his name. Then he saw it. It was black, long and slimy.

It was a sea dog. Surely, not the same sea dog he had once confronted in a time long past. Indeed, this looked to be more snake than fish.

And then, from the water, again, came the call, *"Otahkohsoa' tsis!"*

"I am coming," Red Hawk called out, and wading out into the deeper water, he submerged himself. It required no small degree of stamina to confront the large, snakelike creature. Still, he swam toward it until at last he came right up to it.

The sea dog opened his mouth to show two sets of fangs. At once, terror filled Red Hawk's soul, but he remained steadfast, and he said, in thought, "I am here."

"Otahkohsoa' tsis," began the creature, "behold, I have taken pity on you. I have watched you all this day through, swimming about in my lake, searching for guidance. Only one who is brave and true dare enter my lake, and for this, your bravery, I will bestow upon you my power of cunning and prodigious thought. The Thunderer is great, for he is a god, and he is angry at you, at all your people. Know *Otahkohsoa' tsis*, that your time to act for your people is near. You will be given two chances, one to end the curse for your people, and one to render the anger of the Thunderer less. If you are lucky, you will accomplish both. Now listen, for here is what you must do . . ."

Effie's two wagons were easy enough to find. At present the group was camped on an open meadow. To the north and south of the place were jutting mountains, while to the east and west were hills of a much tamer nature.

They had pitched camp next to a stream, one that housed a few cottonwood trees, as well as a willow or two, and several bushes. One of the wagons was parked beneath an enormous willow, all but hiding it from view. Red Hawk crept up to that wagon first.

It was empty.

Unwilling to announce his arrival to one and all—for Red Hawk hoped to catch Effie alone—he slipped up next to the other wagon, which, though much more exposed to view, was empty as well. However, clothes, pots, pans, even the water and food supplies had been dumped, and were strewn where they lay. What had happened here?

In the center of the camp, voices were raised, and leaping as noiselessly as possible into the interior of the wagon, Red Hawk paused to listen.

"I think this evidence clearly points to the fact that your Indian scout is trying to steal the artifacts from you."

Red Hawk could see John Owens and Fieldman standing before Effie. In Owens's hand, and dangling from it, was an Indian-made choker of blue and white beads. It looked familiar.

Belatedly, Red Hawk reached up to feel around his neck. Sure enough, his choker of glass beads and leather was gone. He hadn't noticed.

Meanwhile, Carl advanced toward Owens and, picking up the choker, examined it carefully. "It is Red Hawk's," he said, as though confirming Red Hawk's guilt.

Madeline had followed her husband, and reaching out to touch the necklace, she said, "There could be some other explanation."

"Perhaps," said Carl, frowning at his wife, "but what other accounting could there be for such a drastic action?"

Carl's statement seemed innocent, and when Madeline's face filled with color, it seemed to be out of place for the situation. But her reaction was soon explained when Lesley said, "Carl, your wife is not at fault here. I'm sorry, but I heard the two of you arguing a little while earlier, and I think I should tell you that Madeline was with me when this happened. While you were out hunting, we went . . . swimming. Now, Father, where did you say you found this?"

"In the most incriminating place possible," replied Owens. "Beside Miss Effie's wagon."

"Well, that's all I need to know," said Lesley. "I for one

agree with Father. It seems that our guide has betrayed us." With hands on hips, Lesley turned to Effie. "What are you going to do about this?"

"Nothing at the moment," replied Effie, "since he's not here."

Red Hawk watched Effie's face intently, as she stepped toward them, and reached out a hand to finger the choker. She paused before she said, "Mr. Owens, Lesley, Carl, thank you for bringing this to my attention, but really I think it's nonsense. We all saw Red Hawk leave. He's probably miles from here right now."

"How do we know that with any degree of certainty?" asked Owens threateningly. "We only saw him leave. What if he doubled back, only to search through your things? I've said it before, and I'll say it again, you can't trust these Indians."

"I agree," said Lesley, her stance challenging. "In fact, I'm beginning to wonder if you are qualified enough to be in charge of this expedition, Effie."

"That was unnecessary," said Madeline.

Carl nodded. "Miss Rutledge has done fine so far. It's not her fault that several mishaps have—"

"Well, if there's any more," said Lesley, "I'm going to throw my lot with Father. I'm beginning to believe that he is the only one who can find the missing artifacts."

Silence followed this rather intimidating disclosure.

At that moment Henry stepped into the gathering. Where had he been?

"What's going on here?" he asked.

"Miss Effie's Indian friend has tried to steal the artifacts," said Owens. "And where have you been?"

"Washing off the deer we killed in the stream," replied Henry. "And I don't believe you about Red Hawk. I could swear that the man is trustworthy."

"I, too, believe this to be so," said Effie. But Red Hawk saw her frown.

"Miss Effie," Owens said sternly, "do not think we are deceived. I have seen you wear his feather in your hair, and I have witnessed that you have a particular attachment to the man, but I think you should look at this logically, as any *real* scientist would do. Someone went through your possessions tonight, while we were all away from the camp."

"Yes, yes, but—"

"This is the third attack upon this group, Miss Effie," said Owens, "and as I understand it, the assaults started occurring around the time when you hired this man . . . Hawk, I believe is his name. Twice, I have been told that there were items found that would implicate the Indian, and I for one believe—"

"But don't you see," interrupted Effie. "That's just the problem. If it really were Red Hawk doing these things, he would never leave anything behind. He's too well trained a scout."

"Bah!"

"Oh, come now," said Effie. "Have you never noticed how meticulous Red Hawk is about everything? He observes even the tiniest of peculiarities, and he misses nothing. The weather conditions, not only of today, but of months previous, he knows them all in perfect detail so that he can know how long ago tracks were made. He paints himself like the environment to avoid detection. He can tell from a single track if the trail is made by an enemy or a friend. Given that, I must ask you and your daughter to consider your words wisely. Do you really think someone so fastidious would be clumsy enough to leave such obviously personal items behind?"

"Miss Effie," said Owens at once, his countenance

contorted with the beginnings of rage. "The man is Indian, and as such, is inferior to us in every way. Do you really think a savage has the reasoning ability that you grant him?"

"I do," proclaimed Henry.

Carl frowned. "I have to admit that I agree with Effie on that, as well."

Effie shook her head gently, before smiling. Then she said, "Yes, Mr. Owens. I would have to agree with Henry and Carl. I think Red Hawk has this sort of ability. Now, please, all of you, I need some time alone. I need to think about this. But most of all, I need to gather up my things."

"I'll help," said Madeline, stepping up to Effie and placing an arm around her shoulders. "And you will, too, won't you, Carl?"

Carl nodded.

"Really, John," said Madeline, "it's bad enough that Effie has to find all her things without *you* adding to her problem. And Lesley." She frowned. "Whether you think Effie competent or not, I think you should help us collect up her things."

John? thought Red Hawk, raising his brow.

Lesley, however, was frowning. "Yes," she said, "just because I think she has a soft spot for the Indian is no reason not to help her. Of course I'll help."

The three women set off toward the prairie, where even now, Red Hawk could see many of Effie's things blowing in the wind.

Interesting. Slipping from the wagon, Red Hawk disappeared from the camp by means of shadows and the cover of the greenery. Of course he knew that someone on this wagon train—or someone following them—was attempting to steal the artifacts that Effie carried. It was interesting that he had been the scapegoat . . . this time . . .

It did make him wonder exactly who was doing this. Was there more incentive behind these attacks than the mere confiscation of artifacts?

These questions, and a good many others, he could not answer. However, he did intend to find out where John Owens and Fieldman were going, for they had not headed in the direction of their tent.

He found them easily enough. But what were they doing? There they were, hunched over in the water with pans held tightly in their grip. This action looked familiar.

Ah, the gold seekers. Prospectors.

Why would Owens and his manservant be hunting for gold en route to an expedition? Such behavior was very strange indeed.

Shaking his head, Red Hawk turned to make his way back to the wagons. This time, however, he would not bother to disguise his approach. He would be leaving camp soon anyway, as he would need to scout the trail ahead of them for the morrow.

"There he is!" he heard Henry shout, and Red Hawk lifted his right hand, palm open, the Plains Indian sign to show that he held no weapons, and came in peace.

"Red Hawk has returned," he heard Madeline say.

"Red Hawk?" asked Effie, and he saw her drop whatever things she had been holding as she set out toward him.

"Red Hawk, you're back!" she shouted with glee. "You have been gone so many days, and we were all afraid something horrible had happened to you."

Red Hawk smiled, for he knew, with the exception of herself, Henry and possibly Carl, that this was not so.

She raced up to him, and stopped. *Haiya*, how he wanted to open his arms wide and welcome her into them, but he held back, for others watched.

Instead, he grinned at her and said, for her ears alone, "I thank you for defending me, my wife. And now, let us talk about that marriage."

He watched with amusement as she grimaced.

CHAPTER 19

The archaeological site—one month later

Effie let down the wooden tail flap of her wagon, and put down an unfolded map of the archaeological site. The map, which was in essence a drawing of the entire area surrounding them (including every rock and tree and shrub), would serve as a guide to each place they chose to exhume.

"Come close," she said to the rest of her crew. It was about midmorning on their first day of digging, but the noon hour fast approached. Using her hands to press down on the map, she pointed to a spot on it.

"Carl," she said, "did you place a marker here so that anyone interested in digging in this area again can more easily find the place?"

"I did."

"Good. Madeline," continued Effie, "did you mark out the site where we will begin our preliminary digging?"

"Yes. I'll point to it on the map."

Effie at once placed a red mark to indicate the location. "That's where we will begin our digging, first to get a reliable look at the strata of the land, so that we can observe what the terra firma was like before man entered the scene. Now," she continued, "do you all have a shovel and a trowel, as well as journals and papers in which to keep your records?"

All those present nodded, and, looking up, Effie silently assessed each piece of equipment.

"This all looks to be in good order." Turning, she smiled at each one of them. "And now, at last, let's begin digging."

There were murmurs of agreement, even a few cheers; most of the crew headed toward the spot where the preliminary digging would occur.

"Mr. Owens," said Effie, "might I speak with you for a moment?"

"Of course."

Effie and the others had set up the site of their work in an area that Red Hawk called *Mahkwiyi Istikiop* or Where the Wolf Fell Down. Known to the white man as Wolf Creek, their site was situated in the shadow of a cliff, which in ancient times had been used as a buffalo jump, or what Red Hawk called a *piskan*. Here legend had it that a wolf, that had been following on the trail of a buffalo herd, which was being lured by the Indians, fell over the cliff along with the buffalo.

It was a fine legend, and an aptly named spot. In truth, it induced a feeling within her of being close to the ancients.

"Mr. Owens," she said, by way of starting. "Need I tell you that I am so glad that you are here?"

"As am I, Miss Effie."

"I am flattered to have such an experienced person for my field supervisor. I'm sure you realize what an important position this is, for you will be directing the type of excavation to be done. I'm very excited to have you here, and I'm assuming that your friendship with my father must have been the determining factor that led you to be a part of this dig."

Effie noted that Owens's gaze was directed somewhere between her nose and her chin. Instead of looking her directly in the eye, he avoided her. It was a little disconcerting.

"Your father was, indeed, a deciding factor, Miss Effie. Our friendship, as you of course must realize, knows no bounds."

"Yes, I am aware of that," said Effie, "and I am most thankful for it. I know you are more experienced than I in the standard procedure of an archaeological dig, and I am hoping that you will not object too much to questions I might need to ask from time to time."

"Not at all, Miss Effie. Not at all."

"Very well. I have tried to determine this from you several times since your arrival, and since we have been on the trail, but it seems that oftentimes either you or I were indisposed. I realize I could find this out myself easily enough, but perhaps we should discuss it anyway. If I remember correctly, I often remember you and my father discussing such things." She smiled.

Owens nodded.

Effie continued, "How have you arranged the personnel for the dig? I'm assuming that—"

"Don't worry your pretty little red head about such details, Miss Effie," Owens interrupted. "I'm sure you have much more to attend to than worrying about things that need not concern you."

Need not concern her?

"Know that my experience has teamed the best people together. Because I was here with your father several years ago, he thought it best that I come along and ensure that the dig went smoothly. *I* am the expert, after all. I think he feared that, though he loves you dearly, you might turn out to be incompetent." He smiled at her, although Effie felt like he had stabbed her in the heart.

Her smile remained in place, as though frozen. But suddenly and irreconcilably, she felt as though she had been dropped from midair.

Still, calming herself, she said, "That will be fine, Mr. Owens, but—"

However, he turned his back on her, and was walking away.

Her mouth still open, Effie watched him for some moments, wondering vaguely if he had meant to appear so patronizing. How could he? He was her friend, her father's friend.

Or was she reading too much into this?

Tilting her head as she surveyed his disappearing figure, some rather condemning facts came readily to mind. Wasn't it true that her father could have picked Owens as the director of the project? Was there some reason why he hadn't?

Also, initially, hadn't Effie been concerned about Owens's possible jealousy? Although her father had initially reassured her that Owens would be happy to act as her second in command, hadn't the situation been enough of an anxiety that she had mentioned it once to Lesley?

Could it be that Owens resented her presence here, on the project? It seemed more and more probable that he did. John Owens was most likely envious of her, the age-old story of the elder being overlooked in favor of the younger.

But if that were so, why was he here? Why hadn't he declined the invitation? Loyalty to her father perhaps? Or was it the lure of one final dig that brought him here?

Effie realized that in the days to come, she would have ample opportunity to dispel Owens's resentment of her. She'd never feel comfortable putting these questions to him, for they were too direct, but if she were able, she could at least show herself to be competent. And if all went well, he should be her friend again.

Meanwhile, she would put this most recent exchange behind her. Yes, that was best. After all, the man was her father's best friend.

As she had said earlier, it wouldn't be too great a strain to simply view the arrangements that had been made. It wasn't as if it required any genius. There could only be two teams, and observing what groupings had been assigned was not a great mental exercise.

Effie grabbed hold of the map again and studied it. Putting it down, she reached for a ledger and began to write. Goodness knew, she had ledgers to fill, journals to make and an accounting of all the funds used so far on this trip. That should be enough work to fill her time and her thoughts for the next several days.

Besides, there was the grid to make. As she and Owens had agreed beforehand, their teams would use the grid system for quarrying the area, a procedure that checkerboarded the excavation site, providing little squares for digging. In this way they could ensure that the entire site had been unearthed.

Ah, here would be a chance to demonstrate her competency to Owens, she thought. And perhaps in the process, she might also prove that her father had indeed placed his faith correctly.

Dear Lord, but it was hot. Hot and dry. And though off in the distance thunderclouds could be seen, with lightning strikes falling to the ground, no rain fell here. In fact, it had been so long since there had been a summer shower, she wondered if the country might not be experiencing a drought.

Enough speculating. Reaching up to remove her hat and wipe her forehead, she set to work.

In the days that followed Effie began to believe that she had made a mistake. It was one thing to think that she could work her way into John Owens's good graces. It was another to do it.

In reality, it appeared that the more control she exerted over the project, the more critical Owens became of her. Indeed, the entire dig was fast becoming an exercise in who would rule the excavation site, much to Effie's disappointment.

The first incident had occurred after Effie had spent upward of five or six hours producing a workable grid. Immediately upon presenting it to the crew and setting them to utilize it, Owens had changed his mind. The crew would now work the site in the vertical-face method of excavation.

When Effie had objected, due to the amount of time she had put in on the project, Owens had said, "But Miss Effie, do you see that the lay of the land goes steeply downward?"

Effie had been ready to answer, for she, too, had taken that into account when she had made the grid. But she hadn't been given a chance, since Owens had laughed at her, and then gone on to say, "The grid method will make it harder on those at the top of the incline than those at the bottom. Therefore, it makes sense to switch to the vertical-face method."

"But, I already—"

"Here give me that." Owens had grabbed the grid out

of her hands and had torn it into little pieces. Then without even a hint of an apology, he had walked away, again leaving Effie with her mouth gaping open.

She hadn't known how to respond, how to go about restoring her authority. In the end, she had done nothing about it. Nor had she told anyone about the incident at all.

Who would believe her? John Owens was a well-respected archaeologist. Secondly, she was not inclined to gossip, no matter the provocation.

So she capitulated. This time.

In truth, even as director, she'd had little choice in the matter but to yield to him. As field supervisor, Owens had every right to change the method of excavation, if he deemed it necessary, no questions asked.

But Effie felt more and more as if she needed a defense against the man, for she found him to be hurtful. She couldn't very well continue on in this manner; the upset ate away at her.

The change had finally come in an alteration of her tactics. She decided it best to simply stay out of Mr. Owens's way, a system that proved more than soothing to her nerves.

And so the days had passed relatively peacefully.

Effie still recalled the first time one of their team members had discovered something of worth. It had been Henry, who had been doing the digging.

"I've found something!" he had called out. Unfortunately, in his enthusiasm, he had tried to run with the find, almost dropping it.

Effie had hurried forward, as did the others, but none were fast enough to save the piece. Luckily, Lesley was a little more experienced than her husband, having grown up around archaeological digs. She had dived for the piece and had caught it after Henry had inadvertently dropped it.

"Thank you, Lesley," Effie had said, offering her a hand up. But Lesley had refrained from taking the proffered hand, and had gained her footing without aid.

The artifact had turned out to be a carefully carved cup, made from the horn of a bull.

Effie now spent her time checking each excavation site for the type of artifacts discovered, since more were uncovered every day. She also carefully supervised the cleaning of each piece, if only because the cleaning required a delicate touch.

Sometimes she helped with the digging. But her biggest duty, which kept her adequately busy these days, was cataloging each artifact found, while comparing them to similar finds from previous digs. In this way, the age of each piece could be determined.

It was not the most physically demanding work. But because it was being done in the heat of the day, even this was exhausting.

John Owens, however, except for an occasional spurt of activity, sat beneath his awning. Occasionally, he cataloged findings. But for the most part, he did little work, except to fan himself and to read occasionally.

Although it was true that due to his age, as well as his experience, Owens should not be required to actually dig, there was so much else to do on an excavation project like this, and so little of it required physical exertion, that it was hard to justify his inaction.

Not even Owens's manservant, Fieldman, lifted a hand to help. Instead, he catered to his employer, with an ever-ready supply of cigars and brandy.

Not once, however, did Effie complain about Owens, or Fieldman. Instead, she tried to understand. In his youth, Mr. Owens had had his day; he'd done his work. Perhaps it was his right now that he was older to do nothing more than watch the operation, as well as give each one of them suggestions on how to do their work better.

Perhaps there were other reasons. It had certainly been a gruelling, though exciting, journey here. Maybe they each one deserved a rest.

Effie sighed, and taking a break from her work on the records, she glanced around their campsite, as though she expected to see Red Hawk there in front of her, teasing her, making himself a nuisance. She missed him. In truth, she had become so used to his presence over these past few months that no day seemed quite right without him.

Red Hawk had told her he was visiting relatives, and was resting in their camps, yet she wasn't certain this was the whole truth. Certainly, at first he had seemed rested, but now, each time he visited, he looked more and more exhausted. And she couldn't help but wonder if this "rest" wasn't bad for his health.

But if visiting relatives wasn't all he was doing, then what else was occupying his time?

In vain, she searched her memories for a clue as to what else he might be doing, but it was useless.

However, her musings brought to mind one of the most spectacular experiences of her life. Smiling, she recalled vista upon vista of unprecedented beauty—the place known as the Gates of the Rocky Mountains, an area of the Missouri River that sliced through stark cliffs and pine-covered mountains.

It had been slow going through those mountains, made longer because of Red Hawk's reluctance to push too far during the daylight hours. He had said to her, "Once my people know that I am here and that I lead these wagons, there will be no trouble. But I must alert the Blackfeet to your presence."

"Why?" she had asked him. "If your people find us, couldn't you simply tell them that we are friends?"

"I could," he had said, "but I fear that the warriors will shoot first and ask questions later. I could be wrong, for scouts will reveal my presence here. Still, I would rather not take the chance."

And so they had moved tardily through that beautiful area, though strangely no one had objected. Now, looking back on it, Effie wondered if the overwhelming views, as well as the feeling of independence this place imparted, might have been the cause of such acquiescence.

However, since the moment when they had arrived here, and had set up a more "permanent" camp, Red Hawk seemed disinclined to remain. Certainly he ventured into the campsite often enough to bring fresh meat, but he was soon gone, and with the exception of a few stolen nights, he might as well have been a stranger.

Their group was at present in their second week of excavation, and a loose schedule of sorts had been set up. In the mornings, the women cooked breakfast, while the men washed up. After eating, the men set to work, while the women bathed, joining their partners about midmorning.

Although the women oftentimes dug within the site, it was more generally accepted that the men should take on the physical aspects of the work, reserving the cleaning and recording of any artifacts found to the women. In the evening, they all retired to the river for a swim before supper. All that is except Effie, who usually continued to clean and catalog, well into the supper hour.

On this day, Effie had missed her supper altogether, easy enough to do, since the sun set so late in the night sky. The light was beginning to fade when Madeline brought her a plate full of food.

"You really should eat more, Effie."

Effie glanced up at the other woman and gratefully

accepted the extended plate. "It's just that there's so much work to do, and if I don't do it—"

"Then we'll just have to stay here a little longer."

"Yes," said Effie, "that's true. But our resources are stretched as it is." Picking up her fork, she began to eat. After awhile, she observed, "It seems incredible that I don't know more about you than I do. Here we are, alone so often, and yet . . . Let's see. What do I know? That you and Carl are happily married, that you both share a love of history and archaeology and that you are a kindhearted individual, one I should like to know better. Tell me a little bit more about yourself. How long did you know Carl before you married? How did you know it was love?"

Madeline shrugged. "There's not too much to tell, actually. Carl and I fell in love when I was only fifteen. That was five years ago. Our parents encouraged us to get together, as our two families were friends. We married fairly young. I was only seventeen."

"Lucky you," said Effie. "I wish I could have married so young."

"Yes," agreed Madeline. "Lucky me." She glanced away from Effie.

"Do you have any interests outside of archaeology?"

"I like to dance," she said, gazing back at Effie and smiling. "At one time my parents made it possible for me to receive classical ballet lessons."

"Really? I didn't know that," said Effie. "But I should have guessed. You are so graceful."

"Thank you."

"Do you and Carl plan to have any children?"

"Oh, yes," said Madeline, "though I don't seem to be doing well in that particular regard. We have tried to have a baby, but so far, we have not been successful."

"That's too bad," sympathized Effie, but then on another

note, she said, "but what fun you two must be having in the meantime . . ."

For a moment Madeline looked startled to think that their director might suggest such a thing. But then she smiled, as did Effie. Before long, the two of them were laughing, just as though they were grand old friends.

CHAPTER 20

"You will come no farther!" shouted Red Hawk to the Thunder Being, as he stood his ground on the prairie, his lance lifted upward and his bow held ready. "I know that you stalk my wife. I know that you are trying to keep her from being successful, because she might help my people. But *I* will not let you near her. So long as I exist, I will keep you from her."

Stepping forward, the Thunder Being laughed at him. Then he roared, "Each day you challenge me, little warrior. Each day you walk away. You talk big. You do little."

"Stay away from her camp!"

"Or you'll what? Walk away? Again? Yell at me?"

"Do not tempt me. Were it not for the love for my grandfather, and for his people . . ."

"I am tired of your words," said the Thunder Being. "Let us begin this fight. Long have you sought your revenge. Now, come take it."

Again, the Thunder Being beckoned Red Hawk forward.

But Red Hawk stood his ground. "I cannot do it and save my people, and well you know it. So I will show you mercy, instead." His lips spat out the word, "mercy" as though it were a nasty one.

The Thunder Being merely laughed, although he did retreat. And taking his black clouds and his lightning bolts with him, he set his path for somewhere besides Effie's camp. At least for the time being. Tomorrow would be another day.

"Haiya!" Again, Red Hawk used the word as though he were swearing. The Thunderer baited him. And though Red Hawk would stand his ground and show mercy, as he must, everything within him rebelled.

"Someday," he said to the heavens. "We will battle. I swear it."

It must have been around midnight by the time the sky finally darkened. However, this place was so far in the northern regions of the country, that even when night finally fell over the land, it seemed no more dusky than a dim version of early evening.

At last, Effie blew out the light of her candle, and setting down her pen, she stretched. There was still much to do, for this site abounded in artifacts, many of them quite old.

So far they had found several ancient arrowhead points, most of which were made from bone or flint. There were also various buffalo skulls and bones, some beads, some well-preserved hides, knives made of bone and flint, and yesterday, Madeline and her husband had found some awls fashioned of bone, as well as one buffalo-horn spoon.

The last had been quite a find, and Madeline had asked to clean it, which Effie had been only too glad to allow.

However, to date nothing had been found that even resembled the artifacts that she still carried on her person.

Effie was beginning to wonder if she and the others were on a wild-goose chase.

Amazingly enough, the heat of the day remained with them into the evening. It was an unusual circumstance here in the far reaches of the Montana Territory. Because the area wasn't known for its humidity, once the sun retreated from the sky, the atmosphere and the land usually cooled.

Maybe she had become too accustomed to it doing so. Whatever was the case, Effie suddenly yearned for a midnight swim.

Ah, to feel the gentle rush of water over her heat-soaked body. She only wished that Red Hawk were here. But he wasn't, she reminded herself, and she wasn't going to restrict herself because of that absence, either.

It would be a perfect chance to bathe, since at this time of night, everyone else was usually asleep. Surely she'd be safe enough to allow herself a quick dip, and perhaps, if she were brave enough, a brisk bath in the nude.

Sighing, she rose up from her desk, shuffling through her papers and placing the more important notes neatly inside folders, which she promptly stored away. Then, grabbing hold of her shawl, she left her tent.

Glancing up toward the sky, she looked for the Big Dipper to tell her not only direction, but the time. If she were right, she thought, it looked to be well after midnight. Perhaps, to another, midnight was not such a perfect time to swim. To some, the evening might hold shadows, phantoms and fears.

But Effie had become accustomed to the trail, to the wild, and had found that the late evenings, instead of frightening her, endowed her with a feeling of independence, to say nothing of allowing her privacy.

Besides, something in the air tonight pulled at her, encouraging her to let go, to come to the water.

Drawing in a breath of the warm, night air, she stepped toward the great Missouri River, heading toward a particular pool that was caught off in a nook. One that was surrounded by willows and pine. In her youth she had used it often, it being the same place where she had first met Red Hawk.

The grasses were dew covered, wet and cool against her slippers, and she fretted that the bottom of her dress would pay the price for her tête-à-tête with the river. But she wasn't about to let a little dew stop her.

At last she arrived. As she bent down to test the water with her fingers, she heard a deep voice behind her say, "I thought you were never going to come. Because I saw you working, I decided not to disturb you, but I have waited here the evening through."

She gasped and jumped, but she wasn't frightened, if only because she was well aware of exactly who had spoken to her. As she drank in the sight of him, she said, "I wonder if I shall ever get used to your sneaking up on me."

He didn't answer. Instead, he opened his arms wide.

As though one were the magnet for the other, they fell into each other's embrace. While he rained kisses over her face and cheeks, he ran his hands up, down and over her back, her hips, her neck, her hair.

"I have missed you," he said.

"And I, you," she responded. "I had begun to worry that you had forgotten about me."

"Forgotten? Could a mountain forget her streams and forests? A lake her fish and currents? You are as much a part of me now as these things are to a mountain or a lake. How could I ever forget you?"

She sighed. "You have been gone so long."

"Fourteen or fifteen suns. That is all."

They sank to their knees.

"That is a long time for me," she said. "Have you finished visiting your relatives?"

"I have."

His lips then captured hers. She welcomed his taste, his touch, his tongue.

Her shawl had long since hit the ground, and his fingers fumbled with the buttons on the back of her dress. He murmured against her lips, "Again, you wear many clothes."

"As do you," she rejoined, indicating his shirt, his buffalo robe, breastplate and leggings.

"The robe is to cushion you against the harshness of the ground."

"Oh," she said, but her insides were throbbing with need, and her stomach seemed to be performing somersaults and handsprings.

He whispered, "I intend to make love to you, my wife."

The endearment sent her pulse soaring. "Please do. Please make love to me, Red Hawk. Now."

They should have finished undressing. Goodness knows their clothes would be mussed by their activity, but need drove them both.

Throwing his buffalo robe over the ground, he lowered her onto it, kissed her and raised her skirts. He said, "I am glad to see that you have given up wearing leggings beneath all these clothes, but are you certain you do not need them, because of these things tied to your waist?"

"It has been hot."

He grinned at her. "For that I am grateful. Are you ready?"

She nodded.

And he joined himself with her, without preamble. They wanted each other. It was enough.

His thrusts were deep inside her, exactly what she needed, although she found herself responding as though, even skin to skin, body to body, it wasn't sufficient. She yearned for more. She moved with him, against him, straining, for the pleasure was too good, too splendid to stop.

He kissed her neck, her lips, her cheeks, her ears, her eyes. With his lips, he adored her.

Rising up sightly onto his forearms, he thrust into her and out, again and again, watching her face.

He said, "You are so beautiful, and if I could, I would look at you as you meet your pleasure."

Not knowing how to respond to such devotion, she increased her action, instead of talking, and pushed her hands through his hair, pulling him down to her. Only then did she whisper, "I love you, my husband. I truly love you."

Her confession seemed to send him over the edge.

Indeed, he murmured against her again and again, his thrusts becoming deeper and deeper. Though he seemed incapable of speech, he managed to utter, "I love you, too."

And with that, while she welcomed him, he shuddered, and spilled his seed into her.

Effie decided that watching him was a little like capturing a bit of heaven into her own little universe. Moreover, she followed his rise into bliss, and with short gasps, she soon met her own pleasure.

Ah, it was truly pure enchantment.

The water beckoned them both.

He removed her clothing, piece by piece, kissing her delicate skin beneath. At the same time, she tried to remove his shirt, her hands sliding over each and every muscle in his chest, his arms, his stomach.

However, she discovered that she was not as adept at removing his clothing as he was with hers. Soon she found herself completely naked, while he was still almost fully dressed.

"Hmmmm," he groaned, sliding his chest—which was bare, except for the necklace she had once given him—over hers. "Hmmmm," he moaned again. And then, "I want you anew," he said, as he moved his hips over hers.

"I, too," she agreed, although her response was almost unnecessary. He had already joined with her.

He strove against her over and over. She opened herself to him, receiving him, tightening her inner muscles to secure him better. And each time she tightened, he whimpered all over again.

"'Tis good," he uttered huskily.

"Yes."

He came up to his knees, bringing her with him. Pulling her legs into position around his neck, he leaned into her, boring against her in their quest for pleasure.

It was a good position. They could gaze directly into each other's eyes as they strained against the tide of passion.

His movements all at once became frenzied, and staring so deeply at her she thought he might be looking into her soul, he said, *"Kitsikakomimmo."*

She met his passion with her own, and as he lost himself to her, she gave herself to him, straining, driving, pushing toward that one plateau. They were almost there, almost there, and then . . .

They burst, their bodies paying complete tribute to one another. So intimate was it, so close were they, she felt that at that moment it would been hard to tell where her spirit left off and his began.

It was as though a part of her had merged with him. She felt complete. Utterly, wholly, complete.

As her body, racked with pleasure, began to relax, she felt herself move away from the body, looking down on them both from above. Interestingly enough, he was there with her . . .

Together, they soared.

"Perhaps, my wife," he said, "there will come a time when we can see, perchance even feel each other's naked bodies, without at once having to make love."

"Perhaps," she agreed.

"But that time is not now."

"No," she conceded. "That time is definitely not now."

"My wife," said Red Hawk, coming onto his elbows, and leaning over her. "I have news."

"And what news do you bring me?"

"There is only one way that I can bring this news to you. I must show you. But do not fear. You will like it, I think."

She sighed. "Do I have to put on my dress?"

"*Saa*, 'tis better that you do not."

"It must be in the water you are taking me, then?"

"*Aa.*"

"All right," she said. "Lead me to it."

CHAPTER 21

In the end, with the artifacts still tied to her waist, she donned only her chemise. Hand in hand, they stepped into the cold, refreshing water. As soon as the water came to their thighs, they plunged into its depths, both of them diving well under the surface.

Red Hawk took the lead, which was good, Effie decided, for she could barely see within its dark void. Though the moonlight cast beams softly into the flowing currents, it was still murky beneath the water's surface, making her more than a little uncomfortable. How long they remained underwater, she didn't know, but after awhile, she caught up to Red Hawk, tapped him on the foot and pointed upward.

They surfaced at once, each of them treading water. As soon as they had both caught their breath, she said, "Though I love bathing here in the evening, swimming underwater at night is a little spooky. And I am scantily dressed. Do you think I should return and clothe myself?"

"We could, if you think it best," he said. "But the way is not far from here. Besides, with this thing on you," he indicated the material of her chemise, "you are well clothed for swimming."

"Perhaps I am," she said. "But could you at least tell me where you take me, since the way seems to be farther than I had reckoned."

"I can tell you a little. We go to the place where I believe you will find those things you seek."

"You mean the artifacts?"

"*Aa.*"

"How can this be? How do you know of this place? And if you have known about it, why haven't you mentioned anything to me before now?"

"I have only learned of this place this very day."

She frowned at him. "Today? But I didn't know you were in camp. I thought that you had been visiting—" She stopped. So this is what he had been doing with his time. She sent him a puzzled frown. "I don't understand."

"You will." He took her hand. "Come, follow me, and if you are frightened, don't let go of my hand."

Effie didn't need to be told this twice, for she *was* frightened. She grabbed hold of him, and on signal from Red Hawk, they again dove beneath the water's surface.

Soon they came to a channel that was shallow and narrow, the water coming to just above their knees. This must have been on the far side of the pool, for the place was unknown to her, and she had often explored this pool in her youth. Pine trees grew on both sides, casting long shadows, lending the spot an eery atmosphere. Occasionally the moon shone through the trees, however, dispelling the gloom, if only momentarily.

Still clasping Red Hawk's hand, she set her pace to keep up with him, thankful that the bed in the channel was cushioned in sand. It was an odd feeling, traipsing through water, at night, in only her calf-length chemise, her hand in that of her husband's.

"Red Hawk, what's this all about?" she asked in a voice barely over a whisper.

" 'Tis only around the bend here, the place where I am taking you. 'Tis located in what the white man calls a 'tributary' of the river, or an 'inlet.' There has been a drought in this part of the country this year, so we are lucky. What I am to show you is quite commonly covered with water."

"Oh," was all she said, not knowing how else to respond.

At last, they trod into a completely different pool, only this one's bed was made of rocks.

"Ouch!" she uttered, as she stepped on something sharp.

Red Hawk turned back to her. "We shall go slower that you may search for good footing before placing you feet on the river's bed."

And so they did. Soon, however, the water was deep enough that they could paddle along with the current.

Within a few short moments, he stopped. They both stood up in the water, which was no more than waist deep.

"Look to the shoreline." He pointed to their right. "Do you see it?"

"No, what am I supposed to be observing?"

"Look closely."

She did. "All I can make out," she said, "here in the moonlight, is the face of a canyon wall, with a . . . Is that a cavern?"

"It is," he said, and he smiled at her. " 'Tis an underwater cavern, and so has remained unseen to the eye of man. It is here that you will find that which you seek."

"Here? How do you know that?" She was already pacing slowly out of the water, that she might catch a closer glance at the canyon wall.

"I cannot tell you how I know. All I can relate to you

is that this is where you will find the missing artifacts, because—"

"*Otohkat! I have sent him.*"

The voice, which came from behind them, was deep, masculine and loud. Effie dived behind Red Hawk's nude body for protection.

"What's happening, Red Hawk?" she whispered from behind him. "Who is that?"

"Do not fear," he said. "It is my spirit protector."

"Your what? Did you know someone else would be here when you brought me?"

"*Saa*, I did not, and I will explain later who and what my spirit protector is. For now, simply listen."

Something smooth and sleek dove in and out of the water—out there, in the deep places of the pool—but it caused barely a sound or a ripple against the current. As it rose out of the water once again, it said,

> "*Four golden images,*
> *When all in a row,*
> *Slaves, his people will be,*
> *No more.*"

"Red Hawk, is that a snake talking to us?"

"He is a sea dog."

"That's no dog."

"Sh-h-h. Listen."

> "*What you seek is here, water being.*
> *But beware.*
> *Once you find what you seek, you must not share.*
> *For there are those among you who will steal what*
>   *you have.*
> *And use what is here not for good, but for bad.*"

Had she lost her mind? Was a snake not only speaking to her, but reciting rhyming riddles?

She said, "I don't understand this, Red Hawk. In truth, I'm a little frightened."

"Sh-h-h. Just listen."

And the sea dog continued,

> *"Four golden images*
> *You both alone must seek.*
> *When at last they are together*
> *The spirits shall meet."*

And then, with a splash, the creature was gone.

Both Effie and Red Hawk stood silent for a moment. Both lost for words.

Effie shivered, and Red Hawk took her in his arms. But once she started shaking, she seemed unable to stop.

Cradling her in his arms, Red Hawk led her into the cavern, then gradually he fell to his knees, where he proceeded to run his fingers through her hair, up and down her back, as though by friction alone, he would restore warmth to her.

She sobbed, but at last she was able to speak, and she said, "Why did you bring me here?"

"Because this is where you will find the artifacts. I did not know that my spirit protector would be here, and I did not know it would speak to us this night. I meant only to show you what I have found. It has been an exciting day for me, because I have been looking for this place since we have arrived here."

"But you told me that you have been visiting relatives."

"*Aa*, I have done that . . . and another thing of some importance. But all the relatives that I have here are adopted, and so the time with them was short. What I have been doing is swimming in these waters for many days, along with that other matter that takes a great deal of my time. I have been in the Big River itself, in our little pool, in every outlet of the river that I could find. It was my spirit protector who led me here; it is my spirit protector that will help you find the things you seek."

"Your spirit protector? Led you here? Your people? You go too fast. And I . . . I still don't understand."

"Have you forgotten that I am of the Lost Clan?"

"No, of course not. It's only that . . . I love you. I have fallen in love with you . . . and since that time, I have been distracted by you, by our love. I think of you as . . . well, as you . . . And I . . . Maybe once, I might have thought purely of nothing but extracting information from you, because of who you are, but . . ."

"I understand," he said, holding her, bringing her in even closer to him. "Love can change many things. So now, let me bring more understanding to you. Let me begin at the beginning . . ."

Red Hawk had changed positions, had settled them both into a comfortable location, there in the cave. At present, he sat with his back against the cavern wall, while he held Effie in his arms. Her backside was against him, his legs were around her, engulfing hers.

"Let us begin with a spirit protector." He drew in a deep breath, then, "When a man reaches a certain age, his mind often turns to war, and to making a name for himself. A warrior will seek a vision and a helper from the animal kingdom to aid him in attaining his goals, for he would strive to have power over his enemies. Since the Creator does not take sides, one must seek the goodwill of a spirit helper to ensure his success. Most often these helpers take the form of an animal."

"Oh, I see. Thus a 'spirit protector'?"

"*Aa*. Now, my helper, who is the sea dog, has not long been aiding me—not until recently has he visited me. I had thought I had no vision, no protector, and might never have a vision. But the problem was that I was seeking my dreams in the wrong places. It was not until I looked for my vision in the water that I came face-to-face with my helper. It was you, the memory of you, who led me to the water. It was my spirit protector who brought me to you, the water being."

"Water being?"

"That is what the sea dog calls you."

"Really? Water being . . . I like it."

"As do I. Now, the poem that you heard tonight, 'Four golden images, when all in a row. Slaves, his people will be, no more,' is the same verse that was given to me within my first vision. Though I did not understand it at first, I have now come to embrace it. There are four artifacts. But these are not merely images in stone. These are the children of the Thunder Being. Somehow—although I do not grasp exactly how—when these stones are at last together, my people will go free."

"I see. It's interesting because my father told me a similar story. He said that the images in the stone were not carved, but were in reality the Thunderer's children."

"It is so."

"I have never believed it, though."

"And now?"

"I still find it hard to believe." She paused, then, "Is this why it was easy for me to convince you to help me?"

"Partly."

"Is it also why you have wanted to marry me? Please say 'no.'"

"*Saa*. Of course it is not. Some time in our near future,

I am going to buy you a white man's mirror, that you never have to question me on this again."

She seemed to ignore what he'd said, and went on to say, "However, it would fit, wouldn't it? If you knew that I was committed to finding these things, then it would be in your interest to make sure that I would give them to you."

He shrugged. "Perhaps it might seem to be so. But it is not true. You know that I have loved you since the first time I saw you. Besides, I have been seeking what you seek. It has never been my intention to take these things from you, only to free my people."

"Yes," she argued, "but then perhaps to free your people, you will need to take them from me. Have you thought of that?"

"*Saa.* I do not believe that stealing is a part of my vision. The Creator would not make it so."

"Maybe not, and my worry is unfounded. But I should tell you that my father has instructed me to keep all four of the artifacts together; he has told me I must give them to no one . . . but the Lost Clan."

"And so you will," he said. "Through me."

"But how do I know that's true? The Lost Clan should consist of many people, not just one. I love you, I want to believe you, and do what's right for you, but someone is trying to steal these artifacts from me, for purposes of their own."

"Do you think I do this?"

"No, but . . . My father told me when the time comes, I will know what to do. It may be that I cannot give them to you. I . . . simply don't know."

"*Aa*, I understand. We will have to wait, then, and see what happens when we finally locate the missing two pieces. Perhaps it will be clear to us then."

"Perhaps. I can only hope that it is. And Red Hawk?"

"*Aa.*"

"If it's only you and I who are to dig for these things, as the sea dog has instructed, when will we be able to do this without the others knowing? If I am gone for lengthy times each day, others will get suspicious. They might follow me. Must we work at night?"

"Perhaps," he said. "Or we might work in the early hours of the morning, when there is at least a little light. Perhaps sometime during the day tomorrow, you can sneak some of your digging equipment to our pool, and I will take those things to this site. But remember, the others must not know what we do. You do grasp that whatever a vision says we must do, must be done?"

She shrugged. "I do. It seems only right anyway. But why must a person do as the vision instructs?"

"To my people," he said, "a vision is the voice of the Creator, speaking through a man's protector. To fail to do as asked is to go against His wishes. It is rare that a man would abuse this. Now you are an unusual woman, because women are seldom given visions. You do realize that you, too, have had a vision? One that we share?"

What has happened here tonight is what's called a vision?"

"*Aa,*" he said. "'Tis so." Leaning forward, for he still held her within his arms, her back toward him, he first rubbed his cheek against hers, then planted a kiss on the side of her face. Then he repeated. "'Tis so."

CHAPTER 22

And so it began. To bed early, up in the wee hours of the day, long before the sun was due to rise. Each morning Effie and Red Hawk would meet by their pool. Each morning, by the light of a thousand stars, they swam to the cavern, there to dig. It took them no less than a week to uncover an area that was approximately seven feet by seven feet square.

But there was no trace of the artifacts to be found. They had discovered a few bones, and of course dirt and sand. But that was all.

"Are you certain this is where we're supposed to be digging?" she had asked one night.

"I am confident of it."

"But there is nothing here."

"They are hidden," he said. "If it were easy, they would have been found many seasons ago."

She could find no reason to argue with him on the point, so they continued. In many ways, Effie felt as though she were living a double life. One was that of the staid and proper site director, the other that of unannounced wife and digger.

Of one thing she had complete certainty. The double life offered very little sleep. Alas, it was becoming almost impossible to keep her eyes open during the day—a fact she tried her best to hide.

Indeed, Lesley had commented on this only this morning.

"Effie, is something wrong?" she had asked. "You have great shadows beneath your eyes. The look is hardly becoming on you."

Effie had grimaced, had murmured something, but for the life of her, she couldn't remember what that was now. She only hoped she had been convincing.

Once again, she had slipped out of camp around three o'clock in the morning. Once again, she met up with Red Hawk at what they had come to regard as their own private lagoon. But now, instead of her bulky dresses, she had taken to wearing her red swimming costume. It was the most comfortable of her clothes when wet.

By the light of a single lantern, they dug for many hours, until daylight made the artificial light unnecessary. In the beginning, they had often played in the water, their antics usually ending in only one way. But as time had worn on, and still they met with no success, by mutual agreement, the playing had almost ceased. Now more attention was reserved for the single purpose of finding the artifacts.

Crack! Lightning split through the air close to them.

"Haiya!" said Red Hawk. "Will he never leave me alone?"

"Who do you speak of?" asked Effie.

Red Hawk appeared suddenly overwrought, as though overcome with anger. It was an emotion Effie had rarely witnessed in him.

Soon and in a calm voice, Red Hawk said, "'Tis the Thunder Being."

She placed her hand over his.

He said, "Do not tell me that you do not believe what I say is true."

"No, it's not that, I—"

"He is following me; he is following you and your colleagues, as well. I have done my best to keep you safe; I have done all I can to prevent him from coming into your camp. But it appears he wishes to see me yet again."

"You don't have to go."

"If I do not, he may try to take your life. I must go. You stay here. The confrontations between myself and the Thunderer are not often long. I will return as soon as I can."

"Very well," she said. "If you must go, I understand. But please don't be long. Please. Without you here, this place frightens me. Besides, I will worry."

Nodding, he leaned over and pressed his lips to hers. "I will come back here as quickly as I am able. I promise."

And with these words, Red Hawk climbed out of the seven-foot-deep trench they had dug, and set off to do battle with the Thunderer.

Clank!

Effie's shovel hit something, and it didn't sound like a rock. Could it be?

Calming herself, for she dared not raise her hopes too high, she fell to her knees. Bringing the lantern, as well as her brush and trowel, closer to the spot, she mumbled to herself, reciting the words her father had often said to her, "Remember to go slowly. Never use metal on an artifact. If you think you've discovered something, use all caution. A brush and your hands will often suffice."

But it was one thing to say the words, another to pay attention to them. If this were it . . .

Excitement had her hands shaking. Yet, as calmly as possible, she used her fingers to brush away the dirt. Slowly she worked at it until, at last, she could see her way clear to pull the thing out.

"Are you ready for this?" she asked herself. "For it may not be what you're seeking." She inhaled on a deep breath, and then mumbled, "On the count of three."

"One, two, three."

She pulled at the stone, lifting the piece out of the ground rather easily. Setting it down on the dirt before her, she shone the lantern over it. It was quartz; it was also the right size. Picking up her brush, she stroked what looked like a golden nugget removing the evidence of being buried for perhaps a thousand years.

She barely dared to breathe.

And then, there, beneath the light of her lantern, the piece shone. It glowed, as though alive beneath the dirt and grime that remained covering it.

"Oh, how I wish Red Hawk were here." He'd be happy. And she'd be delighted right along with him.

The other piece might be here, too, she thought, lying close by to where she'd found this one. And so she continued digging, reminding herself to go carefully, slowly.

Minutes later she hit something that made the same sort of sound. Was this it, then? Was she to have all four artifacts on her person? Could she end the curse? This morning?

Again, she scolded herself, mumbling, "Don't use any more metal on it. Be gentle, yet thorough. Brush the dirt away."

One slow stroke after another, the thing was finally

ready to be pulled from the ground. She did so with care, taking the piece into her hand.

This was it! It was the missing piece.

She had done it. She felt like screaming, like running out of the cave to find Red Hawk and show him this morning's bounty. In fact, that's exactly what she was going to do.

Getting to her feet, she twirled around and around with glee, as though she danced on a stage instead of being in a trench. "I've done it!" she said to the air around her. "I have all four artifacts!"

"You should say had *when you say that."*

Oh, no. It was that horrible, gritty voice again. She would never forget it. Fearing what she would see when she gazed upward, yet knowing she had to, she looked up toward the top of the dig.

It was the man in black, and this time, he had a pistol pointed directly at her.

"I'll take those artifacts now," said the man, gesturing toward her hands, where she still held the nuggets. "Pass them up to me."

When she didn't instantly comply, the man again said in that terrible voice, "Pass them to me now, or I will shoot you."

It occurred to her that she could extinguish the light, at which time no one would be able to see. They would then be on equal footing.

However, the man might shoot first, and think later. And he might accidently blast one of the artifacts.

"Hurry."

"Yes, yes," said Effie. "I am coming with it."

"Now!"

"Yes, all right." With one artifact held in her hand,

Effie stretched up her arm. The man reached down, and as soon as he grasped hold of the thing, Effie pulled with all her might. Never, in her wildest dreams, had she thought she might be successful.

But she was.

The man fell into the pit, and Effie, knowing exactly where the shovel was, took it in hand and hit her assailant on the head.

At once, the man sank back on the ground.

Breathing out on a sigh, Effie realized she would have to tie him up. When he awoke, he could cause trouble again.

Grabbing hold of some rope, which sat next to her, Effie tied the man's hands and legs. Then she impatiently hauled off her assailant's black mask.

Immediately, long, ginger-colored hair spilled forth. *No! Not her!*

"Madeline?" How could this be? Gentle Madeline? Sweet Madeline? But it was Madeline nonetheless; Madeline, who had tried to kill her, three times.

As though the sound of her name awakened her, Madeline opened her eyes, only to find her hands and feet tied.

She let out a scream.

"Shut up," said Effie, "or I'll have to gag you, too."

"You won't get away with it, you know."

"Away with what?" asked Effie.

"Stealing, that's what."

"Stealing? I don't know what you're talking about."

"Then what are you doing here, digging in a site that you have not told anyone else about?"

"I can explain that," said Effie.

Madeline screamed again.

"Don't do that."

She screamed anyway.

Sighing, Effie realized she was going to have to muzzle

the woman. "I'm sorry I have to do this, but I can't have you howling like this."

She gagged her.

Then, grabbing up her tools, she set them at the top of the site—for she didn't want them available to Madeline should she manage to free herself. Then, clasping hold of Madeline's gun and the artifacts, Effie climbed out of the digging site.

She needed to find Red Hawk. And as soon as she did, together, they would end this curse, and set things right.

Moving to the mouth of the cavern, Effie was about to step foot in the water, when—

"I'll take those," came a gruff voice behind her.

She turned around. This time, however, it wasn't Madeline standing before her.

John Owens held a gun pointed directly at her.

Where was Red Hawk? was her first thought.

"Hand them over," said Owens.

"No, I don't think that I will," said Effie.

"Then I will kill you," he said. "I have no qualms about it."

"No qualms? But . . . you are my father's best friend."

"*Was* your father's best friend," he said. "But then that poor excuse for an archaeologist went and appointed you director of this project. *You!* It should have been me. Haven't I waited all this time for my chance to get at those artifacts? Haven't I indulged a man, who is supposed to be a scientist but who instead has chosen to follow a dream? Well, there is no Lost Clan. Scientifically, it's impossible. There are only the artifacts, and they are worth millions. If anyone deserves to have them, it is I. And I mean to have them. Now give them to me."

"But . . ."

"Yes?"

Was her only chance to keep talking?

Perhaps. And so she said, "But how could it be you? It was Madeline who assaulted me in Virginia City. You weren't even there."

"How do you know about Madeline?"

"She's in the pit."

"In the pit? What have you done to her?"

"Nothing, she's just tied up."

"Ah," said Owens. "I will have to fix that."

"Then it's you *and* Madeline who have been doing this?"

"That's right," said Owens. "I must admit that it has taken a bit of work on my part. But Madeline is an ambitious woman, who is married to a worthless young man. She wishes to better herself. *I'll* provide that for her."

"But you're married. I know your wife."

John Owens chuckled. "Of course I'm married. But a man, such as myself, is entitled to have his mistresses."

Effie felt rather sick, and before she could stop herself, she said, "You're despicable."

"I'm a man."

"I'm not so sure."

"Doesn't matter what you think. Hand them over. All four of them. I know you have the other two on you."

"No, I don't, and no, I won't," she said, admitting nothing.

"I know you have them on you. You wouldn't take a chance and leave them behind."

"I might. How did you find out about this place?"

"Madeline observed that you leave to go somewhere early in the morning. She thought for awhile, it was only to meet your Indian lover. But this morning, she followed you here, and I came after her."

"I see," said Effie.

"Now, give them to me."

"No."

"Then you will die, for I know you have the other two on you."

But he didn't shoot. Instead, without so much as pausing for breath, he set upon her, wrestling the artifacts out of her hands. One by one he grasped hold of them, placing them to the side, while he held her hands. "Now where are the others."

She turned mute.

"Come on, if you won't give them up, then it will be my pleasure to find them. You're no more than a whore anyway. You, taking an Indian lover."

"He is my husband."

John Owens laughed. "There is no such thing between a white woman and an Indian."

Without a hint of conscience, he lifted her skirts and tore off her pantalettes. He had no more than set upon her, when he beheld the satchels, tied around her waist.

"Ah," he said, "there they are." And he ripped them off of her. Standing up, he said, "And now I have all four. Thank you, Miss Effie. I'm sorry I have to do this," he said with a cold smile.

Without even a pause, he pointed the gun at her.

CHAPTER 23

"Leave this place! Get away from here!" shouted Red Hawk, waving his arms at the Thunder Being.

As lightning shot through the being, he laughed. "Come, make me leave!"

"You will not tempt me!"

"Do I not?" said the Thunderer. "If I do not tempt you, why are you here, when your wife is in danger?"

"You lie!"

The Thunder Being merely laughed.

Again, Red Hawk yelled, "You lie!" But he couldn't be certain. *"Haiya!"* Was this frustration never to end?

Turning his back once more on the Thunderer, Red Hawk stalked away. But his parting words were, "One day, I will have my revenge."

Again, the Thunderer laughed.

Red Hawk raced back toward the cavern. Had he been wise in leaving Effie alone? He had not scouted out the area before he had left, nor had he looked for an enemy or an interloper. What if someone had followed them?

Could the Thunder Being have been telling the truth? After all, he was one of the Above Ones.

Suddenly, urgency filled Red Hawk's soul.

It seemed to take him forever to reach the cave, and when he did, he approached the place from the cliff above it. Coming down onto his stomach, he edged toward the end of the crag and looked down.

He could hardly believe what his eyes saw. John Owens held a gun on Effie, who lay on the ground at his feet.

Worse, in Owens's hands were the four artifacts, the means by which Red Hawk could end his people's curse.

"Help the enemy. Show mercy."

What? Show mercy to John Owens when he held a gun on his wife?

Yet wasn't that what was required of Red Hawk if he meant to end the curse?

Then he heard Owens say, "I am going to kill you. Good-bye, Miss Effie."

With those words, any confusion Red Hawk might have harbored left him. Curse or not, Grandfather be spared, Red Hawk would *not* let his wife die.

"I'm sorry, Grandfather," he mumbled to himself as he shot up from the ground, and, speeding off the cliff, he bounded onto Owens, wrestling him to the ground.

In the excitement, the gun went off. Red Hawk hoped it had exploded harmlessly, for he could not pause to look. The two of them rolled over and over, onto the beach, into the water, first one of them on top and then the other.

Wet and struggling, they came up to wrestle with each other, the water being only thigh deep. Then they sank, as each one of them grappled for supremacy. Owens was oddly strong for a man his age, but as they fell farther and farther down into the water, looking into Owens's face,

Red Hawk realized at once that he had the advantage. Owens could not hold his breath underwater.

They continued to struggle, Owens now gone wild. At last, having no choice, Owens gulped, but instead of air he breathed in water. Not long after, his body went limp.

Grabbing hold of him, Red Hawk surfaced at once. The man was probably still alive, and could be brought around, if anyone cared to try. Since he had been a friend of Effie's father, Red Hawk would let her make the decision.

As Red Hawk emerged from the water, leaving Owens's body on the shore, the sea dog surfaced; it grabbed hold of Owens, and before anyone could object, the sea dog slinked away, into the deepest part of the lagoon.

Tragic, yet it was hardly a loss, thought Red Hawk. He turned away. Only then did he look for Effie.

What was this? Was that Effie's still body on the ground?

No, it couldn't be. Rushing toward her, he pulled her up into his arms.

"Effie! Effie!" he called.

Was she injured? Had she been shot? In her hands, she clutched two of the artifacts; two others had fallen to the ground beside her. But he ignored them. Opening the top of her bathing costume, he felt for a heartbeat. There wasn't one.

"No!" He cried out.

Then all at once, as though she would not let her life slip away so easily, she gasped in air, gulping. At last, her chest rose and fell.

"Effie!"

She opened her eyes, and stared directly at him. "Are you all right?"

He laughed with relief. "I am fine. I do not think I can say the same for your father's friend, however. The sea dog has him. And you, are you all right?"

I think so, although I seem to have lost feeling in my left arm."

Looking there, he saw that she had been injured with that shot, but it hadn't touched her arm. It was merely a graze on her chest, but it had come dangerously close to her heart.

He laid his hand over the injury. It seemed to be only a graze. She would be all right.

She would be all right.

Laughing, crying, he took her in his arms.

And so it was that he was unaware of his surroundings, when from behind him came a voice, and it said, "Poor Orphan, you have done what most of our people thought was impossible. You have broken the curse."

Red Hawk knew that voice, and raising himself up away from Effie, he said, "Grandfather?"

At last, Red Hawk looked behind him.

"Grandfather, it is you. It is you!"

"So it is. You have done well, my grandson."

"Grandfather, I welcome you. Grandfather," said Red Hawk, kneeling down toward Effie, "this is my wife, Effie. Effie, this is Grandfather."

All the people from the Yellow Shawl Band had gathered around Effie and Red Hawk. Had they been able, a council would have been held at once. But it was not possible. Though Effie, Red Hawk, Grandfather, the chief of the Yellow Shawl Band and White Claw were all present, all was still not well.

Thunder sounded above them. Lightning struck the ground to the right of them, to the left. Like fast-whirling storms, the black clouds rushed toward them, and in fear, all the people retreated into the cavern.

"It is the Thunderer," said White Claw, the tribal medicine man.

"I know," said Red Hawk. "He has been following me and making trouble. Now that my people are freed, I will meet him. I will do battle with him. I will have my revenge."

"No!" cried Effie.

But Red Hawk was steadfast in his belief, and he strode to the cavern's entrance.

"You might do battle with him," the medicine man addressed Red Hawk. "It is your right."

"No," said Effie, wiping away the stifling tears that she had no intention of shedding. And though her voice shook, she continued, "No. I have had enough fighting for one day. I have not come through this only to lose you, Red Hawk. The artifacts are mine. I found them. And though I may incur your hatred, and that of your band, I have decided I will give them to the Thunder Being."

Red Hawk swung around to face her. Though his face was contorted with anger, all he said was, "I cannot let you do it. He will kill you, as he killed my parents."

Rising to her feet, Effie paced toward the cavern's entrance, coming up behind her husband.

She said, "And yet I have the right to do with them as I see fit. Do you remember me telling you that?"

Red Hawk turned his face from her, before saying, "So you did." He paused. "But I cannot lose you either."

"I don't think you will." White Claw had stepped up behind them, and he continued, "Do not confuse the past with the present, my son. Had the Thunderer been inclined to kill you, he would have done so already."

Red Hawk nodded. "Very well," he said, "It shall be done, as you want it to be done. But I would ask that you let me give the artifacts to the Thunder Being, he who is my enemy. I promise you that I will do no more than that."

Effie nodded and without even a backward thought, she handed him the treasures.

Effie watched as Red Hawk stepped from the cavern, directly into the storm outside. Striding with purpose toward the shoreline of the lagoon, he set the four stones in a row, and said, "Here they are, Thunder Being. Your children are returned to you. Take them, and go in peace."

Some moments passed, and then came a powerful voice, which said, "You would give them to me without a battle?" It was the Thunderer.

"*Aa*, I would," said Red Hawk. "My wife found them. My wife has determined that they belong to you. I agree. Take them. Let there be peace between us."

Nodding once, stepping toward Red Hawk, a gigantic man, half blue, half black, moved before the cave. Bending, he took up the artifacts, handling them as he might a precious child. And in truth, they were children. They were *his* children.

Effie watched the Thunder Being retreat into the blackened storm clouds; he became a bird once again. And as the clouds engulfed him, they retreated from the sky, leaving in their place a beam of light.

A thing that Red Hawk had once said came to her: "All must pay for their ill actions against others."

Indeed, she thought. The Clan had paid their price, the Thunderer had, too.

Thank goodness, she thought, *that Red Hawk had not done anything he would regret.*

Turning, Red Hawk took Effie in his arms. "I love you," he said.

"And I love you, too. Now let us go find that preacher."

Together they retraced their steps to the cavern.

CHAPTER 24

In the end, it was a happy occasion, yet sad. One from amongst them was gone. Worse, that person had been someone whom Effie had considered a friend. Owens was Lesley's father; her own father's friend, as well.

How was she to tell Lesley all that had occurred? It seemed impossible, and yet, she knew she had to do it.

And then there was Madeline. What was Effie to do about Madeline? A few people in the Yellow Shawl Band had found Madeline and had untied her. And it was well to say that Madeline was looking more than a little shocked from her adventure.

Which brought another problem to mind. What was Effie to say to Carl, if indeed, she should say anything. Should she let Madeline go with a slap on the wrist? Shouldn't the other woman be made to atone for her mistake?

It was hard to know what to do.

Effie turned to Red Hawk. "Before anything else happens today, I must go back to my own camp. I have to tell Lesley what has happened."

He nodded. "I will come with you."

"I would like that." She sank into silence. And then, "Red Hawk?"

"*Aa.*"

"What am I to tell Lesley and Henry? What am I to say to Carl? How can I relate what has happened?"

"I do not know, but together we will find a way. Wait here, while I tell my grandfather and the medicine man where we go."

She nodded.

Effie watched as Red Hawk approached White Claw where the elder sat in council. Red Hawk squatted next to the old man and murmured something in his ear. But instead of rising up to accompany Effie back to her own camp, Red Hawk remained where he was, looking mildly surprised.

A few more words were spoken between them, then Red Hawk nodded and motioned Effie forward.

"You must hear this from our medicine man yourself, my wife."

"What is that?"

"Come forward and you will understand all as White Claw explains."

Effie stepped toward the group.

White Claw said at once, "There is no need for you to visit your friends in camp."

"But I—"

White Claw held up his hand. "The one you know as Owens is not dead, for the sea dog is not a killer. Though some think he is a monster, he is not. He simply escorted the man to another shoreline, hoping the man would have a chance to change the hatred in his heart."

Effie nodded. "Indeed, I imagine the experience might have caused him to have a change of viewpoint."

"*Aa*, I believe that he did." White Claw smiled, then he said, "I have been to see your people for I had to ensure that Madeline was reunited with her husband. It gave me the opportunity to explain to them what has happened, and if you like, they may come here and be a part of our council. But I believe that already they are making plans to leave here and go home. You will probably want to go and talk to them. Know that all is well with them."

"Then I . . . I don't have to explain?"

White Claw shook his head.

Effie breathed out deeply. "Yes, I will go and see them. Thank you, Mr. White Claw, sir."

White Claw nodded, and Effie and Red Hawk rose and left soon after to tread back to the excavation camp. It was wonderful to discover that, after all, things were exactly as White Claw had described.

What was even better, however, was that all of them—Lesley, Henry, Carl, Madeline, Mr. Owens and Fieldman—were pleased to congratulate Effie and Red Hawk on their marriage.

All, it seemed, was well.

Several days later

It was White Claw who had performed the wedding ceremony between Effie and Red Hawk.

At present, a camp had been set up in the excavation site, and a council had been called. All were present who needed to be there, Red Hawk, Grandfather, Effie, the chief of the Yellow Shawl Band and White Claw. The pipe had been smoked and passed; the necessary rituals had been properly executed, and at last White Claw said, "We welcome you, Water Being. Thank you for your help. We also welcome you into our tribe, and into our hearts. But come, I think you and your husband have questions. I am here for a little while longer that I might answer them. I would ask that you be first to question me, Water Being."

Effie smiled. She was becoming used to her new name, and was beginning to enjoy its notoriety. She said, "I do have questions, actually."

White Claw nodded.

"Sir, I am wondering what will happen with Madeline and Carl. Will they work through their problems?"

"It is a good question, and I may tell you this. Your friend, Madeline, was misled by the evil intentions of another. She thought you were doing wrong, and so she acted, as of course Owens had meant her to do. Madeline's husband suspected that it was she who was doing the ill deeds that beset you. He tried to protect her."

"I see."

"They have gone back to their parents," continued White Claw, "where it is hoped, they will learn to live with one another in a better way."

Effie nodded. "And what of Lesley and her father?"

"As you know," said White Claw, "Owens had a change of heart. He has apologized to Madeline and Carl, to his daughter, and he goes now to make peace with his wife. I do not believe he will cause any further trouble. It was his greed that was his demise. That greed is now gone."

"I am glad," said Effie, "but what I don't understand is how Madeline and Mr. Owens ever came to know one another."

"I believe they met through your father, not so long ago," said White Claw. "It was he who first introduced them. Since she and her husband were to accompany you on your work, your father felt it best that his friend come to know Carl and Madeline Bell. It was then that Owens gave in to a lust that had been festering within him for many years. It was he who tried to steal the artifacts from your father. When he met Madeline, he realized that through her he could attain his selfish desires. He chose the wrong spiritual path. Had it not been for the sea dog, he would have lost his soul forever."

"Then perhaps it was good that this all happened. One more thing, please. Do you know anything about the sheriff of Virginia City? Do you know why he broke into my room?"

White Claw nodded. "I am here to answer your question," he said. "The sheriff suspected you had something of value. I believe that is all. Had he found your stones, he would have taken them from you, I think. And now, is there anything else that you wish to know?"

"Yes," she said. "Is it true that some of your people are still lost, enslaved in a half existence?"

"It is, indeed, true," said White Claw. "But most are now freed. There is but one band of the tribe still imprisoned in the curse. But there is a year left. We have hopes for them."

"What will happen to Red Hawk's people? They are from the past, and do not know the ways of our current civilization."

"This is another good question," said White Claw. "It is hoped that both you and Red Hawk will help them to learn about this new environment. Perhaps they can learn from you, and you from them, for I think you are curious about them."

"Yes," said Effie. "That would be most agreeable."

"And now, Poor Orphan, you who are now known to us as Red Hawk, I would answer your questions. Have you any?"

"*Aa*, that I do."

"Proceed."

"Do you know how I ended the curse? I thought I was doing wrong, for I put my wife's life over the needs of the Clan."

"It is a strange thing, since the Creator instructed us to show mercy. But perhaps that is exactly what you did, my son. After all, you did pull Owens from the water. In this, you did show mercy."

Red Hawk nodded. "But I only did it for my wife's sake."

"I understand that," said White Claw. "Love, it is said, is a powerful thing. Perhaps it guides us in acting in ways that we should, despite the deception of our illusions. It is to be hoped that when the last of the Clan is released from the mist, the Creator will show us what we have failed to grasp, for I feel I should tell you that the other champions have told me much the same as you."

"*Aa*," said Red Hawk. "Let us pray this will be."

"And now," said White Claw. "I have good news. It is told to me by the spirits that you will both live long and well. Know, Water Being, that your parents will love your husband, as do you. Share with them. Your father and mother await you both."

Effie and Red Hawk nodded.

"And so I wish you well," said White Claw. "Now, I must end this council, unless you have other questions."

He waited.

"Being that as it is, I will return to those of the Clan who are still enslaved, although I think I might visit a friend who lives in the East before I return. Live long, be well and know that sometimes to love *is* the answer."

Rising up from his seat, White Claw took his leave of the others.

It is said that Red Hawk and Effie became the stuff of legend. It is also said that their love carried the Yellow Shawl Band through many hard times. Always, were they an inspiration to all the people, and to their families.

GLOSSARY

Because there are some technical terms as well as Blackfeet words used in the story, the following is provided for the reader for ease in reading.

Aa—A Blackfeet word meaning "yes."

Annisa—A Blackfeet word meaning "That's it/okay now."

Anthropology—A study of man and his societies, his way of life, his myths, etc. It differs from archaeology in that an archaeologist is concerned with man's past societies.

Archaeology—The study of past societies by means of finding human-made objects and using these to draw conclusions about that past society.

Artifact—A relic from the past. It is something that is made by man. Thus, a rock, though it might be old, would not be an artifact.

Collector—A person who collects artifacts. He does not share them with the world for their greater knowledge. It is looked down upon for a professional archaeologist to become a collector.

Conservator—A professional in the field of archaeology who acts like a guardian for the artifacts found. Often such people work in a museum.

Grid—In archaeology, a method used to excavate the area to be dug. A grid (or map of the excavation site) is drawn up in what might be called boxed areas, and the area is then dug in sections. The other method of excavation is the vertical-face method.

Haiya—A Blackfeet expression used mainly by males.

Hannia—A Blackfeet expression used as though to say, "really."

Ho—Another Blackfeet common expression.

Ikksisitsi'tsi—A Blackfeet word meaning "understand."

Oki—A Blackfeet word meaning "hello."

Omaniit—A Blackfeet word meaning "be truthful."

Omaopaat!—A Blackfeet word meaning "stop."

Otahkohsoa' tsis—Blackfeet for Red Hawk.

Poohsapoot—A Blackfeet word meaning "come here."

Puncheon logs—Wooden logs, roughly trimmed; one side is hacked flat.

Saa—Blackfeet for "no."

Soka'pii—Blackfeet for "good," usually said at the same time that the right hand, palm down and at chest level, is sent out in a quick motion forward—sign language for "good."

Vertical-face—An excavation method used by archaeologists that is done in a horizontal direction. The general rule is to pick one side of the site and excavate across the site. The other excavation method is the grid method.

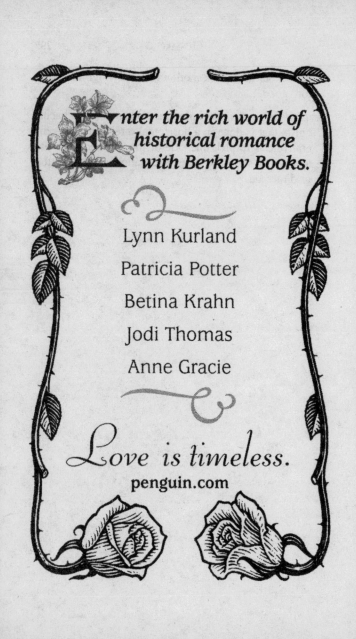

Enter the rich world of historical romance with Berkley Books.

Lynn Kurland

Patricia Potter

Betina Krahn

Jodi Thomas

Anne Gracie

Love is timeless.

penguin.com